Homeless in Heaven

Connie Shelton

Books by Connie Shelton

The Charlie Parker Mystery Series

Deadly Gamble
Vacations Can Be Murder
Partnerships Can Be Murder
Small Towns Can Be Murder
Memories Can Be Murder
Honeymoons Can Be Murder
Reunions Can Be Murder
Competition Can Be Murder
Balloons Can Be Murder
Obsessions Can Be Murder
Gossip Can Be Murder
Stardom Can Be Murder
Phantoms Can Be Murder
Buried Secrets Can Be Murder
Legends Can Be Murder
Weddings Can Be Murder
Alibis Can Be Murder
Escapes Can Be Murder
Holidays Can Be Murder - a Christmas novella

The Samantha Sweet Series

Sweet Masterpiece
Sweet's Sweets
Sweet Holidays
Sweet Hearts
Bitter Sweet
Sweets Galore
Sweets Begorra
Sweet Payback
Sweet Somethings
Sweets Forgotten
Spooky Sweet
Sticky Sweet
Spellbound Sweets - a Halloween novella
The Woodcarver's Secret

The Heist Ladies Series

Diamonds Aren't Forever
The Trophy Wife Exchange
Movie Mogul Mama
Homeless in Heaven

Children's Books

Daisy and Maisie and the Great Lizard Hunt
Daisy and Maisie and the Lost Kitten

Homeless in Heaven

Heist Ladies Mysteries, Book 4

Connie Shelton

Secret Staircase Books

Homeless in Heaven
Published by Secret Staircase Books, an imprint of
Columbine Publishing Group, LLC
PO Box 416, Angel Fire, NM 87710

Book layout and design by Secret Staircase Books
Cover images © Franciscah, Droidworker, Natalija Hahalishvili, 1971yes, Jara3000

First trade paperback edition: July 2020

First e-book edition: July 2020

* * *

Publisher's Cataloging-in-Publication Data

Shelton, Connie
Homeless in Heaven / by Connie Shelton.
p. cm.
ISBN 978-1945422898 (paperback)
ISBN 978-1945422904 (e-book)

1. Heist Ladies (Fictitious characters)—Fiction. 2. Arizona—Fiction. 3. Religious scams—Fiction. 4. Women sleuths—Fiction. 6. Con artists—Fiction. 7. Mystery caper—Fiction. I. Title

Heist Ladies Mystery Series : Book 4.
Shelton, Connie, Heist Ladies mysteries.

BISAC : FICTION / Mystery & Detective.

813/.54

Dan, Stephanie, Susan, Shirley—each of you contributes and makes my writing life so much easier and so much more complete. Deepest gratitude to all.

Chapter 1

The drive out to Apache Junction took slightly more than twenty minutes on US 60 the first Saturday morning in December. What traffic there was seemed headed the opposite way, into the metro center where the shopping malls would be jammed.

"I'm glad you talked me into this," Sandy Werner said, as the landscape opened up and paved parking lots gave way to dirt ones. "I need to do something more physical than sitting at my desk in the bank."

"Not to mention it's a great cause," Mary Holbrook told her. "Trini says they're hoping to get this new addition to the shelter opened before Christmas. I never realized, until I ended up at Heaven Sent, how many people are on the streets this time of year."

Sandy nodded. It was true. Although she saw people in need of money, the bank branch she managed in Scottsdale didn't exactly draw a poverty-stricken clientele. She'd been shocked, two years ago, when Mary had come in to withdraw her last few hundred dollars, admitting to the sudden downturn in her own financial life.

Now, Mary was a physical trainer and partner in a successful gym in Chandler. And since her experience with homelessness she'd given generously of her time and money to help—first by teaching self-defense techniques to the women residents, and now by spending her Saturdays to help build and enlarge the Apache Junction branch of the shelter at the eastern end of the sprawling Phoenix metropolis.

Mary pulled her little red Ford into a parking lot filled with vehicles, including a delivery truck from a local hardware store.

"Wow, good crowd already," Sandy said as Mary maneuvered to a parking spot at the fringes of the lot.

"People in this city are used to getting up early for work, so what's one more pre-dawn alarm setting?" Mary reached for her paper cup of coffee, checking that the top was securely in place.

Sandy stuffed her purse beneath the front seat and reached for the zip-up sweatshirt she'd brought. They locked the car and walked toward the building. A sign greeted all who came: HEAVEN SENT—A SAFE PLACE. Someone had strung Christmas lights around the edges of it, and a big red bow decorated the front door.

A woman with gray hair in a cute pixie cut stood out

front, directing the volunteers. She sent a group around the left side of the building and then spotted Mary.

"Hey, you made it!" The woman pulled Mary into an embrace and held her, rocking gently side to side.

"Trini, this is my friend, Sandy Warner. She's—"

"Sandy! I've heard lots about you. Welcome, welcome. Trini Newton." She held out her hand.

"Thanks, Trini. Great to meet you. I hope I can actually be of help. Construction isn't exactly on my list of skills."

"If you can handle a paint roller, you are in the perfect place today," Trini said with a warm grin that accentuated the lines around her eyes. Smiling had apparently been a lifelong habit.

Mary seemed surprised. "You're already painting?"

"Hey, we don't mess around. We've made a lot of progress since you were here last week." Trini led them inside through the front door.

"I love the decorations," Mary said. She pointed to a tall Christmas tree in the corner of the small lobby and strands of tinsel hanging from the reception desk.

"We're trying to round up some more," Trini said, leading them down a hallway toward the back of the building. "People bring stuff and we put it up wherever it fits, mainly here in the women-and-children area. These kids need something to brighten the holidays for them. The men's area is across the hall." She waved toward another closed door, farther along.

She opened the wide door in front of them and they stepped into a large room filled with cots. Curtains hung from the ceiling between the beds to create privacy. Some of the curtained 'rooms' held one bed, others had two or three.

"We try to give families a space to themselves so, for

instance, a woman and her kids will have a cubicle. This is the purpose for the new addition. We'll have it structured so husbands and wives with kids actually get a bit of space to themselves."

"You've done a very nice job with it," Sandy said.

Leaving the women's area, Trini led them to the end of the long corridor. "Communal bathrooms and showers are here—ladies on the left, men on the right. And the kitchen and dining hall are back here. We provide a couple of computers where residents can get online to check job listings and housing opportunities."

Mary noticed no one at the computers, but the dining tables were filled. Today's breakfast seemed to be a choice of oatmeal or scrambled eggs, dished up by volunteers where a buffet of sorts was set up along the back wall. From her own experience she knew breakfast was meant to give a good start to the day. By lunch time residents were expected to be out looking for work, and dinner for those who chose to stay the night would be a soup or stew and bread. Nothing fancy, but it kept starvation away.

They trailed behind Trini as she bustled through the dining room and pushed a door open at the east end, revealing the newly constructed space, a room about the same size as the women's quarters they'd just visited. The scents of unfinished drywall and newly laid vinyl tile greeted them. Stacks of paint cans and roller trays waited near an exterior exit door, and strips of wooden molding lay in a pile on the floor.

"Mary, I know you're good with a nail gun," Trini said. "All that trim needs to be put up around the door frames and baseboards."

"I can handle that."

"Bob Perkins over there will help with measuring and

cutting, so you should be able to keep up a pace just by nailing."

Mary ran a hand through her spiky reddish-blond hair and reached into her hip pocket for the pair of gloves she'd brought along. She headed toward the elderly man with the tape measure and they began to confer.

"Sandy, painting?"

"I love to paint." She'd already been eyeing the cans and rollers. "And I wore my grubbies just for the occasion."

"Go for it." Trini flashed a quick smile before someone across the room called her away.

Apparently, the hardware store had provided everything. Sandy found painter's tape and masking paper, which she quickly began to apply to the window frames.

"I love the way they designed this," Mary said, walking by with an eight-foot strip of baseboard molding. "Looks like there will be a small window for each section, once they hang the privacy curtains. It'll give nice light in the mornings."

"Thanks for talking me into coming," Sandy told her. "I'm glad to be part of the project."

Conversation came to a halt once the bam-bam-bam of the nail gun began. Within half an hour Mary had framed the door into the main building and the two outside exits. Mr. Perkins helped by carrying lengths of trim to her and she quickly attached the baseboards around the perimeter of the room. Sandy had begun painting the ceiling, working her way with the roller to the wall sections Mary had finished. Two other women in paint-spattered overalls joined her, and by noon the entire room had one coat of cheery pale yellow.

"We can take a break while this dries," Mary suggested as Sandy stood back, looking for spots she might have missed. "Trini says Gino's Pizza just delivered a huge stack of boxes for us."

"Good idea. A little lunch and I'll have the energy to come back and apply the second coat."

They washed their hands in the women's bathroom and returned to the dining hall where most of the volunteers were taking advantage of the pizzas while they were still hot. Grabbing a couple slices of pepperoni, Sandy followed Mary to the last two seats at a table near the door.

"Ah … my shoulders are gonna be speaking to me by tomorrow," Sandy said as she finished her first slice.

Mary looked as though no amount of physical labor daunted her, and no amount of pepperoni ever seemed to go to her waist. Not for the first time, Sandy thought about taking her friend up on the offer of a complimentary gym membership.

Mary was picking up her third slice when the door to the corridor opened and voices drifted through.

"You people are responsible for this," a man's voice shouted. "I follow the rules and I'm still robbed—that was my grandfather's watch!"

"Micah, slow down." Trini's voice rose to get his attention. "Show me where you were."

The rest of the conversation was lost as the speakers moved away and the door closed again.

Mary and Sandy exchanged a look. What was that all about?

Chapter 2

When they next saw Trini they'd finished lunch and tossed away their paper plates. Sandy was prying the lid off a fresh can of paint. Mary was ready to pitch in, but wondered whether she might be needed elsewhere. She was about to walk outside to see what the exterior crew was up to when she spotted Trini coming into the new room from the dining hall.

"How's it going?" Trini asked, eyeing the bright walls. "Looks good."

Sandy smiled and said she could get the second coat done by midafternoon.

"Trini—we couldn't help but hear the voice of that man who was so upset earlier. What's going on?"

Trini glanced around to be sure no one else was in earshot. For the moment, the three of them were the room's only occupants. "Another missing item, a family heirloom, and Micah is understandably upset."

"Sure. Anyone would be."

"We try to tell them not to bring valuables to the shelter, but most of them don't own anything of value. And if they do, what else will they do with it? It's not as if they have safe deposit boxes. If they had a home, they wouldn't be here." She ran her fingers through her hair. "We have a small safe in the office behind the reception desk and we always explain that they can leave money or small items in it. We keep it locked."

"But they don't do that?" Sandy asked.

"It's hard. They've been on the street and they're so untrusting. Some even wheel in grocery carts full of, basically, junk and they want to sleep with it right beside their bed. When space permits, we let them."

Mary spoke up. "You said *another* missing item. So this has happened before?"

Trini nodded sadly. "Unfortunately. In the past three months, I'd say a dozen items have been reported to me. Micah says it's his grandfather's gold pocket watch that's missing now."

"The police? Have they been called?"

"At first, I did. They take one look around and see ragged people with hopeless faces, and basically they just roll their eyes and remind me that the missing items can't be worth much. They take a report, but I don't get the feeling any effort goes toward recovering the lost items."

"Do you think it's another resident stealing these things?" Mary asked. "Who's new here?"

"Pfft—everyone's new. You know how it is. Some stay one or two nights, some come and go over the course of months. They aren't allowed to move in permanently, but some we think of as our 'regulars' and others we never see again."

"A gold watch sounds like something of value."

"I never saw the timepiece. It could have been a twenty-dollar thinly plated thing from the discount store, for all I know. As I mentioned, they never want to trust us to keep their stuff under lock and key."

"So Micah has imagined this as an heirloom?"

"I have no idea. It might actually be. People hang onto things until they absolutely have no other choice. One woman had a diamond ring her mother gave her. It wasn't anything spectacular, but it might have paid the rent on an apartment for a month or two. But she wouldn't part with it. Said it was the last item of her mother's, said it reminded her of a time when life was better. I couldn't push the issue. I was just happy she let us lock it in the safe until she was ready to move on."

"So sad," Mary said. She noticed Sandy had tears in her eyes.

Trini took a deep breath. "Look, I'll let you get back to your painting so you can go home at a reasonable hour. Thanks so much for all you're doing."

They both hugged her. "Do you need help again tomorrow?" Sandy asked.

"Sure—if you'd like to hang curtains and set up beds, it would go a long way toward moving people in once we get our occupancy permit."

By three p.m. the large room glowed with its second coat of pale yellow, and the workers had peeled off layers of clothing, down to T-shirts now as the day had warmed to the mid-70s. Mary had grown up here in the Valley; Decembers that felt like spring seemed normal, but many of the volunteers were snowbirds from the upper Midwest and they reveled in the mild winter temperatures. Those who felt the Christmas season wasn't complete without snow simply went back home to spend the holidays with family.

"You've been kind of quiet," she said to Sandy as they walked out to the Ford.

"Thinking about what Trini said about the thefts at the shelter. I can't believe someone would steal from homeless people."

Mary pulled out of the lot onto Superstition Boulevard and aimed toward the 202 Loop to deliver Sandy back to Phoenix. "They're not all sweet and honest and simply down on their luck, you know. There's a strong survival instinct among them. If a shiny object looks like it might bring a few bucks at a pawn shop, and if that money could buy meals for your kids … or, and I hate to say this, a bottle of booze …"

"Maybe so. I just wonder why this rash of thefts all at once. Surely Trini has seen that kind of thing a lot in the years she's worked here. But she specifically said these thefts of valuables had happened over the last three months."

Mary nodded. "True."

"So, what if we were to do a little investigating of our own? She said the police are basically blowing it off. Maybe we could learn something and catch the thief."

"Sure. Let's ask around when we go back tomorrow."

Sandy sat back in her seat, already thinking of questions she would ask Micah if she could catch up with him in the morning. By the time Mary dropped her off she had several things in mind.

"I'll drive tomorrow, if you'd like," Sandy said as she got out of the car. They set a time and Mary headed toward her own apartment.

* * *

"What's all this?" Mary exclaimed the next day, sliding into the passenger seat. "Looks like Santa's sleigh exploded in your car."

Sandy laughed. "The dollar-store folks were happy to see me last night. The gift bags contain little stuff for kids—socks and undies, along with some crayons and puzzles and stuff. I'll give them to Trini to hand out as she sees fit. The boxes … well, I went on a little sorting-and-cleaning binge among my holiday decorations. You can't believe how much I've accumulated over the years."

Mary glanced over her shoulder into the back of Sandy's Mazda. "Uh, yeah, I think I can."

"So I figured, who needs more than one Christmas tree? A lot of the garland and tinsel is stuff that I used to put up all over the house, back when I was younger and more energetic. I haven't used it in a few years, so someone else might as well get some enjoyment out of it. I just hope Trini doesn't see it all as a pain in the neck and a bunch of junk to store away after the holidays."

"She'll love it, I'm sure," Mary said.

Thirty minutes later they pulled up to the front door at Heaven Sent. Trini greeted them and exclaimed over the bounty. "Just put all the decorations in the reception area," she said. "I'll stash the presents in the storage closet behind the desk. Won't it be wonderful to have things for the kids as the big day draws closer?"

After the fourth load of decorations Mary turned to Sandy. "Are you *sure* all this was just spare stuff from home?"

"Well, okay, I admit it. I called Pen and Gracie when I

got home, and they each came up with a bit more."

Mary laughed as they stacked the last of the boxes. "Well, you certainly were a busy lady last night. And a great organizer!"

The new dorm room at the back of the building revealed its own sort of bounty. Mattresses and box springs were stacked against the walls, and metal bedframes lay on the floor.

"I put a few of the muscular men to work this morning, carrying all this in from the storage building out back," Trini said. "All we need now is to bolt the frames together and set them up."

"Easy-peasy," Mary told her. She had a couple of open-end wrenches at the ready.

"Trini, is there any news about Micah's missing watch?" Sandy asked, holding two sections of metal frame in place while Mary inserted the bolts.

"Nothing."

"Were the residents' possessions searched? Well, if that's even ethical to do."

"No, and it's not really cool to go through people's things. But I did ask if anyone knew anything about the watch last night when we had most everyone assembled for their dinner of beans and cornbread. No one admitted knowledge of the theft. A few seemed upset that it happened to Micah—he's been helpful and friendly to everyone."

"Something as small as a watch or piece of jewelry, wouldn't the owner keep it on their person all the time?" Mary asked.

"Normally, yes. They'll wear their rings into the shower, even, but that's hard to do with a watch, especially an older, non-waterproof one."

"So, if someone watched until Micah went into the shower ..."

"The stalls are two-part—there's a place to lay clothing on a bench and keep it dry, then the shower itself, with a plastic curtain dividing the two spaces. The outer door to each stall locks for privacy."

"So it would be unlikely, but not impossible, for someone to sneak through the shower room and rifle through the clothing while the resident is behind the curtain."

"If they don't lock the stall door, then I suppose so. I can't think of any other time they can't keep an eye on their stuff, unless it's while they're asleep. But again, the valuable item would most likely be clenched in hand, hidden under a pillow, or worn pinned to pajamas."

"We're assuming another resident is stealing these items," Mary said. She had completed bolting the four sides of the first bedframe and set it in place. "Maybe outsiders come and go during the day?"

Trini shook her head. "Not normally. But we've had lots of volunteers around during the construction, and we don't always have someone at the reception desk. Depends on who I've got for help."

"Can I talk to Micah?" Sandy asked. "Maybe he's got some idea of who took the watch."

Trini looked skeptical as she took over Sandy's position and they moved to the next frame. "Sure. He was here at breakfast, but you may have to look around. During the week he usually goes out, but this being Sunday I'm not sure where he'll be. He's about five-ten, clean shaven, wearing a blue Patagonia jacket."

Sandy found him at one of the computers in the dining hall. He looked up when she took a chair next to him. She noticed he'd been browsing real estate listings.

"Micah? Hey, I'm Sandy. Um, I happened to overhear what you were telling Trini yesterday about your missing watch."

"Yeah? You know something about that?" His brown eyes narrowed.

"No, unfortunately. But my friend and I were hoping to help. We're sort of amateur detectives and we've helped recover some other things." She didn't say that a pocket watch didn't exactly fall into the same category as a million dollar diamond necklace; to this man his heirloom might be every bit as valuable. "I just think it's rotten that anyone would steal from people who—"

"People who are homeless. You can say it." Micah ran a hand through dark hair that had grown over his ears and to the collar of his shirt.

She noticed his shirt was of fine quality and his slacks still held creases. The jacket was a good brand and showed no wear. This guy had not shopped at the Goodwill store, and he'd probably not been on the streets.

"You're right. I don't belong here," he said, noticing that she'd given his clothing the once-over. "Until three months ago I was living in Scottsdale, had a thriving real estate business and a family."

"What happened? Sorry—maybe you don't want to say."

He shrugged. "Real estate market went bust, banks took away everything. One by one, my investment properties foreclosed. Wife stuck with me until they came after our house, then she packed up the kids and took off for her parents' place in Iowa. At least the kids will get a white Christmas this year." His voice grew rough and he cleared his throat.

"Wow, I'm so sorry. Everything's gone?"

"I kept my car, but cops are suspicious of a guy living on the street in a BMW. Sold it for barely enough to pay off the balance."

"And your grandfather's pocket watch was kind of the only thing of value you had left."

"Yep, both my parents are gone, no siblings. In-laws weren't too sympathetic—they told Cassie I didn't know what I was doing with my investment strategies, and they were happy to take her and the kids as long as it was without me." He paused. "I'm not here long term. I find the right deal and I'm outta here. I'll rebuild everything I once had."

Sandy let a moment pass, hoping the bitter words would leave the air. "The watch. Do you know when it was taken? I mean, was there an opportunity for someone to pick it up?"

"I kept it in my coat or pants pocket all the time. Locked the door when I showered, slept with it under my pillow. Yeah, I know, like a puppy when it leaves the litter and you have to put a clock in bed with it for company. The tick-tick was reassuring somehow."

"Could someone have picked your pocket?"

"Possibly," he admitted. "I worked enough in downtown Phoenix to be pretty aware of people pushing against me or bumping me. But I don't know. Can't swear to anything. This place is open all hours during the day. I think they lock the doors at eleven, but anyone can come and go. Trini needs to keep someone at the front desk all the time, keep a log of who's walking in. I told her that."

A stooped woman with frizzy gray hair and a shopping cart filled with blankets, rags, cardboard, and aluminum cans pushed past, eyeing the now-closed breakfast buffet tables hopefully.

"Okay, maybe it wouldn't be easy to get *every* person to sign in."

Sandy shifted in her chair. "We'll ask around, see if we can find out anything about your watch. I'm really sorry that happened."

He gave her a look that said, *yeah, whatever.*

Chapter 3

Sandy passed the grocery cart woman who was muttering something under her breath.

"Sorry the breakfast service is finished," she said, handing her a cereal bar she'd stuck in her pocket for a mid-morning snack. "Maybe this will tide you over."

The woman snatched the packet without meeting Sandy's eyes, then wheeled the squeaking cart back toward the open doorway to the hall.

In the new room, Mary now had four bedframes assembled and two other volunteers were setting box springs and mattresses on them.

"Did you find Micah?" she asked.

"I did. Didn't come up with anything substantial in the way of clues. He seems different than a lot of the residents, although it's a story I've seen and heard before. Played the real estate market on borrowed money, overextended himself, and lost it all. We saw it happen a lot at the bank, and unfortunately the banking laws allowed it to happen. We made loans we shouldn't have, let people borrow more than they should have. I regret that—a lot."

Trini walked up just then. "Regret what?"

Sandy waved it off. "Irrelevant to what I wanted to learn today. The only clue Micah could provide was the possibility that his pocket had been picked. Did you and he discuss that at all?"

Trini waited until the other volunteers had walked outside, and she kept her voice low. "He ranted a bit about how we need to do more to track who's in and out of here. He's ready to pin the theft on any of the other residents."

"But you don't think so."

"I'm not so sure. There seems to be a sort of code of honor among the homeless we see. All of them are down and out, and they know what the others are going through. There's more empathy than competition among them. Micah comes from a world where everything was about the *stuff*, about how much you accumulated. It's probably natural that his first reaction is to believe someone with less than he has would want to take his prized possession. It's sad, yes, but I'm reserving judgment. Since Micah got here we've had a constant parade of construction workers, delivery people, volunteers such as the cooks and cleaners. I'm not pointing a finger at anyone, but you can see there are a lot of possibilities." She patted Sandy's shoulder and walked toward the dining room.

"True," said Mary. "It's a transient population all the way around. It'll be hard to trace this one small item."

Sandy slumped. "I know. But it's more than just one, according to Trini. I don't want to give up already." She looked around the large room. "Looks like your assistants have abandoned you. Shall we go out to the storage building and bring in some more mattresses. We can have this job knocked out in another couple hours and I'll spring for lunch, your choice of restaurant."

"Deal." Mary stuck her wrenches in the back pocket of her jeans and they headed toward the south-side exit door. "The storage building is around back."

Sandy followed and they came to a tan-stuccoed building with two double-sized garage doors and a walk-through door facing the drive that circled the main building. With ample space, it served as the receiving area for deliveries. The women could easily see how Trini had her hands full, trying to be everywhere and keep an eye on everything at once.

"Obviously, theft is a concern out here, too," said Mary when she tried the door and found it locked. "I guess we'll need to track down Trini to get in."

Backtracking to where they'd last seen the director, they found the dining hall empty but they caught the sound of voices from the front. Trini stood at the reception desk, facing a couple who must have just come in.

The man wore deep blue, loose-fitting pants and tunic with two strands of white crystal beads and some type of amulet hanging from them. His dark brown hair hung to his shoulders in soft waves. At more than six feet tall, he cut an imposing figure.

The woman stood about a foot shorter, dressed in emerald green and, despite the hippie image, Mary had a feeling the blonde highlights in her waves had been carefully applied, as had her makeup. She placed both of the pair in their early forties.

"Sorry—we didn't mean to interrupt," Sandy said.

"It's okay." Trini looked somewhat relieved at the break in conversation. "Meet the neighbors."

The man stepped forward. "Hello, gracious souls. I'm Orion. This is Sunshine."

Of course she is, thought Mary.

The pair stepped forward with a prayer-hands bow.

"Neighbors. You live out here?" Mary asked.

"We founded the Rising Moon, located on the adjacent property," he said.

"Oh, we don't live in the Temple," Sunshine piped up. "Our home is out back. We love to be close to our followers."

Mary detected a distinct hint of the South in Sunshine's voice, perhaps the overdrawn syllables of west Texas.

"Do you have a spiritual home?" Sunshine asked. "Our doors are open to all."

"I'm fine on that count," Mary said.

Sandy turned to Trini. "We were going to bring in some more mattresses, but the storage building is locked. I assume you're the keeper of the keys?"

"I am." Trini practically leapt from behind the desk. "Let me give you a hand. Sorry, Orion, Sunshine. We've kind of got a lot going on here right now. If you'll excuse me."

She gestured toward the front door until they had no choice but to take the hint and leave.

"Talk about excellent timing," Trini said as the three women made their way through the kitchen and out the back door. "You rescued me from those two. The minute they walk in they start bending my ear. It's happened constantly ever since they rented the empty building over there and parked that ratty old bus."

For the first time Mary noticed the view from Heaven

Sent looked into the neighboring property and a huge paved parking lot. Taking up four slots, an old school bus, painted sky blue and decorated with images of planets and stars and the moon, sat near the building. An extension cord and water hose apparently provided utility hookups for the makeshift housing. A chain link fence separated the properties but did nothing to hide the view.

"Tacky, huh." Trini reached into her pocket for keys to the storage building. "I mean, we jumped through all kinds of hoops to get city zoning to allow a homeless shelter here, gave tons of assurances that our place wouldn't degrade the neighborhood—and look at that thing!"

Sandy spoke up. "Your building is beautiful, Trini."

"Because we make the effort. We keep the shrubbery trimmed, the building clean, and we don't allow anyone to sleep outside or park their carts where they can be seen from the street."

"Have you talked to the zoning department about the bus?"

"I have. I was told they'll send someone around, but if the vehicle can't be seen from the street there's most likely nothing they can do about it. This isn't a high-class neighborhood anyway, so I doubt anyone else has complained."

She flipped on a light switch and pointed to the area where plastic-wrapped new mattresses had been stacked. Sandy and Mary grabbed each end of one and started the trek back to the new addition.

"So, what is this Temple of the Rising Moon, anyway?" Sandy asked as they set the first mattress on its frame.

Trini rolled her eyes. "I went over and attended one of their services when they first moved in. Too hippy-dippy for my taste. The one useful thing they are claiming is that they're raising money to build housing. I suppose sort of a copycat of Habitat for Humanity, maybe? They put on quite a spiel, but I don't know—something about it feels *off*."

Chapter 4

Lunch turned out to be salads at Brennan's, a casual place, since both women still wore their work clothes.

"Something Trini said has got me wondering," Sandy said after taking her first sip of iced tea. "The hippies, for lack of a better term, moved in right about the time the thefts began at the shelter. Maybe there's a connection."

Mary raised an eyebrow. "I don't know … For all their flowy clothing, earth-child names, and long hair, Orion and Sunshine don't strike me as underprivileged—I should say, as poor *enough* to steal from those who have nothing."

"But they seem to come and go from the shelter any time they want. Trini admits she can't watch the front desk all the time and the volunteers tend to only monitor the door during times the homeless people are showing up to claim beds for the night." Sandy stabbed a chunk of lettuce from her Chinese chicken salad.

"And they draw huge crowds. Trini told me the parking lots—front and back—are filled at least three nights a week. We have no idea what types of people they're bringing in. Maybe some of their followers are wandering over and rummaging through the people's possessions at the shelter. It wouldn't be hard to do, sneaking in while everyone else is in the dining room." Mary's eyes glittered. "We could become spies! Dress down and hang out a bit. See who comes and goes."

"We'll need more than just you and me if we plan to watch people in the temple and at the shelter."

"Bring Pen and Gracie and Amber into it, you mean?"

"Why not?" Sandy gave a huge smile.

The group of friends had caught an investment scammer, a cheating ex-husband, and had taken down an international jewel theft ring. Surely this couldn't be any more complicated than those cases. The Heist Ladies would go into action again!

"I'll call them now," Sandy said, pushing her nearly empty plate aside.

* * *

Penelope Fitzpatrick's spacious home on Camelback Mountain in Scottsdale was the chosen meeting place. Pen had stashed away the boxes of Christmas decorations she'd intended to spend the evening with. There was no need to clean—living alone meant her tasteful furnishings rarely accumulated more than a micron of dust. As an added treat she had come up with an array of snacks and wine for her guests.

"My publisher sent two lovely bottles when my last

book reached the top of the charts. It's a good Bordeaux," she said as she opened the first. "I needed an occasion and some friends present so I could justify opening it."

She poured the rich red wine into glasses and Sandy handed them around as the others reached for the selection of fine cheeses.

"After the day I've had with my kids, I'm ready for this," said Gracie Nelson, raising her glass. She had pulled her long brown hair into a messy bun at the top of her head, and her lack of makeup suggested she'd rushed from the house after turning the two teens over to her husband.

Mary glanced around at the faces of her friends. "Are we ready to take on a new case?"

"Tell us about this," Pen asked. "Sandy, you mentioned thefts at a homeless shelter?"

"That's how it began," Sandy said. She went on to explain what little they knew about the thefts and then told about the oddball neighbors next to the place. "Trini Newton, the director at Heaven Sent, said her first thought about the newcomers was that they're just another pair of snowbirds with an unusual twist to the reason for their stay. Could be—maybe they'll be gone by May when the weather turns hot again."

"Or, maybe they're onto a hot moneymaker with this idea of fundraising to build low-income housing," Gracie suggested.

"We also had that thought," Mary said, "although they're living pretty low-key in a converted school bus parked at their rented 'temple'."

Amber Zeckis, the youngest member of the group at twenty-four, spoke up. "I'm kind of intrigued with this angle—the couple and their religion thing. They sound like some of the friends my parents tell me about, people they knew before I was even born. I'll go to this temple and see what the deal is, if you want me to."

Gracie laughed. "Just promise us you won't get roped in."

Amber gave her a sassy look. "Huh-uh, not my thing. You know I'm skeptical of anything that can't be broken down into computer code."

"I think it's brilliant," Pen said. "Amber's got the correct look—those curls of yours can't be tamed, no matter what—and you're the right age, I'm guessing. You shall play the role perfectly."

"Pen's right," Sandy said. "I can't see myself there—all corporate-looking with my neat little blonde bob—or Pen, who is far too elegant to pull off a part at either a homeless shelter or an ashram. Amber is what Goldilocks would call 'just right.'"

Pen huffed a little. She had, after all, donned disguises in the past and managed to conceal her British upbringing, her perfectly turned out makeup and hair, and her designer wardrobe.

"We'll keep you in the background, for when we need a woman of the right age and elegance."

"Based on the glimpse of myself I caught in that mirror over there, I could pass for homeless," Gracie offered. "I mean, if that's needed. Just saying."

"So, we're agreed? We'll team up and investigate these thefts?" Mary asked.

Nods all around.

"Good. So, I've made up some assignments." Mary had already started a notebook. "Amber—church service, or temple, or whatever that place is. They hold their gatherings on Tuesday, Thursday, and Saturday evenings."

Amber gave a thumbs-up.

"Sandy and I will take the first shift as volunteers at the shelter. While one of us mans the front desk, the other will quietly hang around the sleeping quarters while everyone is at dinner, looking out for anybody who might be sneaking in to pilfer something. Depending on how it goes, we can enlist Gracie. If somebody is watching us watching them, they may be less suspicious if there are different faces from time to time."

"Pen, you are our ace in the hole who will be ready when we need your very special touch."

"We can start tomorrow," Mary said.

Pen raised her wine glass. "In that case, here's to us and our success. May the Heist Ladies solve this crime and bring the dastardly culprits to justice!"

Chapter 5

The next afternoon when Sandy and Mary arrived, Trini seemed ecstatic to have the extra help.

Pulling out a spiral bound notebook, she said, "We try to get everyone to register—and I use the word loosely—just so we know who's here for the night. It's not mandatory. Some are very uncomfortable giving their names, some give first names only and that's okay, and there are some cases where I wonder if the person is actually literate enough to write his or her name. Handle each with compassion and if they won't sign the book, just make a little note with the basics—male or female, approximate age, clothing. We had a kitchen fire once and it was crazy and scary trying to round up everyone outside when we evacuated the building. I'm not trying to pry into their lives, but I need to know that we get everyone out safely if something like that ever happens again."

"Makes sense," both women agreed.

"If one of you wants to take that job, I can use the other to help serve dinner from five o'clock until seven."

"I'd be glad to do the food," Sandy said, "but I'd also like the chance to keep an eye on the sleeping quarters, to see if anyone is poking around where they shouldn't be."

Trini thought about it for a moment. "For tonight, until they get used to seeing you around, how about if I do the dorm room duty? In a day or two, we can switch places on that."

Mary stepped behind the desk, wrote the date at the top of a fresh page in the notebook, and turned it to face incoming visitors.

"Food service starts soon, and they'll come rolling in quickly," Trini warned. "Sandy, this way with me."

She led the way down the hall, peering into the empty men's dorm and then the women's where she asked a young mother with two kids to sign in at the desk before supper.

"We've got chicken pot pie tonight, always a favorite," she told Sandy. "It's baked in large flat pans, so you'll dish out a portion to each person. Try to make them about equal in size, like so, although anyone is free to come back for more after everyone has had some. Shouldn't become an issue—they're used to the way we do things here. Plus, thanks to a generous donation from the farmer's market, there's salad and rolls."

The young woman and her children were the first to appear, and four others came in close behind. Sandy picked up a plate and began serving the fragrant dish. Another volunteer added salad and a roll to each plate. Nearly every resident said thank-you when handed the meal.

The third person in line was Micah, the fourth a man

Sandy hadn't seen before. He had a day's growth of beard and his clothes were decidedly dirty and tattered. She wanted to give him a larger portion of the food but wasn't certain how many other hungry people were yet to come.

"What's your name?" she asked.

"Ron." His voice was rough and he wouldn't meet her eye.

"Well, Ron, if there's extra food after the others are served, you're welcome to come back for more. If you want to."

Her fellow server gave her a look. Maybe the offer shouldn't be done. She looked up to see the next person in line, a young woman with bright orange hair.

More than two hours later, her feet and legs aching, Sandy hauled the last of the empty baking pans to the kitchen where someone else took it and dunked it into a sink full of soapy water. Sandy washed her hands and went to find Mary.

"Still a few checking in," Mary said, "but it looks like the beds are pretty well filled."

Trini had come in and overheard this last. "That's good. I like it when we get everyone inside early in the evening. I'll set up the TV in the dining hall with a movie. Most will stay to watch but some just prefer to get to their beds and read or get some extra sleep."

"Mind if we hang around and compare notes afterward?" Sandy asked.

"Exactly what I had in mind." Trini bustled away but returned fifteen minutes later.

"Okay, things should be quiet for awhile." She opened the door behind the reception desk to reveal a furnished room. "Welcome to the manager's abode."

It was a tiny bed-sit with a couch, dresser and television.

A small desk in the corner held Trini's personal computer, and another door apparently led to a private bath.

"You actually live here?" Sandy asked.

"During my shift. I do have an apartment in Phoenix, but while I'm working my ten days on duty, I sleep over. The sofa bed isn't too bad, actually. My co-director works the next ten days, then I'm back on for ten. It gives each of us a nice break, a chance to experience what for us is 'normal' life. I can't complain. None of our residents has another life to escape to. Those dorm rooms—those *are* their normal."

She pulled out the desk chair and invited the others to choose between it or the sofa. Mary had carried the spiral notebook inside with her.

"In the slower moments I looked back through the pages," she said. "You marked the dates when the thefts were reported, so I thought I might find a pattern of who was here each of those dates. Then I quickly realized it wasn't going to be quite that simple."

"There's a lot of coming and going," Trini admitted. "Sometimes we have the same residents for a week or two, other times they'll stay one or two nights, leave, and come back a month later."

Sandy piped up. "How about if we put the data on a spreadsheet? A pattern might emerge that way."

"Great idea, as long as you have someone with the skill and time to put that together," Trini said. "It's not me, for sure. I can write a fairly decent business letter and make my way around Facebook. For computer skills that's about my limit."

Mary grinned. "We have just the girl for this."

"During dinner, did you notice anything unusual going on in the dorm areas?" Sandy asked.

"Just the normal amount of settling in. They claim a bed and leave something to mark it, a jacket or duffle bag, sometimes a shopping cart. We could pop in now while they're watching the movie, take another look around."

On the pretense of making sure every bed had enough blankets and a pillow, they tapped on the door to the men's dorm and walked in. Two men were inside, one lounging on a bed, the other rummaging through a backpack that had once been yellow but was now a grimy shade of gray.

"Hey, K.C., how's it going?" Trini greeted. "Want an extra blanket tonight?"

The grizzled old man was skinny enough to blow away in a stiff breeze, but he was apparently content with his layers of clothing and the single blanket on his bed. He grunted and shook his head at the offer. The man on the bed was perusing a battered copy of *Road and Track* with ripped covers. Sandy recognized him as Ron, the one who had come through the food line early in the evening. He had kicked off his boots but the grimy socks he now rested on the bedding weren't much cleaner. Aside from his filthy clothing he looked reasonably healthy. She wondered if he was actually reading the magazine or just browsing the pictures. He, too, declined a blanket although Sandy could feel his eyes following as they circled the room. She supposed newcomers stood out.

In the women's dorm, more of the residents had opted out of television and were settling in. The young mother had settled her two little daughters into one bed. Even with limited resources she had made certain their faces were clean and they changed from their street clothing into pajamas. Between them, they cuddled a teddy bear that was missing an eye and a lot of its stuffing but both girls were talking to it as if it were their best little friend.

Walking outside as they were leaving, Sandy and Mary paused to get Trini's assessment.

"Old K.C., he's been on the streets a long time. We only see him at the shelter on the colder winter nights or the very hottest of summer. He grabs little handyman jobs where he can. A lot of AJ residents know him and I suspect someone allows him to sleep in a camper or shed a lot of the time, so he's halfway self-sufficient. Ron's in and out, a semi-regular here. He sleeps here one or two nights a week, doesn't say much. People say he's on the corners a lot, cardboard sign, scrounging quarters and dollar bills when he can. He travels light, and I suspect he makes the rounds of the shelters in the area so he doesn't wear out his welcome at any one place. I can name a dozen more of them who kind of follow that pattern. As the nights get colder, I just hope they're not sleeping on the street."

She paused. "Cicely and her kids … I'm pretty sure she's fleeing an abuser. She was completely freaked out the first night she showed up. I've hinted that she find a battered women's shelter where she can get counseling and some help to find a job, but she seems content here. When her thirty nights are up, I'll need to see if I can help her with a better alternative but, for now, it's good that she's here. Most likely she rode the bus as far as she could get from the husband, and this is where she landed."

"Wow. So many stories. I can't believe what a soft life I've led," said Sandy.

Mary gripped the spiral notebook. "I'll make copies of this so Amber can put the data on computer and we'll get the book back to you."

Trini nodded solemnly, gave each of them a big hug, and thanked them for their help.

Chapter 6

The ping of the alarm on Amber's watch brought her out of her haze of data entry. Hours of inputting dates and names into a spreadsheet, and she hadn't even taken a break for lunch. But she was nearly done and should soon be able to play around with the data and, hopefully, come up with the cross-references Sandy hoped to find.

Meanwhile, the alarm reminded her to get ready in time to drive out to Apache Junction and find this Temple of the Rising Moon. From what Sandy and Mary had said, the evening service promised to be an interesting experience. She rose from her chair and did a few stretches to get the kinks out, shut down her computer, and headed for the bedroom.

Her normal taste ran toward stretchy fabrics and exercise wear, but a scan through her closet showed she still owned a voluminous broomstick skirt her mother had sent one year for her birthday. It made her feel squatty and even shorter than her petite five-foot-one, so she never wore it. A perfect disguise. She pulled it off the hanger and added a T-shirt, covered by a blocky ribbon jacket—another gift from Mom—and the outfit seemed okay.

She put everything on, shook her hair out of its bun, and took a look in the mirror. With her caramel skin, curly hair, and the ill-fitting clothing she might come close to blending in at this 'moon temple' or whatever it was. At least no one who knew her would recognize this version. She added three strands of beads for effect and left her apartment.

How far out in the sticks *is* Apache Junction, she began to wonder as the miles peeled away. The population of the metro area grew by the year, and in winter it became almost overwhelming as snowbirds crammed in and the traffic became impossible. Her parents had been after her for years to move back home to Santa Fe, but that wasn't really her style either. She'd loved living in a young, hip college city where jobs for computer geniuses were plentiful.

Her GPS informed her she was arriving at her destination in one-quarter mile, and she spotted the massive building before she got there.

Temple? Okay, she thought as she pulled into a crowded parking lot. By all appearances it had probably been a warehouse, but the addition of an elaborate wooden sign and strategically placed up-lighting to showcase the palm trees that flanked the double front doors helped create a certain ambiance.

People were streaming into the building, and a tour bus arrived at the front door to discharge more. Amber cruised rows of parked cars without seeing a single open spot, but a man in an orange vest caught her attention as he directed traffic around to the back of the building.

This is a bigger deal than I ever imagined.

The back lot was rapidly filling, as well. She parked, locked her car, and filed along a walkway with the crowd to enter the building.

A raised stage had been constructed up front, with deep purple draperies as a backdrop and huge pots of white lilies highlighted by spotlights. Tiers of raised seating meant there wasn't a bad seat in the house. A thousand people would have an unobstructed view of Orion, or Sunshine, or whoever was going to speak to them. Amber tucked herself into a seat in the middle of a row. She was here merely to observe, not to call attention to herself.

The lights blinked subtly a couple of times and the soft background music rose in a crescendo as the lights dimmed fully. The crowd went silent. All movement stopped.

Amber consciously let out her breath. It was as if the entire assemblage had fallen under a trance and not a word had yet been spoken.

Suddenly, a soft pink spotlight came on at the back of the hall. It fell on a beautiful blonde woman in a long white gown. She carried a wireless microphone and when her voice came through, it filled the space with a melodic, soft tone.

"Welcome." She came down the aisle from behind the crowd, floating toward the front. People actually gasped as she passed their seats. Her gown shimmered with ethereal light.

A woman seated next to Amber breathed "an angel" as the vision passed them.

"Welcome," said the angel once more. She glided up a short set of steps to the stage, where she paused to face the section of seats to her left. A deferential bow. "Thank you," she told the people.

Then to the center of the stage and the same reverence for those seated in front. The same words and motions then repeated to those on the right. At last, she stood in the center of the stage and looked up, taking in the entire audience. "Thank you, everyone. We are so grateful for your presence here tonight."

She had every one of them in the palm of her hand.

"My name is Sunshine, and I want to share some amazing things with you this evening. We are doing some amazing things—all of us, you and I. We each have the opportunity to make an incredible difference in someone's life."

She went on in this vein for another minute or two, but not long enough for the assembly to become impatient. Amber caught a flicker of movement at the backdrop curtain, and a moment later Sunshine introduced—with a flourish—her husband, Orion.

From the folds of the curtain, out stepped a tall man, also dressed completely in white—gauzy pants, long tunic, sandals. While Sunshine's gown practically glittered, Orion's clothing emanated an almost opalescent glow. Was it a quality of the fabric or of the lighting? His appearance was completed by long, wavy brown hair that hung to his shoulders and an amethyst-colored medallion, held in the center of his chest by a glittering strand of purple beads. Amber watched in fascination as he raised both arms then brought them down to a prayer position and bowed from the waist to salute his audience.

"We are indeed blessed, especially at this holiday season," Orion began. His voice was low and cultured, with a hint of an accent that hinted at classical theater training.

"I am particularly blessed, my friends, because but for the grace of God I would at this moment be … dead."

He let the word hang in the air long enough for the collective gasp to whoosh through the room.

"Yes, that is true. I died … four months ago."

Sunshine, at least ten inches shorter than her husband, stood to the side, gazing devotedly up into his face. She nodded and blinked back some tears when he made his pronouncement.

"Yes, my good people, I was a dead man but I was called back to continue serving. It was not my time to leave this earth."

He went into a tale of horrific chest pain and being taken to a medical facility. He claimed to have risen from his body and hovered overhead while a doctor pronounced him dead, followed by a vision of a bright light and a voice saying he was not to leave yet for he had more work to do here on earth. His voice rose at the dramatic point and grew soft in all the right places during his story. If Amber had not grown up among the many actors her parents hosted as friends, she might have hung on every word, just the way the rest of the audience appeared to be doing.

Orion ended his story with head bowed, apparently depleted by the telling, and Sunshine took over.

"And so, my friends and loved ones here tonight," she said. "This experience taught us much. One, we are grateful for every day we have together." She took his hand. "And two, we have a calling to do great things. We left that hospital, my friends, and we began our true mission in this life—to build houses for those who do not have a decent place to live. Our first action was to give our own home to a deserving family. Yes, we moved a few necessary items into a bus we refurbished as our home, and we gave away the four-bedroom split-level house in the suburbs of Houston."

A pause for effect. "And now we travel the highways of our great nation, stopping when a place calls out to us, gathering good people such as yourselves to help the cause. In a few minutes we'll pass the hat, and we will cherish and put to good use anything you can contribute to this worthy cause."

As she spoke large screens, which had previously been unseen in the darkness, lit up with a series of scenes. Houses under construction showed smiling people hammering away and erecting wooden framing. Electricians and plumbers gladly gave of their time, volunteers painted the walls, and happy families stood outside finished homes, smiling and hugging.

"*This*, dear friends, is the work we do. We have built homes in ten states with the money we've raised, and we intend to give free homes to needy people in all fifty states before the end of next year!"

Applause began near the back of the auditorium and quickly spread.

"Can you see the goal?" Sunshine called out. "Can you feel it?"

The noise intensified.

"Can I get an Amen on that!" She was pacing the stage now, calling out to the crowd, whipping up their enthusiasm. Her angelic gown flowed, but gone were the subtle moves. Now she was aggressively inviting participation. The music swelled.

Orion walked to the edges of the stage to make eye contact with those in the first rows, hands together at his chest. People who received his blessing began to pull out tissues and wipe their eyes.

The music dropped in volume and Sunshine stopped precisely in the middle of the stage. "Folks, it's Christmas. Can you imagine those poor people who have no homes in which to hang their stockings, no warm hearth, not even a kitchen where they can share the joy of baking cookies with their children or preparing a holiday meal? There's a homeless shelter right next to us here—we can help those folks. Even a dollar, or five, or twenty makes a difference. A hundred or two is a godsend. Help us, please?" Her voice cracked and she carefully wiped an elegantly manicured fingertip beneath each eye.

Precisely on cue men in white pants and shirts appeared at the ends of the rows of seats. Baskets on long poles paused at every seat, waiting until the occupant dropped something inside.

Chapter 7

Sunshine opened a cupboard above their two-burner stove and a box of instant coffee packets fell, hitting her forehead. She flung it aside, landing the box squarely in her husband's lap.

"I gotta get off this freakin' bus!" she shouted.

"Careful, baby … voices …" He set the box of coffee on their tiny dinette table, barely looking up from his tablet where he was tapping numbers into the calculator.

A growl formed low in her throat. "No one's around," she stage-whispered through gritted teeth.

The crowd had dispersed more than two hours ago, and beyond the chain link fence the homeless shelter looked buttoned down, with only a few night lights showing.

"Honey, you know you have to take care of your throat," he cautioned.

"Really? That's the important thing? I have to be able to speak in an angelic voice and can't risk getting a scratchy throat." She opened the cupboard again, pulling out the contents, slamming boxes of cereal and granola bars, a can of green beans, and a packet of peppermint candy onto the table. "I need a drink."

Her mood settled when she came to the bottle of scotch. All the real glasses were dirty—they owned exactly two of each item of dinnerware—so she poured a paper cup half full of the golden liquid and downed a large mouthful.

He sighed and set the tablet aside. When he stood, his head grazed the ceiling, barely missing the dim, forty-watt light fixture. He set a gentle hand on her shoulder and turned her to face him, gathering her in his arms and pulling her close. She couldn't very well keep up the nagging with a face full of his chest hair, and it gave him a moment to make a plan.

"You're right. We both need a break. Let's do one of our getaway weekends," he said, patting her on the back.

She tilted her head back sharply enough to get a look at his face. "Greece? You know how I love Greece."

"Baby, baby … you know this gig is too good to walk away from yet. We've got a potential audience in the millions and we've barely tapped them yet. The snowbirds will be here at least through the spring and we need to make the best of it." He nuzzled her hair and kissed her forehead. "Plus, where else could we go where their idea of a bad winter day is when it clouds up and rains for a few hours? We've got it made here."

She looked at their surroundings. "It's just the damn bus."

"Designed to your specifications. We have to keep the

hippie vibe, but you've got *every* convenience Alonso could work in—espresso machine, microwave, Egyptian cotton bed linens and our custom pillow-top mattress … which we could put to use right now …"

Her expression softened and she entwined her fingers through his.

Too bad she'd changed from her stage gown to these unpeelable Spandex things. There was something he loved about seducing her in angel mode.

"I know how to get you to relax," he said, slipping a fingertip under the edge of the tight bra-like thingy. "And then I'm going to make us a reservation at one of those classy resort spas in Scottsdale, where we will live the high life for a few days."

Her expression told him she'd like to ditch the bus and move into the resort permanently. He planted a trail of kisses across her neck that were designed to remove those thoughts from her mind. As he steered her toward the back of the bus, he kicked the big cardboard box full of tonight's cash under the table.

Chapter 8

I'd be surprised if this is the pair ripping off little keepsakes from the homeless shelter. They took in at least five hundred bucks from the row where I sat, just what I glimpsed. Some people were writing checks."

The Heist Ladies had gathered at Gracie's home.

Sandy punched numbers into the calculator on her phone. "So, *if* they get the labor donated to build these houses, as implied by the smiling faces of all those happy volunteers, and they get materials at cost, as hinted by the corporate sponsor names you said you saw on the screens, they're bringing in enough to build a house every few days."

Gracie plucked two tortilla chips from a bowl and passed it along. "So where are the houses?"

"Good question. What they show in the presentation could be located anywhere. They claim to have built and given away homes in ten states."

"Do you believe it?" Pen asked. She skipped the chips and went for a chocolate cookie to go with her cup of tea.

Amber looked around at their faces. "I don't really buy the pious act. His story of the near death experience is a little too pat, like it came out of a book. I've read some research on the phenomenon, and it's quite rare. Less than ten percent of people who die under those circumstances actually get resuscitated, only one percent of *those* report anything like this. Plus, the whole thing reeks of showbiz—perfect costumes, perfect choreography … But, about the housing and donations, I don't know. They might be using their glitz and style to actually help people. It shouldn't be up to me to make that call. Maybe the rest of you should attend one of these events and see what you think. Pen, you especially would fit in with the high-donor image. I suspect those are the ones who got the front row seats."

Pen held up her hands. "I prefer to do my charitable giving quietly and anonymously. But, all right, I could attend just to watch the show."

"You might get into conversation with some of the other donors and learn something," Gracie suggested.

Mary chimed in. "We're kind of getting away from our mission of finding out what's going on at the shelter. We still want to pursue and catch the thief, right?"

"Absolutely." Sandy looked at the others and received nods all around.

"I'm arranging my schedule with Billy so he'll take my evening shifts at the gym. That way I can be at the shelter to help Trini and keep my eyes open," Mary said.

Amber handed over the spiral notebook. "I've got the data entered, and now I can run some scenarios. I'll let you know what I come up with."

Gracie offered to visit the Temple of the Rising

Moon's website and see what she might learn. "Although I suspect it's only going to tell me what they want the public to know."

"I can go deeper than that," Amber offered.

"Then how about if I go to the county records and see how many building permits have been issued to this organization of theirs?" Grace suggested. "If they're even partway into the home-building process, they will have applied for permits."

"Great idea, and I'll give a quick look to see if, by any chance, they have accounts at Desert Trust," Sandy said. "For informational purposes only, of course."

"Of course," Pen agreed. "Sandy, you cannot risk your job by prying too deeply."

"I won't. I'm at least ten years away from retirement and I've put a lot of time into getting where I am. But, I can possibly verify some things about this couple and, frankly, I'm curious to know exactly how much money they are bringing in."

Amber gave a secretive little smile. As they had learned with their previous cases, people could be creative and devious with money, even when the majority of it wasn't obtained in cash.

Chapter 9

The Who-Is registry was the first and simplest stop on Amber's mission that evening. With information she'd found behind the scenes on the Temple's website, she dug deeply enough to learn the site was registered to a nonprofit organization, Fordyce Charities—whatever that was. The nonprofit status was no surprise. Orion and Sunshine were surely not dumb enough to make their claims of religious teachings and charitable fundraising without that bit of legal cover.

She lightly drummed her fingertips on her keyboard. Where to search next?

Taking the legal title of the religious nonprofit entity, she performed a few more searches. *Interesting* … The results of those queries sent her off in a new direction, and her fingers tapped the keys as she followed it.

The hours flew and next thing she knew it was nearing midnight, a little late to call the rest of the Ladies and report. She yawned, realized she hadn't eaten anything all day, and went to the kitchen for a yogurt.

* * *

Mary walked in the front door at Heaven Sent and nearly bumped into Orion. He and Sunshine appeared to have Trini cornered behind her desk as the guru was in the midst of a mini-sermon on the uselessness of homeless shelters.

"We want these people to have homes of their own," he said, jamming a forefinger at the countertop. "It's why we work so tirelessly at raising money to build houses for them, so they don't have to live in places like this." A sneer lingered barely below the surface.

Trini saw Mary behind the man. "Sorry, Orion, you two will have to excuse me."

Mary discovered she'd clenched her fists as the two walked past her and left. "The nerve! Want me to punch that guy? Throw him over my shoulder?"

Trini chuckled and rolled her eyes. "I've heard it before. Last week, she was the one with the lecture. What do they think destitute people are going to do, even if they're given a brand new house? They have no money for *food*, much less utilities and insurance and all that goes along with owning a house. We can only take things one step at a time. I'd rather work with job placement agencies, retraining programs, and mental health facilities to get our residents the real help they need. There's no one-size-fits-all solution to the problem."

"But don't you just want to scream at those two?" Mary

was still staring through the glass door at the retreating backs of the pair.

"Sometimes. But, really, they're all fluff. They weren't here a year ago, and I'll bet they won't be here a year from now. Let it go. We've got real work to do and real help to offer." She stepped out from behind the counter and gave Mary a hug.

"You're right, absolutely right. I'll wear off my aggressions during my women's self defense class before dinner. Afterward, just let me know what you'd like me to do."

The tasks turned out to be the usual—welcome each person who signed in, assign beds to the new ones, serve dinner and clean up. As Mary carried out two bags of trash around eight o'clock, she saw the crowded parking lot next door. The evening ritual—sermon, fundraiser, lecture, service, whatever they called it—was under way. She wondered if Pen had chosen tonight to attend, and whether the older woman's impressions would agree with Amber's.

* * *

Gracie sat at her dining table, dimly aware of the sounds of an action movie from the living room. Scott and Dylan had either convinced Kylie to go along with their choice, or her daughter was deep into a texting marathon with her friends and entirely ignoring the males of the household.

Before Gracie sat a single page she'd printed at the county courthouse this afternoon. It basically documented the search terms she'd used to locate records of the homes the Rising Moon group had supposedly built. Right off the bat, the clerk informed her she needed more information—

site location, contractor, property owner—anything. Anything except the bare nothing Gracie knew, that the organization was called Temple of the Rising Moon and the couple were known as Orion and Sunshine.

Even to her own ears it sounded lame, and the clerk just shook her head. Clearly, Gracie wasn't going to find anything, but the woman took pity and allowed her to sit at a table with a computer terminal. It was no surprise she'd hit dead ends every way she turned. After an hour she'd given up.

That was Maricopa County. She still had all of Pinal County to search too. Fun. Ugh.

Her head hurt. She reached for her tea mug to discover it was cold and empty.

* * *

Friday afternoon was the first opportunity for the Ladies to get together and compare notes at Pen's house.

"The county courthouses were both a complete bust," Gracie complained. "I really did try, but they need too much information as a starter. If I knew anything at all—who's doing the actual building, where the houses are located—any tidbit would be helpful. I'm sorry."

Sandy's report on her banking searches were similarly empty. "They don't do business at Desert Trust Bank. Or if they do, it's not under any version of their business name that I could drag up. And the first names of Orion and Sunshine didn't exactly net me any results either."

Pen had attended the Temple the previous night and her report agreed almost identically with Amber's, except this time it was Sunshine with the tale of her heartbreaking woes of infertility and the nearly magical way in which she had conceived their child on the exact day foretold by a wise old woman.

Amber asked a few questions, trying to pin down specifics about the story, but Pen swore few details were given.

"It was very much the emotion-driven tale," she said. "They never said where they were living at the time or anything more about the baby's birth, gender, or where it is now."

"I'm fairly certain no children live with them in the bus," Mary said. "Trini has said, more than once, that she sees 'the two of them' staying there. Surely she would have mentioned whether they have kids."

"I'm really feeling at a dead end here," said Sandy. "We just aren't finding much to go on."

Amber raised her hand from the spot where she sat cross-legged on the floor. "I may have something." She went into the explanation of her search for ownership of the Temple's website. "Learning that it was a religious nonprofit organization doesn't really reveal much and it wasn't surprising. However …" a pause for effect "other records about the organization revealed that their real names are Foster and Melissa Fordyce."

Raised eyebrows all around. "Do we know anything about them under those names?" Pen asked.

"Very little, so far, but I have a feeling there's a lot more." Amber consulted her notes. "For instance, I discovered that a Foster Fordyce did have a medical scare a couple of years ago. He was admitted to a Houston hospital with chest pains but released after just a few hours. It could very well be the basis for his dramatic tale of having died and come back to life, if you take the facts and add a big dash of conjecture and other reported cases of 'seeing the light'."

"I'm not going to ask how you learned this," Sandy said, "with all the laws in place protecting medical privacy."

"You're right. Don't ask." Amber gave an enigmatic smile. "And don't ask how I learned that the IRS is poking around in their finances, auditing several years' worth of their tax returns."

This time Sandy's eyes definitely widened. "Be careful, Amber. If the government is looking at this couple, they might easily learn that you are also looking. I don't want to see any of us in trouble over this."

"I'd say that goes for all of us," Mary added. "I'm not afraid of this Orion and Sunshine—Trini's right, they're phonies—but it's not worth getting ourselves in trouble over them."

Pen straightened in her seat. "Still, we must consider the sheer amount of the money they are bringing in. They are using fake stories to draw people into an emotional state and part with their hard-earned money. You've seen the community out there in the east valley—these are not wealthy people. Many of them are giving away hundreds of dollars at a time and quite possibly they cannot afford to."

Mary nodded vigorously. "Absolutely. We began this by looking into small keepsakes belonging to homeless people but, really, isn't it just as tragic to see middle-income people bilked of a few hundred dollars?"

"You're so right," Gracie said. "I don't think we can walk away now that we know this much. We really do need to follow through and see what's going on."

"Maybe it's encouraging to know the IRS is looking at them," Sandy said.

"Possibly. But, even so, would the government return the money to those who've been cheated? Would they even expose the scandal? I find it doubtful. The Revenue Service only wants its percentage." Pen's mouth formed a firm line.

"And we've all heard the tales about how poorly government agencies communicate. There's no guarantee of prosecution on the *real* crime, even if they are sent to prison on income tax evasion."

"Somewhere behind this whole thing I'd bet there is a cohort," Sandy said. "A lawyer or accountant who's helped them set this up. *That's* the person we need to find."

Chapter 10

Melissa floated near the edge of the indoor pool, her arms draped along the concrete edge, eyes closed, her hair up in a bun to keep it dry. A lazy smile played across her mouth.

"Hello, Sunshine." Her husband slipped into the water beside her and eyed the tiny bikini that barely covered anything.

The lazy smile vanished. "You can cut the crap here," she said. "Give me a break from Sunshine and Orion, okay?"

"There's my girl." He nibbled her earlobe and slipped an arm around her waist.

She grinned and turned to deliver a long, deep kiss.

A child's shriek pierced the air, and Melissa saw a family of five enter the pool area. So much for privacy.

"Let's go take advantage of that nice suite upgrade I got us." She took his hand from her breast and stood up.

Melissa always handled the check-in process at fancy places. Her big green eyes never failed to earn them a discount on the room or free spa treatments. At the very least no bellboy had ever felt insulted when she batted the eyelashes at him but forgot to hand him a tip. She was as comfortable scamming people as breathing. The role was like slipping into a familiar old sweater, one she'd owned since childhood.

And she had. Her daddy had taught her, and during the steamy Houston summers his little blonde cutie could finagle complimentary Dairy Queen cones or a free day at the swimming pool for them. She could accomplish those feats with ease by the time she was four. By age eight her shoplifting skills got all Mama's cosmetics free at the local Walgreens, and by fifteen she'd learned that a pretty girl never paid for a meal or a new dress. She did it all with smiles and kisses. Mama told little Missy a girl didn't need to give away her most important assets to get what she wanted.

Missy met Foster Fordyce when she was twenty-one and still a virgin.

He was her age, tall and handsome, and had drifted into their lower-middle class neighborhood where he got a job at a nearby Denny's and caught her eye. For three years he'd been bouncing to and from the two abusive alcoholics he called Mom and Pop. With no job skills, he'd drifted from one diner to another—washing dishes mostly, sometimes cooking, often cleaning the kitchen and mopping the floors after closing. He watched happy families eating burgers with their kids, teenage couples sharing milkshakes, and idealism would take over. As soon as he got fired for not showing up for a shift, he'd go back home where he imagined his parents would have changed and the three of them would become one of those families who ordered restaurant food and laughed over funny stories.

Mom would take him back and point out all the chores he should have been there to do, mostly washing dishes and mopping the kitchen floor. Then Pop would come home with a bottle and the old scenario would start again. Whatever cash he'd brought home from the last job quickly vanished, there was never enough food in the house, and within a week or two he got sick of being their unpaid, underfed servant while he listened to their fights. He would hit the road again and thumb his way to a different small Texas town.

When Melissa walked into that Denny's, Foster was immediately enchanted. From fourteen on, there had never been a girl he couldn't seduce but this one was different. She flirted outrageously, and she openly stared at his trim, fit body, but despite his smooth patter he couldn't convince her to go all the way. They began taking long walks and talking.

Melissa discovered a man who underestimated himself; Foster discovered a girl who was so savvy she scared him. Together, they learned they both had a yearning for the kind of freedom that only big—great big—money could buy.

The cons began small, basically glorified begging, until one evening they came upon an old-fashioned evangelical tent revival. They prevailed upon the minister to marry them on the spot, proceeded to slip a hundred or so from the collection plate, and they were on their way out of Houston. They'd found their life's calling.

Chapter 11

Amber chewed a ragged cuticle and stared at her computer screen. So far, she'd found very little online about the Fordyces, even now that she had their real names. It seemed they owned nothing in their own names, and precious little under the nonprofit entity of the Temple of the Rising Moon. She had seen the money come flowing in. So where was it all?

They didn't have bank accounts, they conducted services in a rented building, and they lived in a bus. No credit cards, no loans, no property. The couple had either perfected a life off the official radar, or they had some superior methods of concealing cash.

She thought back to what Sandy had said yesterday. It could be they were hiding behind layers of corporate entities, and those must have been set up by teams of lawyers and accountants. So far, she'd found no trace of any. Every clue seemed to take her to a complete dead end.

Enough of this, she decided. Her shoulders ached from hours at the computer and she needed a break. She might tackle the mall long enough to find Christmas gifts for her parents and then go to the gym. Mary had told her to come anytime.

By noon she had purchased a gift basket of fruit for her health-conscious parents and was assured it would be shipped to Santa Fe in time for the holiday. Some non-perishable treats for the Ladies, and her shopping list was complete. Congratulating herself for not resorting to a few online clicks, and for handling her list two weeks early, she drove to the gym.

"Hey, Amber," Mary said when she saw her young friend. "What's up?"

"I left home thinking I needed a punching bag to take out my frustrations."

"Oh?"

"Just not having a lot of luck getting the information we need."

Mary led the way into the noisy room that smelled equally of sweat and disinfectant cleaner. "Here's a bag and I'll get you some gloves."

Amber eyed the contraption hanging from the ceiling. It must have outweighed her by a hundred pounds and looked solid as a mountain. A broken hand would certainly crimp her style. "I'm doing better now that I got my Christmas list done," she said. "Maybe a run on the treadmill will do it for me."

The elliptical machines and treadmills filled a quieter room. Mary stepped onto an adjoining one and they trotted along together for a few minutes.

"Any news about the thefts at the shelter?" Amber asked, although she figured Mary would have mentioned it already if they'd caught the culprit.

"Not yet. It's frustrating. The population there is pretty transient this time of year—more so than in summer, I think. Have you had any luck matching the residents with the dates of the thefts?"

Amber didn't want to admit she'd become sidetracked with the search for the Fordyces. She shook her head. Luckily for her, someone called out to Mary and she hopped off the treadmill to help them. Amber plugged in earbuds and started her favorite exercise playlist. Twenty minutes later she'd come up with an idea.

Back home and showered, she eagerly opened her browser and took a new tactic with her search. It didn't take long to narrow down the number of Fordyces in south Texas. She started phoning, using the age-old pretense that she represented a law office calling to discuss an inheritance. On call number six the woman said yes, her son's name was Foster.

"What's he done now?" asked the voice, which sounded hardened by cigarettes.

"I'm not at liberty to go into the specifics. At this point I need a little family history to verify he is the same Foster Fordyce we're looking for. Can you give me his full name, date of birth, and the full names of both parents?"

Myrna Fordyce complied willingly. "Foster don't need no inheritance. He's made it big now. Got his law degree and all. Married some blonde girl we never met. But he sent a picture and they're together still and they seem happy enough. His pop, now, Archie needs help—his liver's about gone. We could sure use that money for the medical bills."

She paused. Amber flinched at the sound of the cough

that came over the line.

Myrna cleared her throat noisily and resumed. "You'd think our own son could help us out. We got problems and he don't give us the time of day."

"So you haven't heard from him in a while?"

"Oh gosh, prob'ly a year or more. He'd called to say he was mailing me a check for Christmas. Measly hundred bucks is what it was. And then he goes on and tells me they had just give away a four-bedroom house! Can you imagine? I got so damn mad I hung up. Just hung up on him, the self-centered little s.o.b."

Amber could see the conversation going along in this vein forever. "I just need a few more details to verify his identity. Can you tell me where he went to school?"

Another hacking cough. "Um, well. Claremont High. That's right here in our neighborhood. He took off shortly after and we'd just see him hit-and-miss. I don't know as I ever got the name of his college where he went to that law school. Archie might remember it if I can wake him up long enough to ask. Want me to do that?"

Law school—that was interesting. Amber was already keying Claremont High School and the name of the town into a search.

"Um, no thanks. That's okay. I think we can work with the information we have."

"Now you call me back once you get that inheritance figured out. Me and his pop, we're due some of that money too, you know. You keep my number and we'll be real happy to pass along the news to Foster when we see him again."

I'll just bet you will. Amber thanked the woman and hung up. *Whew.*

Even as she dialed Foster's old high school Amber wondered what, exactly, she could possibly learn. But she went through with it and found an old-time counselor who'd been there the years he attended.

"You called at the right time," Louise Kinsey said. "I'm retiring right after the first of the year. Thirty years of dealing with teenagers is enough for anybody."

"I'm hoping you remember one boy, a Foster Fordyce. I think he would have graduated about twenty-five years ago. I know that's asking a lot. Maybe the school has records going back that far."

Louise chuckled. "We got records going back to Jesus' day. Well, we would have. Claremont's one of the older schools in the district. I attended here and so did my mother. What do you need to know about Foster? I mostly remember him as this tall, gangly kid who sat through his counseling sessions as if he'd rather be anywhere else."

"His mother told me he went to law school, and I was hoping maybe his high school records would indicate where he planned to attend college. I just need a lead in the right direction."

"College? I'd be very surprised if Foster Fordyce ever went to college. He never was on that track—in fact he never graduated high school, as far as I know."

"Really. Did he stay there in the city?" Amber began to wonder if she'd found the correct Foster Fordyce.

"I don't know. Haven't run into him, not in twenty years or more. Lot of the kids do stick around and I see 'em now and then. One of Foster's best buddies died—tragic car accident when he tried to outrun a train at a railroad crossing. The other kid he hung around with most was Lenny Sassel. Lenny got his girlfriend pregnant, they married and had four more kids, and now he manages the big hardware store out on the old Baytown Highway. I go in there all the time."

Amber was amazed at the woman's recollection for details. She didn't seem to be consulting a computer or any written files.

Louise went on. "But Foster … he was a case. I always thought he had so much potential. Bright kid, but he had this restless energy. If anybody'd cared, he probably would have seen doctors and been diagnosed with ADHD or something. But the parents just let him run his own life. They were dirt poor and whatever money came in, the father drank it up. The mother wasn't much better on that score. It was probably a good thing they only ever had the one boy—a houseful of kids like Foster would have been big trouble. I felt sorry for him, but with close to two thousand kids enrolled here I just couldn't follow up with every one of them."

"Is there anything else that stood out about Foster?"

A short pause. "Hmm … math whiz. He would ace his math tests. Sophomore and junior years, his teachers commented on how sharp he was. You know, if he'd only applied himself he could have gone into any number of careers—finance, engineering, science, computers. Sad that he quit so young. Last time I recall seeing him was about the time he would have been walking down the aisle to get his diploma. Instead, he was mopping the floors at a low-class diner downtown. It was after hours and I spotted him through the window. I just about cried. It all comes down to the parenting, I say. If Foster'd just had better support at home he'd have made it big."

In a way, Amber supposed, Foster had made it big. Certainly not as an engineer or programmer though. As Louise Kinsey wound down her recollections, Amber performed a search of online colleges, using several key words she had gleaned from these two recent conversations.

Graystone Institute came up as a match for all the search terms except 'Texas'. The institution boasted that a person could earn a law degree valid in all fifty states without ever attending a campus class. Everything could be done online, preliminary requirements were minimal, and the average student graduated in fourteen months. The claims seemed iffy and a little scary to Amber.

She clicked around until she found a backdoor way into their student records. No point in getting caught up in another long-winded conversation when she could go right to the source. Fordyce's name was uncommon enough that it was a fairly sure bet she had the right person when his record came up.

Prerequisite courses: Waived

State residency: Waived

College transcript review: Waived

Course(s) of study: Law, International banking

Date of enrollment and date of graduation were twelve months apart. Apparently, Foster Fordyce was as brilliant as his high school counselor had pegged him, or he'd bought his way through. Either way, he did hold a law degree with a specialty in international banking. And that explained a lot of things for the Heist Ladies and their mission.

Chapter 12

He had a problem, and he knew it. He couldn't help it. He would spot a bright object or a doodad with some particular quality, and he just had to possess it. The first time he'd come home with a ladies' brooch after a visit to his aunt's home, he'd received a light scolding and been forced to return it. Aunt Jane called him a little *klepto* and never invited him back again. After that, he never showed Mom his findings again. He simply stashed them, first in an old cigar box under his bed, then in increasingly clever caches where he wouldn't be pinpointed as the thief.

Part of the thrill was the uncertainty about getting caught. In school his locker contained more of other kids' possessions than his own. He learned to be cagey about who was standing around when he opened the door. Every couple of weeks he would scoop his prizes into his backpack and take them home to join the collection in the back corner of the yard shed where his mother never looked. She'd somehow gotten the impression the shed was crawling with black widow spiders.

Now, he pulled a cookie tin from under his bed and sat back on the rug with legs crossed. Raising the lid, he breathed a contented sigh when he viewed the contents. The gold pocket watch was a recent find, an item he'd known he would possess the first moment the man pulled it from a pants pocket to check the time. Subtly picking pockets was a learned skill he'd picked up sometime in his late teens.

He ran his thumb over the watch case. It was carved with images of a steam locomotive and cars. Inside, a name and date had been engraved. The personal touches pleased him.

Last night he'd attended some kind of quasi religious service at that 'temple' next to the homeless shelter. The weirdo couple were collecting money to build houses for the poor. Boo-hoo, he thought as he listened to their spiel. If he could figure out ways to make a living without doing much work, then everybody else should be able to do it too.

Fend for yourself. It was a lesson that went back to the year he turned eight.

Just as he'd fended for himself last night when the collection plate came around. Making a show of dropping in a dollar bill, he'd quickly palmed a twenty. Even the young kid sitting next to him didn't catch the move. He might go back tonight and bring home a little more—a guy has to pay the rent, after all.

Chapter 13

Melissa Fordyce watched her husband's bare backside as he sauntered toward the huge bathroom in their suite. The view of his body never failed to please. If she'd known afternoons could be this much fun, she might have ignored Mama's advice about staying a virgin.

She draped the expensive bed linens over herself and savored the silken feeling. The whole gig with the hippie clothing and bus began to wear on her at times. Even with the niceties she'd insisted upon, the place was just so cramped. Her designer clothes were all in storage while they donned the baggy things she thought of as sackcloth, although even the simple designs had not been cheap and she knew she looked great in them.

"Better get out of that bed," Foster chided as he stepped out of the shower. "We're on stage in ninety minutes."

She sighed and closed her eyes, imagining herself in the floaty white gown and trying to remember if tonight was Foster's sob story or her own. Didn't matter. Sometimes they decided at the last minute, and each of them had some version of nearly meeting their maker and how they'd been sent back into this life to raise money for the greater good.

"Baby—really." He was standing at the bedside now.

"I'm moving." She groaned as she cast aside the sheet and stood.

He ran a fingertip from her mouth downward across a bare breast and then to her belly. "We'll be back here by ten and I promise you another *fulfilling* experience."

She laughed and scampered to the shower. As the hot water coursed over her body she slipped into the fantasy she loved most. The moment when all the collection baskets were carried down the aisles toward them. While Foster bade the audience good night and thanked them for their generosity, Melissa always slipped backstage to make sure none of that generosity managed to sneak out the back door.

In less than four hours she would be standing behind the curtained dais where she would open the lid of a two-foot-square metal lockbox and watch as each of the men in white dumped the contents of a basket. As she rinsed the shampoo from her hair, she sighed at the thought of all that money. The vision never got old.

Foster had already ordered an Uber to take them to the parking lot two miles away where they'd left the dented VW Beetle that was part of the hippie persona, their around-town car in case the people who attended their shows might catch sight of them.

She dressed in linen slacks and a cashmere sweater, casual chic for the resort but low key enough if someone saw them arrive at the Temple. They would change into costume inside the bus. Fluffing her hair, she told Foster she was ready. Privately, she couldn't wait until they decided they'd raked in enough from the Arizona crowd and the snowbirds. They didn't have to go to these lengths when they worked California or the South.

Melissa's original inspiration struck the night she and Foster, the young couple full of dreams, had watched that evangelist in the tent on a sticky summer night in south Texas. Neither of them had much of a religious upbringing so it was the promises of salvation and eternal life that grabbed her attention. How could someone in a shiny suit and slicked-back hair promise she would go to heaven simply by having faith?

She'd watched her daddy con all kinds of people out of all kinds of things—would daddy go to heaven merely by believing his sins were forgiven? Would she? If so, it seemed simple enough. Do what you wanted to all your life and in the last moment utter the words and profess this man's type of faith and—ta-da!—there you were. She was about to walk out when she glimpsed the expression on Foster's young face.

"You buying this stuff?" she whispered.

"Watch, baby. Watch what happens next."

How did he—?

But he was right. The preacher's wife stepped forward, tears in her eyes, and made a plea for generosity in helping them to continue the Lord's work. Magically, men with bowls appeared in the crowd and people began dropping money in. Coins clicked as they landed, and the woman on stage cried out for more.

"We need your help," she begged. "We can feed all the starving children in Africa with this money. Open your pockets and purses, good people. Give what you can."

The clink of coins changed to the swish of dollar bills.

Foster nudged Melissa and nodded toward the exit. Outside the tent they faced each other, eyes shining. "You thinking what I'm thinking?" he asked.

She nodded. This was the motherlode.

They attended every service that weekend, studying. Between times they practiced the spiel, critiqued each other on the nuances of the words and tone. That summer, they followed the circuit of these preachers through the South and into the Midwest, learning the dialogue like lines in a play, studying the pacing and figuring out the precise moment when each speaker turned from giving out promises to asking for money. There was a right time, they discovered, to bring in the most cash. They sneaked to the back of the tents where there would be a small area separated by a curtain, or sometimes a little camper trailer. They spied and listened and were astounded by the amounts these guys brought in.

Melissa could spot the real pros, the ones who had their act down so well they never failed to rake in hundreds, sometimes more than a thousand dollars in an evening. The amateurs either bumbled the timing, or they were genuinely religious and didn't push hard enough to get into the real money. She coached Foster, pointing out what worked in each performance, and what didn't.

Foster, with his head for numbers and lightning quick memory, became the money man. As they spied on the hucksters and watched them dump their collection plates onto a table, he could tell, within a few dollars, how much they'd collected. Their careers were set—no more washing dishes or mopping floors.

Over the years they'd worked the scam in many ways,

from traditional to New Age, and their show became more of a production with the passage of time. Whatever the market would bear, whatever the audiences hungered for—the Fordyces aimed to please.

Housing for the poor was a popular one during the holiday season. Audiences gave generously and everyone knew it took a lot to build a house, so the donations seldom included pocket change. They raked in some real money. Later, in the spring, they would probably head for California, ditch the painted school bus, and set up one of their favorite gigs: psychic mind reader who connected people with their departed loved ones. It never failed to please, especially when done with a sizeable studio audience, broadcast on cable and distributed online. That last part had been Foster's idea.

"Okay, Sunshine baby," he said, pulling the VW in beside the school bus. "We're here. Change into your dress and I'll just check the auditorium. Be there in a minute."

"Of course, Orion. I'll be at my sparkling best because I remember what you promised me for later on." She sent him a wickedly sexy grin.

Chapter 14

Trini stepped inside after taking out the trash and found Mary in the kitchen.

"We've assigned all the beds," Mary said, "and I put the No Vacancy sign on the front door."

"Listen, I've got an idea," Trini said.

Mary's ears perked up.

"The show's on next door and it looks like another big crowd, so I'm thinking Sunshine and Orion will be busy for quite awhile. What do you say we sneak over and take a look in the bus?" She paused and fiddled with the zipper on her hoodie. "Tell me if this is crazy and you don't want to do it."

"Heck yeah, I'm all for it." Mary was practically bouncing on the balls of her feet. "I'd love to find Micah's missing watch and the other items over there."

"I know. Even though the rest of your friends don't think this couple is doing the thieving, I'd just like to be sure."

They were already on the way outside, where they look a long look around the parking area. Six men dressed in white pants and shirts hung near the front door, smoking and apparently killing time until their turn to appear in the show. The women slipped around the end of the chain link fencing and ducked behind a leafy bougainvillea. No one had noticed.

Keeping low, they stayed behind vehicles in the lot and made their way to the side of the bus. The folding door faced the back of the property, away from the back door of the Temple building.

Trini tried the door latch with no luck. Mary backed up, raising a leg, ready to give the thing a swift kick.

"Wait! We don't actually want to break it, do we? They'll know we've broken in."

"They'll know *someone* broke in. Can't really know it was us."

"What if they have a camera mounted somewhere?" Trini paced a couple of steps away. "Oh god this was a bad idea."

"I don't see any cameras. Hang on. I've got more tricks," Mary said, reaching into the pocket of her jacket.

She came out with a keyring and thumbed through, holding up a tiny tool of some kind. Working it at various angles in the lock, she felt something give way, triggering the door release.

"Okay," she whispered. "We're in."

"It's pitch dark in there. Do we risk a light?"

"Is there normally one on in here when they're doing the show?"

"Sometimes yes, sometimes no."

"Let's turn one on. If anyone walks by it'll be less suspicious than a flashlight flickering around."

A switch near the door turned on an overhead light. The women quickly closed the door and made certain all the window curtains were pulled shut.

"Okay, if I were a stolen pocket watch, where would I be?" Trini murmured.

Mary giggled.

"Sorry, it's a trick I use at home to find missing things. Always works for me there."

"Here's a small closet," Mary said. "I'll go through it. You take those drawers."

The closet revealed three white dresses and Orion's flowing stage clothing in white and purple. None of the outfits had pockets, she discovered with a pat-down.

"I now know how Sunshine appears to glow when she comes down the aisle," Mary said, holding one of the dresses under the light. "There's metallic thread woven into the gauzy white material. The spotlights they use in there would bring out the sparkle even more."

"The drawers are jammed with kitchen tools, a candle lighter, some packets of coffee. One has nothing but paper plates and napkins."

"What about those?" Mary pointed to some cardboard boxes tucked under the dinette table. She turned back to the closet, straightening the clothing as she'd found it.

"Holy cow!" Trini sputtered. "Look at this."

She held open the flaps on a box. Inside were neatly banded packets of twenty dollar bills. Mary's eyes widened. "Whoa. Amber was right—they do bring in a lot of cash."

Trini removed a few of the stacks then ran her hand down the inside edge of the box. "It seems to be the same, all the way to the bottom. No little trinkets stashed beneath."

"There's another box. Check it." Mary edged past, heading for the queen-sized bed at the back of the bus. Beneath its platform was a sizeable storage space and she pulled out two smaller cardboard boxes and some kind of machine.

"What's that?" Trini asked, elbow deep in the second box of currency.

"It's a money counter. I guess when you have this kind of haul, it's too much work to sit down and count it manually." Mary shoved the machine back under the bed.

The two small boxes rattled enticingly when Mary shook them, but neither revealed what the women wanted. Instead, one held two pairs of earbuds and some kind of transmitter device. She looked them over and shrugged. The other box contained a banking debit card and two credit cards in the corporate name Moon Temple LLC, and a pair of passports issued to Melissa and Foster Fordyce.

She spread the documents on the floor and snapped a picture with her camera phone, flinching when the flash went off.

"How long have we been in here?" Trini asked, nervously eyeing the door.

"Long enough, I'd say. Do you know what time the show ends?"

Trini shook her head and began repacking the boxes of money.

Mary stepped to the side window and peeked around the edge of the curtain. "Oh no! People are coming out. Hurry!"

She ran back to the bed, shoved the small boxes back in place, and checked to be sure everything looked as she had found it. Another peek out the window showed the burly men in white gathered at the back door. Some kind of security detail for the gurus, she guessed, in addition to being the passers of the collection baskets. She caught a flash of bright purple and saw Orion's long hair.

"Trini, get up! We have to get out before they see us."

Trini noticed one loose packet of twenties, snatched it up, and jammed it into the box. The cardboard flaps were not cooperative as she tried to re-tuck them. Mary had the door open a crack and was practically dancing on her toes to get moving. She stepped outside, keeping watch at the front of the bus, ready to provide a diversion, but Trini stumbled out and pulled the door closed.

They dashed toward the back of the bus, opposite to where Orion and Sunshine were approaching. Pressed against the back, they held their breath until the couple's voices sounded from inside.

"Quick—get around the fence to our own side," Trini said, ducking for the protective bougainvillea once again.

Inside the homeless shelter, and safely in Trini's quarters, they finally dared to speak again.

"That was way too close," Trini said.

Mary let out a pent-up breath. "Yeah." Although she actually remembered a couple of other close calls and figured at least this was one she could have probably talked her way out of. "How much do you think was in those boxes?" she asked Trini, mostly to take her mind off the folly of the mission.

Trini shrugged. "No idea. I'm glad you snapped pictures. At least we have some proof."

"I don't know. Proof of what? Just because they collect all this money in cash, it doesn't prove they don't use it for housing for the poor, just as they claim."

Trini slumped on the sofa. "Right. And we didn't find any of the stolen items from our people here. Kind of discouraging, really."

Mary nodded but didn't say anything. She needed to take the evidence to the rest of the Heist Ladies.

Chapter 15

Foster liked to count the money right after the service each evening. It helped him to keep track of the take, plus he always slept better. Melissa loved his mood afterward, always amorous after a good show with hefty proceeds.

They remained in the bus long enough to change back to their resort wear and for Foster to feed the cash through the money counting machine. It had been a generous crowd tonight, and his mood was high, even though he admonished her for not quite leaving the big boxes of cash neatly tucked against the side wall of the bus.

"What was that earlier, one of the Macks saying something?" she asked as she slipped her white dress onto an empty hanger in the closet.

He shook his head, wanting a moment to separate

checks from currency in the lockbox he'd carried out of the auditorium. "Which of the Macks was that?"

"How do I know? They all look alike—it's why I call 'em all Mack."

In every city they hired new helpers and part of the selection process was the unspoken criteria: Big, dumb, unambitious, and willing to do as they were told. All they had to do was dress in the outfit, look like private security, be intimidating enough to scare anyone who might be tempted but not conniving enough to want to help themselves to the money that passed by them every night. In return, they were paid well at the end of each week. All cash, all off the books.

Foster placed another stack of bills onto the machine and watched them feed through with a satisfying flutter. He paged through the checks, laying them out in a spread on the table so he could deposit them with his phone.

"Hey, here's a nice one—thousand bucks," he said.

"People are so generous around the holidays," Melissa said with a warm smile.

"And they're scrambling to get year-end tax deductions. Great for us." He took the counted stack of twenties, banded it, and set it aside while he placed a batch of tens in the machine. "So what were you asking a minute ago?"

"Oh, one of the Macks took you aside right after you came off stage. What did he want?"

Foster's expression hardened. "Thought he saw some clown palm some money out of the basket. Wanted to know if he should chase him down."

"What'd you say?"

"Same as always. Just watch for him in the crowd, see if he comes back, put the fear into him if he tries it again." He pulled out his phone, brought up the banking app, and began snapping pictures of the checks for a mobile deposit.

Melissa gathered the banded stacks of cash and brushed past her husband to reach the cardboard boxes under the table. One was full to the top already, but the other had some space and she arranged the stacks that had become disheveled and added the new ones. Before they finished their season here in Arizona, every nook and cranny in the bus would be filled with the beautiful green stuff.

Ironic, she thought, how the losers all ended up next door believing money was a scarce commodity. It certainly came easily enough when you had the right pitch. People would give you all you needed. She indulged in the vision of her dream home, a huge place, somewhere with a coastline.

Would there come a day when even an enormous villa wouldn't be enough to satisfy? A tiny wrinkle crossed her brow. What if she and Foster built the villa, had enough piles of cash to do anything they wanted, and it still wasn't enough?

She thrust the thought aside. So what? It wasn't as if there was an end goal in life. They loved the adventure, the con; the show itself was enough, as people stared up at them with adoring eyes and gave generously to their causes. And there was *always* a cause—this year they'd worked the houses-for-homeless-people angle. Next year it might be clean water for African villages or food for overpopulated India.

It was easy to find heart-wrenching photos of skinny kids with big eyes and flies buzzing around their heads. The internet had loads of images to grab and make it look as if you'd actually been there, crying over their plight. Come back to an affluent society and make it sound like you had all the answers, that you could fix it all if only you had the money. So simple. No one ever followed up to find out what was real and what wasn't.

"You about ready?" Foster asked, gathering the checks into a rubber band and jotting the deposit date on top. "The resort has a late supper and there's a dance band tonight. I'm starving."

She squeezed his hand, ignoring the irony of his statement. They both automatically looked around the bus to be sure nothing was out of place.

Chapter 16

The five-dollar bill burned hotly in the hand he thrust deeply into his pocket. He was good at palming things, and folded money was so simple, but he'd caught the stare of the man in white and wondered if he'd been spotted. He adopted a leisurely pace as he left the Temple of the Rising Moon—what kind of stupid name was that anyway?—and neither looked at nor avoided the man in white.

The goon stared at him the whole way but didn't approach, even as he walked past the parked cars and down the street. He'd gotten away with it. Five dollars. No big deal. Not as good as the twenty he'd taken a couple nights ago, but it gave him the thrill of the successful conquest.

Still, he thought as he covered the six blocks to the supermarket parking lot where he'd left his car, it would be best if he stayed away from this neighborhood for a few weeks. The homeless shelter hadn't netted much of value, other than the gold watch. The other few trinkets were just sparkles that caught his eye. The old biddy who ran the place was getting suspicious. He felt sure he wasn't on their radar, but he'd attracted the attention of that burly guy tonight.

Yeah, better to work some other spots—he knew of plenty—and leave Apache Junction alone for awhile.

His car sat exactly where he'd left it, in the less-popular lot at the side of the building. This time of year, shoppers were out until all hours so the lot was never empty enough so anyone would notice a car that remained unmoved for hours at a stretch. He loved supermarkets for that reason. He retrieved the key fob from the small pouch he wore attached to his ankle, under his sock, and unlocked the door.

For the fun of it, he drove through the drive-up at the nearest McDonald's and treated himself to a meal from the dollar menu. Five bucks went fairly far when spent that way. Gloating over the coup, he hit US 60 and headed westbound into central Phoenix.

Twenty minutes later he entered a middle-class neighborhood of homes with stucco in varying shades of tan and tile roofs that were increasingly being covered in solar panels. He thumbed the button built into the car's overhead console, raising the garage door and driving straight inside.

The kitchen was neat and clean, he was happy to see. Once, he'd forgotten and left an unrinsed cereal bowl in the sink when he went to spend two nights at the shelter. When he got back the place was teeming with ants. He could put up with less-than-clean clothing but cringed at the sight of bugs taking over his house.

He emptied the pockets of the oversized jacket he wore for his day job. Leaving the contents on his dresser, he peeled off jeans, black T-shirt, and gray hoodie and draped them over a ladder-back chair in the bedroom corner. The battered running shoes and dingy once-white socks were set neatly on the floor.

The hot shower felt luxuriously good. He let the water course over his body, using a generous squirt of the Old Spice body wash someone had given him last Christmas. The scent contrasted pleasantly with the smells he'd been immersed in the last two days. He massaged shampoo into his scalp and thick sandy hair, then debated about shaving the half-inch of beard growth. Decided not. The holiday season was one of his most lucrative, and he needed to play up his assets.

The hot water began to grow tepid so he shut off the taps and reached for his towel.

Dressed in pressed khaki slacks and a polo shirt, his longish hair combed straight back from his forehead, he picked up each of the items he'd taken earlier from the pockets of the coat. First was a small locket, the kind a young girl would wear, with a pink stone set in an inexpensive gold heart-shaped casing. It opened to reveal tiny pictures of a man and a woman. He'd also picked up a Timex watch with buttons for setting alarms and digital numbers—he might actually wear that. And there was the first twenty-dollar bill he'd taken at the hippies' fake religious service.

He reached under the bed and brought out the cookie box, opening it and lovingly setting each new item inside to join his previous acquisitions.

Chapter 17

Amber gave herself a high-five in the living room mirror when she saw the message from Mary. Finally—something concrete to work with on this search which had, so far, proved extremely frustrating. She grabbed a high-caffeine soda and a bag of M&Ms, prepared to sit in her fleece jammies at her computer half the night if that's what it took.

In his passport photo Foster Fordyce had short, corporate hair and wore a suit and tie. Melissa's blonde hair was up in a casually elegant style with tendrils framing her face. She somehow managed to look like a fashion model. No one looked that great in a passport photo.

"Told you," Amber muttered under her breath. "I knew these two weren't genuine earth-child types."

The banking debit card and the two credit cards were

all issued in the official name of their business, Moon Temple LLC, which explained why she'd had no luck in her prior searches. Now, she could really go to work. Her fingers raced over the keyboard.

By three a.m. she'd compiled enough for a report to the Ladies. She picked up her phone, stopping just short of speed dialing Mary. Although she was wired from all the treats and the new information, not everyone would be up and ready for a meeting at this hour. She composed a text instead:

Let's meet for breakfast. 8:00 @ Chubby's. Got news!!!

The moment it went out to the group, she felt herself crashing. She crawled onto her futon and pulled a blanket over herself.

* * *

Chubby's Grub had been a campus favorite forever. Mary arrived early to grab a table large enough for five; Sandy bustled in, apologizing because she would probably need to leave early for a meeting at the bank; Gracie appeared barely awake, despite the fact she carried her own thermal coffee mug with her; Pen was no less elegantly turned out than ever in winter-white slacks and a lavender sweater, her gray-blonde page perfectly smooth.

"Where's Amber?" Gracie asked. "I wouldn't have come out in traffic this early if it didn't sound—"

Pen pointed toward the front windows, where their youngest member was race-walking toward the door. She sported a hastily put-together outfit consisting of jeggings and an ASU sweatshirt, a froth of dark curls in a band on top of her head, and the ubiquitous messenger bag slung across her shoulder.

"Sorry. I was up 'til three."

"We know," Mary said with a wry grin. "I forgot to mute my phone and the ping woke me up."

"Ohh ..." Amber seemed half contrite, half sleepy.

"Let's get some breakfast," Gracie said. "One coffee isn't doing it for me this morning."

They all ordered the waffles, Chubby's specialty, with a big plate of bacon on the side to share.

"So, I'm eager to hear this big news," Mary said. "Hoping it's something I can report back to Trini."

"Well, that's part of it," Amber told them. "Before I got your photos last night, I worked on the spreadsheet and came up with some names, based on Trini's list of the volunteers and workers who'd been at the shelter at the time of each theft, which I incorporated with the residents."

She reached into her bag and pulled out some printed sheets, handing them around.

"Micah, Lizzie, Ron, Sue, Carrot, and Blue—that's how they signed their names in the register. Those are the residents. Most of the construction workers and volunteers came during the day and left before dinner time, and none of them were at the shelter on the dates of *all* the thefts. Plus, they stayed in the area of the new building addition, so I could pretty much discount them. All the thefts happened when it was mostly residents who were in for the night. I've listed three volunteers who served food and cleaned up the kitchen. Trini said she's already questioned them and they are just as baffled about this as she is."

"So we need to check these on the list," Pen said. "They seem to use a lot of nicknames and first names only."

"Right. That's the challenge."

"I can't even think where to begin," Gracie said as the

waffles arrived. "Maybe my brain will wake up once I've eaten."

They dug into the food and conversation lagged for a few minutes.

Pen ate slowly, looking thoughtful. "Didn't your friend Trini suggest whoever was stealing these items most likely pawned or sold them as soon as they could? I'm not saying we shouldn't continue our investigation, but we must realize it could be a hopeless quest."

Mary nodded. "True. I hate to say it, but we may never know."

"Still, I think it's worth focusing on the little bit we do know," Sandy said. "It would certainly lift my holiday spirit if we could retrieve these heirlooms for their owners, not to mention brightening theirs."

Nods all around.

"I'll be at the shelter again tonight," Mary said, "and I will specifically look for these people among the residents. Trini may be able to help shed some light, now that we have a small list to look at." She pushed her empty plate aside. "Now, Amber, you said something about the photos I sent last night. Were they of help?"

"Actually, yes. The cards were in a corporate name. I discovered Moon Temple LLC was formed as a Delaware entity, which is not uncommon. A company doesn't need a physical address in the state where it's organized, just a representative there. That's usually a law firm but there are companies who set up for the sole purpose of forming and maintaining corporate entities for others."

Sandy was the only one who seemed already familiar with the concept.

"Anyway," Amber continued, "it looks like Foster Fordyce did this one himself. His quickie law degree has come in handy in quite a few ways. For instance, banking. Moon Temple has bank accounts in at least two countries outside the US. Within our borders, they have one. It's a big New York bank, well known, and an account holder really only needs the mobile banking app to conduct business."

"It's the way most banking is done anymore," Sandy said. "You don't have to live in the same neighborhood, or even the same city, as your bank these days."

"So all this money we've seen coming through the Temple here, is it going to this New York bank?" Pen asked.

"Some of it is," Amber confirmed. "But I doubt it's everything they're bringing in. The balance right now is in the mid five figures. I'm guessing at least that much came in during the one service I attended. I suspect the offshore banks are receiving the bulk of it. I just haven't figured out how they get it there, since so much is in cash."

"Obviously, a lot of the cash isn't going anywhere," Mary said. She lowered her voice and told the others of the boxes she and Trini had found under the dinette table in the bus.

"Still, eventually, it must get from there into a bank account—somewhere?" Gracie asked.

"I'm working on it," Amber said, "but that may actually be the million dollar question."

Chapter 18

Melissa plucked a huge ripe strawberry from the fruit plate in front of her. Its juice filled her mouth and she grabbed a napkin to keep it from running down her chin.

"Ah, the good life," said Foster watching her, enjoying his own perfectly cooked omelet.

"Better than what I can whip up on that dinky stove in the bus," she agreed.

"Who would have ever thought Foster-the-loser and little Missy would come this far?" He grinned the same smile that had won her heart the first time she saw him.

"Not my parents, that's for sure." Melissa thought of her father. Too bad he'd stayed such a small-time grifter. He would have loved running the big cons like this. Too bad he never would. Mama and Daddy both died when a tornado took out their double-wide and they'd refused to run for the community shelter down the road. They'd never even gotten to meet their new son-in-law.

"We ought to spend our last day at the pool," Foster suggested, breaking her pensive mood.

"Last day? I want to stay longer."

Normally, her petulant lower lip could sway him to change his mind. She was persuasive that way, either smiling or pouting until she got what she wanted. Nobody—from the contractors who would build their new palace, to the bankers in Switzerland, to the girl who did her hair and nails—could resist Melissa. She simply shrugged, smiled, and made the argument that she had a very clear vision for her life. For whatever reason, it worked. People gritted their teeth, ripped out a wall, removed the fresh nail polish … and changed it. No matter what she requested she got it.

"Baby, we got several hundred thousand reasons to stick closer to the bus for awhile. We've talked about this." About all their hard work vanishing if someone broke in and found the boxes.

She tossed a kiwi slice back on the fruit plate. "I *need* this break, Foster. You know how exhausting it is to be in front of people every night."

"You love it. You feed off the energy of those audiences."

She sighed. "I do. But I need a break from life on the bus. Two more nights? I have a massage appointment this afternoon and a hair appointment tomorrow. I just don't look as good in the white gown if my highlights have faded."

The persistence wore him down. "Fine. I'll go and stick around the bus, at least during the day when that homeless place next door has all those workers around. I don't like that."

Her expression brightened. "That's a great idea, honey. You're so smart to figure these things out."

She ran a fingertip along his arm, a look of promise in her eyes.

Dammit, she'd done it again, taken his plans and turned them upside down.

The fingers leaped down to his thigh and walked upward from his knee until she really had his attention. He scribbled a signature on the check and took her hand, leading her toward the elevators.

An hour later, bedding flung all over the floor, sweat glistening on his skin, Foster tried conversation again.

"I'll be back at five," he said. "Enjoy your massage and get yourself back in character for tonight's show."

She turned away but he reached for her chin and tilted her face toward him.

"We'll cut the Arizona gig short, I promise. Let's make it through the holiday and by January first we'll be on the road again."

"Really? California?"

"It'll be beautiful near San Diego and we'll put the bus in storage and stay in a nice place. Get a condo for a couple months or something."

"That's perfect, sweetie. We can pull off the hippie look there without having to actually live in poverty. Californians expect their New Age types to be wealthy. We can hang out with movie stars. Oh! I know! We get in with the Hollywood crowd and start the Dearly Departed routine. They've all got someone they regret losing—breakups with the family they left back home, tragic kid who OD'd. They lap up our séance routine."

He had already headed for the shower. "Sure, whatever you want to do." It was the easiest way to shut her up. He had enough on his mind already.

Chapter 19

When Sandy phoned the next morning with the suggestion of a girl's day out, some Christmas shopping, lunch, and a matinee performance of *The Nutcracker*, Gracie leaped at the chance.

"It's my last day to do my own thing before I'm wrapped up in the kids' holiday school activities and then having them home full time until January. Heck yeah," she said.

Sandy picked her up and they set off for Arizona Mills. "I normally don't touch that place," Sandy said, "but it's the middle of the week and I'm hoping every other person who finagled a vacation day during the season won't be there at the same time."

"How *did* you manage a vacation day at the end of the year?" Gracie settled into the Mazda's comfortable passenger seat.

Sandy laughed. "Believe it or not, I still had days left from last year, and corporate came down with a 'use em or lose em' policy this year. So, they didn't have much choice."

They cruised toward the busy shopping mall and exited I-10. At the intersection of the off-ramp and Baseline Road a man with a cardboard sign sat at the curb. **My kids need a Christmas too**, said the sign.

"Oh, sad." Gracie looked across the two lanes of vehicles and almost reached for her door handle.

"Too dangerous," Sandy warned. "The light's going to change any minute." She glanced toward the corner and stared. "Oh my gosh, I know that man."

"What? The guy with the sign?"

"Yes. He comes to Heaven Sent pretty regularly. I've spoken with him. I should remember his name …"

A car behind her honked impatiently. The light had changed and she had no choice but to move on.

"He's pretty far from home," Gracie said. "Well, if a homeless shelter can be considered home. This is so sad. I wish there was something we could do for him."

"Trini told me he begs on street corners a lot. At least enough to get bus fare across town, it seems." Sandy stayed with the flow of traffic and they had soon crossed a major freeway overpass. Too late to make a move and turn back to Ron's intersection. That was his name—Ron.

Gracie dug into her purse and pulled out a few dollar bills. "At least I'll be ready if we pass someone else. Or if we go back this way and he's still there." She tucked the money into the center console.

The huge outdoor mall was crowded and the cloudy, chilly day and lavish holiday decorations put the ladies in the spirit. "I could just walk around with a hot chocolate in hand and look at the sparkly things," Gracie said, "without actually setting foot in a store."

"I only need a couple of gifts," Sandy told her. "We drew names for Secret Santa at work, and the woman I picked loves lotions and creams. I thought I'd find something along those lines."

"I know the perfect store for that," Gracie said, pointing toward one of the few non-chain shops. "I met the lady who owns Maggie's Magical Mixes. She's great. She makes all her own soaps, lotions, and candles. And she's got a friend who creates mixes for soups and breads. I'll grab some of those while you look at the bath products, if you're interested."

They headed inside and spent nearly an hour browsing and sampling. Maggie offered tastes of some cranberry muffins she'd baked from one of their mixes. "If you're still in the mall around noon, pop by for a taste of the corn chowder. It's cooking in the crock pot right now."

Noon saw them grabbing a table at a pub, setting their gift bags aside while they indulged in French onion soup and crusty bread, then it was on to midtown for the ballet. Afterward, Gracie's eyes sparkled.

"Scott and I used to bring the kids to see *The Nutcracker* every year," she said as they retrieved Sandy's car from the parking garage. "They loved it when they were little, but I guess they've become too sophisticated as teens."

"By the time they're adults they'll love it again," Sandy told her. "Even without kids to bring, the story enchants me every time I see it."

The downtown avenues had a number of street people, some meandering in their own little worlds, talking to themselves; others claimed a corner, with a beseeching look in their eyes and a hand out. Gracie managed to give away all her dollar bills before they reached the 202.

"It was a fun day. Thanks for thinking of me," she said as Sandy dropped her off at home.

Sandy had her mind on picking up cat food as she pulled into the crowded Basha's Supermarket parking lot nearest her home. She dashed into the store, bought four cans of Fancy Feast, and was on her way back to her car when she spotted a somewhat familiar figure.

The man was dressed in grimy chinos, a knitted watch cap, and an oversized jacket. He carried a cardboard sign down at his side. She would swear it was the homeless man, Ron. He walked with confidence from the bus stop at the corner and into the Basha's parking lot. She watched as he stooped to do something with his shoe, then the lights flickered on a white Mazda parked in the side lot. He tossed the cardboard sign into the back seat and climbed in behind the wheel. The car backed out and headed toward the exit.

Sandy ran to her car and jumped in, starting it and backing out, realizing she'd barely checked her mirrors.

Ron's car made a right turn out of the lot and she followed his moves. What was a homeless guy doing with such a nice car, and where was he going?

Chapter 20

He went off into a neighborhood of little side streets and I lost him," Sandy told Mary as they hung curtains in the new room at the shelter.

"Did you get his tag number?"

Sandy shook her head. "There was no way. He was too far ahead of me before I even got out of the parking lot. But I know that model car—it's a Mazda 3. I had one just like it about six years ago."

Trini walked in. "You getting a new car?"

Sandy filled her in on the conversation. "I swear the guy I saw, thirty miles from here, was Ron, one of your residents."

"Hm. They usually don't get around quite that much," Trini said. "Most seem to end up in a neighborhood and stick close."

Mary spoke up. "Ron's one of the people on the list Amber gave us. There were six residents who fit the criteria of being here when the thefts took place. We were hoping to talk to each of them." She pulled the folded page from her jeans pocket.

Trini looked at it. "Micah was in the shower earlier. Thought he had a lead on a job. He actually cleans up pretty nice." She shot them a smile.

"Carrot and Blue are somewhat of a couple, although they sleep in the separate dorms. I saw them at breakfast. Lizzie is the shopping cart lady you've seen before. She's probably scouting the dumpsters behind Fry's, but I'd bet she'll be back in time for dinner. And Sue … hmm … I don't think I've seen her here for several nights. She got into a little spat with another woman when they both wanted the bed nearest the bathroom. I told them to work it out or I would assign beds. There was some glaring and hissing, like a pair of grumpy old cats. Could be Sue's miffed and that's the reason she's staying away for a while. Ron was here two days ago, but I can't say that I've seen him since."

A young woman wandered in, a girl in her twenties with flame-orange hair. Sandy remembered serving her in the food line.

"Carrot," called Trini, "come meet some new friends."

"Hi, me Carrot," she said, giving Mary an interested stare. "I like your hair."

Mary ran a hand through her spiky strawberry blonde locks. "Thanks. I like yours too. Is it why they call you Carrot?"

She nodded vigorously. "My daddy say, me carrot-top."

"Carrot, where's Blue? Is he still here?"

Another emphatic nod. "Blue put on clean shirt. In his room."

"We wanted to ask you and Blue a question," Mary said. "A man had a gold watch and he can't find it. Have you guys seen it?"

"Watch? We watch TV."

Mary laughed. "You made a joke! That's a good one. This is *a* watch, for telling time." She pointed to her smart watch. "Kind of like this, but it doesn't go on the arm. It's to carry in a pocket. And it's this color," she said indicating the gold-tone casing on hers.

Carrot gave the matter serious consideration but shook her head.

"Can we ask Blue? Maybe he saw it." Trini started toward the dorm rooms and the others followed along.

The door to the men's dorm stood open and a bulky male about Carrot's age was coming out. He sported a well-worn and much-laundered T-shirt—blue, of course. And blue canvas sneakers.

"Hey, Blue," Trini greeted. "These ladies have been working on the new dorm room, and they'd like to ask a question."

Carrot had come along and she took Blue's hand now.

When Mary posed the question about the missing pocket watch, Carrot tapped Blue's wrist where he wore a cheap plastic digital watch with a blue band.

He shook his head. "My watch not missing." He pointed to his own wrist.

"We hunt," invited Carrot, leading the way to Blue's bed.

"Is it okay?" Trini asked Blue.

He nodded and lifted his pillow to prove there was nothing under it. In the next moment he'd picked up a small day pack and unzipped it, dumping the contents on the bed. He had a toothbrush, a comb, four cards from a children's animal rummy game, a twist of blue yarn that didn't seem to belong to anything, and a wadded T-shirt, obviously the one he'd just shed in favor of the clean one.

"Now me, now me," Carrot insisted, taking Mary's hand and leading her to the women's dorm across the hall.

At her bed, she proceeded to fling the covers back and search for the watch before she, too, emptied a small backpack that contained her possessions. She poked among them and seemed disappointed when she didn't come up with the watch, as if it were the prize in a scavenger hunt.

"Thanks for your help with this," Mary said.

"But I not find the prize." Carrot's lower lip quivered a little.

"You won a prize anyway," Mary told her, reaching into the pocket of her hoodie and coming out with two small candy canes she'd picked up at the register of the coffee house where she and Sandy had gone for breakfast. "One for you and one for Blue because you both did a great job with the hunt."

The girl's face lit up as if the reward had been a hundred-dollar bill. "Wow—you nice ladies!" She handed Blue his candy cane and they walked down the hall, hand in hand.

Sandy turned to Trini with tears in her eyes. "Is a homeless shelter really the right place for them? They're so innocent."

"Social services is working on something. They've fallen into the gap between schools for children and facilities for adults with disabilities. Neither has family in the picture. Her parents died in a car crash and had no plan in place for her. Blue's mother just gave up—turned him over to the state to raise since he was about five. We're hoping an adult living facility in Mesa can take them both after the first of the year. They've grown so close, it would be really tough to split them up."

Trini excused herself to grab a ringing telephone at the desk. Mary and Sandy were about to head back to their task with the window curtains when they spotted Lizzie, the cart lady, outside at the front door.

Sandy stepped forward to hold the door for the older woman to push her shopping basket through.

"Pretty chilly out there this morning, isn't it?" she said with a smile.

Lizzie responded with a grunt and wheeled the squeaky cart down the hall. Trini finished her call and Sandy got her attention.

"What about her?" she asked with a nod toward the dining hall where Lizzie had gone.

Trini paused, thinking. "She likes bright shiny objects. Once she brought back a broken flash drive she'd found in the dumpster. Loved it because the silver metal part retracted and the casing was hot pink. Another time she showed me a little box full of foil papers, gold and silver ones. She collects them from Hershey Kisses if she sees someone toss one away. So, it's entirely possible the watch would have intrigued her."

"Do you think she would let us have a look in her cart?"

"Ooh, not likely. She's really protective. I'd try just asking her about the watch. If she has it, most likely she would love to show it off."

Sandy wasn't sure what she would say if it turned out Lizzie did have the missing watch. How would she talk her out of it? But she would think of something.

"I'll go along with you," Trini offered. "She knows me."

They walked into the dining hall and Trini offered

Lizzie a cup of coffee.

"That'd be nice." It was the longest sentence Sandy had heard from her yet.

"Say, Lizzie," said Trini, dispensing coffee from a big urn into a paper cup, "one of the men thinks he dropped a pocket watch somewhere the other day. You didn't happen to come across one, did you?"

Lizzie held the hot cup between her palms, warming them. She worked her lower lip a bit, and Sandy realized she had no teeth.

"Mighta." She raised the cup and sipped carefully.

"If it's the right one, there might be a reward," Trini said.

The words worked like magic. Lizzie set her cup on a nearby table and leaned over her shopping cart. Carefully picking through several layers, she brought out a dented tin box that had once held a fruitcake. Her gnarled fingers worked at the lid until it came open.

Sandy nearly stepped closer for a look inside but didn't want to spook the woman. One by one, Lizzie pulled out small treasures—the flattened foil pieces Trini had mentioned, a dime, a two-inch length of copper wire, a small gold-tone photo frame with some serious corrosion, a gold blazer button, the top to a lipstick case. She set the box aside and beamed toothlessly at her collection. No gold watch.

"Thank you for checking," Sandy said. She jammed her hands into her pockets, wishing she could pull out a candy cane reward, as Mary had done, but she had none. Wait, there was a coin. As luck would have it, it was a fairly new penny and the copper color shone beautifully.

"For you," she said, handing it to Lizzie. The coin went immediately into the treasure box.

She joined Mary to finish the curtain project. "Well, looks like three of our possible suspects are probably innocent. And, considering one of the remaining people was the victim of the theft, the list is getting much shorter."

"Have we actually given much thought to Micah himself?" Mary asked.

"What—that he would steal his own watch?"

"Or claim someone did, hoping the shelter carries some kind of insurance or something."

"But what about all the other missing items? Micah's watch was only the latest."

"So, maybe that's the perfect cover-up for the crime."

Chapter 21

Foster didn't like the way the door looked, as if someone had messed with the locking mechanism. Had it been that way yesterday? Or last night when they changed clothes and left? He rattled the door, testing. It seemed tightly locked. And when he went inside and checked the boxes of cash they looked exactly as he'd left them.

"Gotta get all this to a more secure place," he muttered to himself.

Things were too unsettled right now for his taste. The four-bedroom house in Texas was gone—giving it to their maid had probably been a stupid move. One of Melissa's grand gestures, but dumb when they hadn't yet built a new home. Having a home base always gave him somewhere to stash the cash. In the Houston house he'd entirely filled one of the spare bedroom closets with cash. Boxes, just like these, stacked floor to ceiling and marked "Books" so anyone taking a look would think they'd simply not unpacked everything when they moved in. When they'd vacated the house, they'd taken the boxes along but that proved cumbersome so they'd left them in a storage unit in Amarillo.

He needed to rent a unit here—planned on it if they stayed until spring, but now it looked like they'd go to California instead. Unsettled. At least a bus with books packed in boxes didn't raise many eyebrows, even that time when they'd driven across the border on a whim because Melissa was certain the margaritas would taste better in Mexico.

He'd sweated the border crossing, both directions, when officials wanted to take a look. But the drug-sniffing dogs hadn't pointed to the boxes and since there actually were books on top of the money, a cursory glance didn't reveal anything and they'd made it through without a hitch.

But now the bus was filling up. There were boxes under the bed at the back, boxes in the overhead cabinets, small boxes in storage cubbyholes near the generator and spare tire compartment, and now the space beneath the dinette table was becoming crowded. He needed a place to send some of the money.

Having a business which dealt almost exclusively in cash was a great thing, no doubt, but he hadn't thought through the logistics of dealing with it, especially when they had no permanent location. The banking laws that required reporting any cash transaction over ten thousand dollars made it tough.

He paced the length of the bus, crammed the boxes a little tighter, and forced his mind to calm down. He would figure out something. He always did. The beauty of their non-profit religious status—there was a perfectly logical explanation for so much cash.

And that was the answer. Beginning with tonight's take, he would simply deposit most of it. He made a phone call, reaching out to a man at the bank where one of the Moon Temple LLC accounts was located, a low-key institution in Delaware, unlike the large New York bank where he deposited the checks. And this one had international ties.

His contact at FEBG was an acquaintance he'd met through an online study group formed for fellow law school students. While the others chummed it up, studied together, and networked like crazy, Foster had looked only for those who could truly be of use and Richard Templeton turned out to be the one, mainly because he had a slightly sneaky way of approaching things.

A banker with flexible ethics was exactly what Foster and Melissa knew they needed. As a founding partner at FEBG, Richard could do whatever he wanted. Or whatever Foster wanted him to. There was the matter of a little indiscretion on Richie's part; knowledge of it gave Foster leverage no other customer of the bank would ever have.

"Hey Richie! Foster here."

The response was friendly but cautious. Good. Foster liked it that way.

"I'm FedEx-ing you some boxes of books this week. I know how you love those James Patterson and Lee Child novels." Code for *dangerous action with some sex thrown in*, which described the banker's careless move a few years ago that now held him under Foster's control.

"Good!" Richard said it with such false cheer that Foster knew someone else was in the room. "Your holiday gifts are always so great. You have my home address, right?"

"I do. By the way, I'm impressed with the interest rate

on my account right now. Love to watch my balance climb."

The whole conversation would pass unnoticed by anybody from a banking regulator to a casual eavesdropper. What it really meant was, *I'm sending the cash to your house by FedEx. Deposit the money to my account in small increments and it had better all add up. I'm watching.* They ended the call with a bright "Happy holidays."

Foster pulled boxes from the nearest hiding places and stacked them on the table, where he proceeded to tape them securely closed and fill out shipping labels. He would drop them at a FedEx office on his way to pick up Melissa. By the end of next week their bank account would have grown by another two hundred grand.

Melissa was in a mellow mood when he pulled into the parking lot at the resort. Not wanting to go through the rigmarole of switching the VW with an Uber and all that, he'd texted her to meet him out front. She spotted the little car and took her sweet time about walking over to him.

"Good massage, huh?" he asked, steering out and heading east.

"It was lovely. I will have no problem being my most angelic this evening," she said with a smile. "Especially since you said we could stay here a few more nights."

"One or two," he reminded. Of course, now that he had much of the money on its way to the bank, he was less stressed about being away from the bus.

"While I was under the capable hands of Francine in the massage room, I had a great idea," she told him, closing her eyes to block out the crazy traffic maneuvers that were happening on the freeway.

"What's that, baby?" His attention perked up. Her ideas almost always proved to be lucrative.

"We do the commune-with-the-dead routine next

week. Invitational only. We'll pull names and contact info from the donor checks. Anybody who gave over a certain amount gets invited. Might be good to throw in a few local celebrities too. If there is such a thing out here. Apache Junction isn't exactly where the rich hang out."

"Yeah, the locals tend to bring in twenty bucks or less a head. But I've been paying attention. A lot of A.J. winter people come from elsewhere, and they must have decent retirement funds if they can afford to winter in Arizona."

"*Celebrity* might actually be the local weather girl but, hey, everybody will know her face."

"Just remember, we can't afford to bring in some hotshot reporter who wants to make his career by exposing a scam."

She tilted her head and gave him a look. "Foster, I know."

She might be shallow about her clothes, makeup, and hair, but he had to remember how smart his wife was when it came to working a crowd. She had a deeper understanding of human nature than most of the over-educated psychologists he'd ever met.

"Sounds good," he said as he pulled into the Temple's parking lot. "I'll round up the money types, and you dig up background on them."

She beamed him a brilliant smile. Since social media, her part of the job had become *so* easy. She used to have to hang out with the queue of people waiting to get into the show, chatting them up and memorizing hundreds of little facts about them. Now they fed her all the personal information she needed, once she had their names.

Death of a loved one or beloved family pets were nearly always announced online now. Exactly what she needed to glean from this type of audience. Especially around the holidays when emotions about the departed were running high, it was easy to get information and then to play on the empathy of the whole crowd. Give away a message of comfort to two or three of them and you'd sold the package to everyone.

Every so-called 'medium' or street corner psychic used the technique. Nail a few key points, then claim it will take several future visits to reveal more—all at a much higher price. She giggled happily and went inside to change into her gauzy white gown.

Chapter 22

"How did they get your name?" Gracie turned over the thick cream envelope and looked at the handwritten address, then back at Pen. She had dropped by the older woman's home to bring a tray of cookies she and the kids had baked and found Pen puzzling over the odd item that had arrived in her mail.

"It came to my post office box, which is the address given on my author website. That part isn't terribly difficult. But how they came up with my name, I can't think—" A light dawned in her eyes. "I spoke to the woman sitting next to me at the *show*, for lack of a better word. This person was writing a check for a donation and practically flashed it in front of me, saying how impressed she was with this couple's work and that she was happy to contribute to such a worthy cause."

"And ..." Gracie knew she would need to let the story unfold.

"Before the program began, this woman had mentioned she was reading a book she really enjoyed and when I asked the title, it was one of mine. It's a bit awkward when that happens, but when she pulled the book from her bag I admitted I was the author and she begged me to sign it."

Pen dropped the invitation card onto the hall table and led Gracie through to the kitchen.

"It's absolutely the only way I can imagine anyone in that room knew I was there and the only way they could have tracked me to send this invitation."

"Pen, you're a bestselling author. Surely people recognize you all the time."

"Actually, almost never. All right, writers such as Stephen King or James Patterson—perhaps their faces are that well known. But, Penelope Fitzpatrick—I'm certainly not a household name." She'd put the kettle on when Gracie called earlier to say she was coming. Now, she brewed tea, poured them each a cup, and they helped themselves to cookies from the plate.

"So now you're invited to a special, invitation-only event at the Moon ... place ... temple ... whatever it's called. And what did the invitation say this event is?"

"Quote 'a special evening during which we will reach out to departed loved ones, hosted personally by Sunshine and Orion'. Aren't all their shows hosted personally? Really."

"Are you going?"

"Of course I'll go," she said with a laugh. "My only departed loved ones would be my parents and they've been gone quite some time, but I suppose I could make up someone for them to locate. If nothing else, this could provide some real 'inside' research for a future book."

Gracie picked up a second snickerdoodle. "Sounds interesting … I wonder how many people will be there. Surely not as large a crowd."

"The invitation mentions an intimate setting, but I can't imagine that large auditorium of theirs becoming exactly cozy. I suppose I shall find out."

"Just don't take your checkbook with you," Gracie teased.

"Oh, rest assured. And you can be certain I shall have a full report for you and the Ladies."

"Very good," Gracie said, standing. "I gotta go. Amber and I are working to find proof of this couple's good deeds, so I have an assignment for the afternoon."

* * *

Pen arrived promptly at seven p.m. According to her spy on site, Mary, the Temple of the Rising Moon had been closed for services last evening and there had been considerable bustling about with props and draperies. A sign out front advised visitors that tonight's service was by invitation only, and one of the Men in White, as she'd come to think of them, was at the door to check invitations. She showed hers and was ushered inside to be greeted personally by Sunshine.

Tonight's gown was much more subdued—a rich purple tunic that went to the floor, voluminous on Sunshine's small frame. Her golden hair glowed in contrast and she wore a crown of entwined willow branches with small purple flowers woven throughout. If Pen put her in a novel she would play the part of a wood nymph or sprite.

"Welcome, Ms. Fitzpatrick," Sunshine said. "We are so

pleased that you have come. The gentleman will show you to the reading room. Sit anywhere you like." Her beautiful face shone with benevolence.

Another of the Men in White waited beside a dark curtain which had not been there on Pen's first visit. He held it open to reveal a double ring of chairs facing a smaller version of the stage. Dark curtains hung from the ceiling, enclosing the space which—at a quick count—was designed for an audience of thirty. The lights were low and sitar music played softly. Pen almost expected to see a table with a long cloth and a crystal ball. She chuckled under her breath at the cliché image.

"Oh, Penelope! Um, Ms. Fitzpatrick," said a chipper voice. "Sit with me again."

The woman from the other night waved her over and Pen saw no other choice. Most of the chairs were filled already, and people were chatting quietly among themselves.

"I've brought another book, and I wonder if you would mind signing it? To Anna." She reached for her tote bag. "Oh—I'm sorry. Is that too presumptuous of me?"

"Not at all," said Pen with a smile. She took the book and pulled a pen from her purse. A fan was never an interruption, she had decided long ago, and she was always happy to sign books.

Anna talked while Pen wrote a short inscription.

"I was so excited to be invited tonight," she said. "I really, really hope they can give me a message from my dear Eddie. He passed six months ago."

Pen made the appropriate consoling comment and handed the book back.

"I just need to know he's okay. On the other side, I mean. To know he made it to a good place and is happy would mean everything to me."

Pen was saved from further comment when the lights dimmed. All chairs were occupied now, all invitations apparently accepted.

With precise timing, the house lights dimmed and a soft light came on, filling the stage with an almost iridescent glow. The pinkish tone flattered Sunshine's skin and clothing as she stepped out from a space between the curtains.

"Welcome, greetings, namaste, prayers and well wishes to all of you," she said with her hands held together in front of her heart. "This is a very special evening, and I must tell you we do not do these very often. Once in a great while, when we have been in a location for some weeks, we begin to sense an *otherness* about a few of the people. For those, something of great import has happened in their lives."

A few nods around the room.

"I have to tell you," she said, adopting a more casual tone, "Orion and I have both commented on this feeling we've had for about a week now. We know"—a fist pressed to her chest—"we *know* each of you has suffered losses. I understand, the holiday season brings out so many memories, wonderful ones and some not so wonderful."

More nods, more vigorously.

"And that is why I am here to share with you my husband's most incredible gift—his ability to communicate with those in the afterlife. We *so very much* want to put you in touch with the person or persons you are thinking about right now."

She had stepped to the very edge of the stage. "So, close your eyes and fix a picture of your loved one in your mind. Right now. Do it now." A thirty-second pause. "All right. You may open your eyes."

Pen noticed a few dabbing with tissues.

"Open your eyes and let me present …" An arm waving toward the curtain. "My own dearest one—Orion!"

He stepped through the curtain, wearing a dark blue tunic and pants, his waves of brown hair cascading over his shoulders. He raised both arms, then brought his palms together and gave a small bow.

"I have been in prayer all afternoon," he said quietly, "because there is something very mysterious in the air today. A vibration that has put me in touch with the deepest secrets of the universe. And I am so thankful," his voice cracked a little, "this was the evening we chose for you to be here. Very important things are about to be revealed."

He took a deep breath, closed his eyes, and said. "There is someone named Kirsten in the room. Kirsten, where are you?"

He opened his eyes. Sunshine had noticed the young woman's reaction and had stepped over to her side. Pen recognized Kirsten Nichols, one of the morning show hosts on Channel 6.

"Kirsten, we have never met. Is that true?"

Kirsten shook her head, managing to take in the rest of the audience with her public smile.

"Kirsten, you have lost someone important to you. Someone young. Someone you loved more deeply than anything. I'm seeing a number … the number seven."

The newswoman's face crumpled. "My little Oscar, my Chihuahua. He died, seven days ago." She couldn't hold herself together. Tears flowed, marring her perfect makeup.

Orion raised his hands and spoke. "Kirsten, my dear woman. Your pain is so great. But I have welcome news. Oscar is happy and he is free of pain. He's doing well." He raised his eyes to the ceiling. "I see him, running through an open field of grass and flowers, playing with another little dog. They are having a wonderful time. He is thinking of you and hoping your heart will heal soon."

Kirsten nodded and sat down. Sunshine stepped to the back of the room.

Orion closed his eyes again. "I'm hearing a name. Ed … Edward …?"

Beside Pen, her new friend gasped. "Eddie!" she called out. "Are you talking to my Eddie?"

Sunshine stepped over to them, leaning across Pen to encourage Anna to stand up. She held a microphone so Anna could share her story.

And so it went as a half-dozen of the audience members were called upon and received amazing stories of how their deceased loved ones were faring. At one point, Orion mentioned the name of Pen's mother. He looked at her as he spoke. It would have been easy to react and be drawn into the show, but she didn't. When no one responded to the name, he deftly turned it into a similar name. Marion became Marianne and a man jumped up when he heard it.

After forty-five minutes came the ending and the pitch. Orion began to appear fatigued on stage as the effort of communicating with a distant world became overwhelming. Sunshine rushed to his side and helped him to an upholstered chair that happened to be waiting behind him. He slumped onto it, his head hanging low.

"I'm afraid that's all for tonight," she announced. "His ability to hear so many voices often wears him out. When he's tired the voices begin to fade."

Plus, forty-five minutes is about as long as you can hold an audience's attention without their becoming restless or looking for faults with the performance, thought Pen.

"For those who were fortunate enough to connect

with their loved ones tonight, bless you all. If you wish to speak further with Orion, to see if he learned more or if he later heard again from your dear one, we have some appointments open tomorrow. Despite his weary state, now he will retire to his private quarters and write down everything that came to him."

On cue, one of the white-clad men showed up to take Orion's elbow and lead him away.

"Transcripts of his writings will be available tomorrow, as well. For those who did not connect with someone you wanted to hear from, do not give up. Please speak with me later and give a little information. If Orion heard anything, if he recorded anything for you, I am most happy to set a personal appointment or pass along his written words."

As the audience began to shift in their seats, Sunshine added quietly, "And of course we appreciate all donations toward our housing project."

Pen had to give the pair points for brazenness.

Chapter 23

The evening had grown chilly, and Pen drove away from the Temple feeling exhilarated over what she had learned and too keyed up to immediately go home to sleep. She phoned Sandy and asked if the group would be up for a drink somewhere.

"O'Malley's would be an easy detour for me," Sandy said. "I'm just leaving the Mesa Community Center. I'll call the others."

Traffic was light and Pen arrived twenty minutes later. Amber, Sandy, and Gracie had already found a corner table, and Mary walked in a minute behind Pen. All agreed that the hot mulled wine sounded like an excellent choice. The server brought baked brie and a sliced baguette to go along with it.

"Quite interesting, the show—reading, séance—

whatever you would call it. The technique became obvious to me, given that Mary had already told us about the existence of the earbuds." She ran through the events, including the fact she'd actually spotted Sunshine's communication device when she leaned in to speak to the woman in the next seat. "I felt sorry for her, this Anna. She clings to the hope that her deceased husband is out there somewhere and will speak with her."

"Do you think she's one of those who will pay extra to go back and learn more?" Sandy asked.

Pen nodded. "I fear so. Others were even more desperate. A woman who lost a child was sobbing and clinging to Sunshine's arm when I left. I feel for them, and wanted to tell them none of it was real. But people need something ... some shred of hope that a loved one is not really lost to them."

"None of us really know, do we?" Gracie asked, cupping her mug of hot wine between her palms.

"We don't. It's just so sad when people like the Fordyces, who are very adept actors, instill a belief in innocent ones," Pen said.

"And where those innocents have paid money to back it up," Mary said. Her mouth was set in a firm line. No one asked, but Pen got the feeling Mary had personal experience along this line.

Pen patted her hand. "The money is the sad part. As I left, several of the attendees were hovering around Sunshine and I heard her hinting about the costs for private consultations. They'll pay dearly and receive only whatever scripted lines Orion chooses to give them." She let out a pent-up breath. "So—that's my report, sad as it may be. Has anyone else found something more positive?"

Amber and Gracie exchanged a look.

"Not sure if this falls under *good* news or not," Gracie said, "but Amber and I decided to look into the claims that the Moon Temple duo are building houses for poor people."

"They show all these photos of happy people standing out in front of new homes, but where are they? Are they even for real?" Amber said. "So, I began digging through their website, parsing the exact words, and I came up with three houses I could match to a location. Then I used Google Earth to actually go there …"

She pulled out her phone and touched an app. Stretching the picture and playing with the angle of it, she showed a small house with white siding and blue trim.

"Supposedly this is one," she said, clicking over to a different page in her browser. She showed it all around. "But, when Gracie went to the tax records for this town it turns out the house at that address has been there twenty years, and the same owner has been paying the property taxes on it the whole time."

"I called the owner," Gracie said. "They bought the house when it was a new subdivision. Gave me the name of the builder who did the whole neighborhood. They've never heard any of the names we know to be associated with the Fordyces."

"Maybe it's not the same house?" Mary asked.

"Or some quirk of misinformation," Amber said. "So I checked the others. Similar stories. The pictures and addresses the Moon Temple folks claim match up, but the owners never heard of them and they certainly didn't get a free house."

Mary was drumming her nails on the table top. "So, if the money isn't being used to build houses, where is it going?"

Amber got a gleam in her eye. "I'm working on that. And I *will* find out."

Smiles all around. They knew she could do it.

Gracie yawned and Mary piped up. "Before we call it a night, I want to give a quick report on my findings at the shelter. Sandy and I took Amber's list of the residents who were there all the times a theft happened. So far, we've only been able to question three of the six. One of the others was a victim—Micah—but I plan to get to the others soon. I'll be going back there tomorrow."

"Don't forget our little party at my house on the twenty-third," Pen said as they left the table. "Spouses, dates, others are included."

They split up in the parking lot, but while the others got into their cars, Sandy pulled Pen aside.

"This is starting to look a lot more serious than I'd guessed," she said, pulling the lapels of her sweater together against the chill breeze from the west. "I thought we were looking at a couple of hippies who talked all love-and-helpfulness and lived in an old bus, but it looks like some big money is changing hands and a lot of false claims have been made. Isn't there something we can do about it? I feel awful for people like that lady, Anna."

Pen looked thoughtful as she fingered her keyring. "I agree. I'm not sure what laws they're breaking, especially if people are willingly handing over their money."

"A good case for fraud, I'm thinking, and that's just for starters. What about tax evasion? Any bets on how much of that money is being reported to the IRS?"

Pen nodded. "I shall talk to Benton. He's not in the District Attorney's office any longer, but he's been a wealth of information in the past. And I owe him a dinner." She winked at Sandy. "I shall report."

Chapter 24

"Great job, everyone," Mary said as she dismissed her self-defense class.

Some of the women at the shelter had been on the street long enough they already knew how to look out for themselves. Lizzie, for one, looked at the participants as if they were stupid or crazy. Others, such as the young mother with the two little girls, were clearly grateful for the tips and techniques. Mary picked up her small towel and wiped the dampness from her neck.

She had promised the Ladies she would continue making inquiries about the stolen items, but she was getting discouraged. She could pretty much rule out Carrot and Blue. They had such an open and innocent attitude, they seemed completely incapable of deception. Lizzie, too, had willingly shown her collection of shiny objects, and it was obvious that the rest of her shopping cart contained only old clothing, cardboard boxes, and aluminum cans.

Two men were on the list—Ron, the grungy guy, and Micah who claimed to be one of the victims of a theft. Mentally, Mary had added the word 'claimed' for some reason she couldn't pinpoint. Micah was different.

His story included big successes in real estate, bitterness toward the banks who'd foreclosed his loans, and now a lot of computer searches as he attempted to rebuild his lost fortune. She had an easier time believing he'd once owned a gold watch than she could believe he was comfortable living in a homeless shelter.

This morning she had intended to talk to him before the self-defense class but he'd vanished. It was right after he walked past the reception desk where she and Trini had been talking. It almost felt as if something about their conversation prompted his disappearance. But when Trini had looked in the men's dorm, Micah's things were still on his bed. He intended to come back.

Mary slung her gym bag over her shoulder. Maybe she could locate either Ron or Sue, the other two on her list of residents who had been here the dates of all the thefts.

"Ron hasn't been around for several days," Trini told her when she stepped into the dining hall to help with the tables and chairs Mary had moved for her class. "That happens, especially with him."

"He panhandles on the street corners, doesn't he?" Mary remembered Sandy saying she'd seen the man.

"Yeah. It's probably why he doesn't come around all the time. Maybe he collects enough to stay in a motel or something."

"How about Sue? Is she here? I don't think I know her."

"Always wears a yellow windbreaker and a red scarf wound around her neck. She was at breakfast, but I haven't seen her in a couple hours." Trini set two plastic chairs in place at a table. "She's quiet, keeps to herself, hardly talks to anyone, and goes away during the day. I have no idea where."

Mary looked around. "I saw Micah this morning and wanted to talk to him."

"Hmm … he might have found something of interest on the computer. He was right over there while the others were eating."

"He walked past us. When I arrived this morning, and you and I were talking at the front desk—do you remember what we were talking about?"

Trini laughed out loud. "Gosh, I'm doing well if I remember to comb my hair in the mornings. Too much going on to remember every conversation. I think I had asked you if your friend Sandy was coming back—maybe that was it? Sorry to be so vague."

"It's okay. Not important." Mary decided to drive around the neighborhood a little, see if she could spot either Sue or Ron.

If not, she ought to get back to the gym and give Billy a break. December tended to be a slow month, and he'd been so cooperative about her taking this much time away. Come January it would be a different story when their members got all virtuous again and decided to lose the extra holiday pounds. Classes and equipment would be full.

She started her car and pulled out of the parking lot, noticing that the temple next door was quiet and there was no sign of the gurus out near their bus either. She spotted a bright yellow garment at the bus stop on the next corner, but it wasn't Sue. And although she cruised the area for another fifteen minutes, she didn't see Ron or anyone else with a cardboard sign.

She headed back to Tempe and her business, and was nearly there when the scene popped into her head—she and Trini talking about Sandy. It was the moment she'd told Trini that Sandy's job at the bank was limiting the number of hours she could volunteer. She'd said something like, "Desert Trust has some big manager's meeting this week," and that was the moment Micah walked by. His whole demeanor had stiffened and he walked out the front door without a word. It must fit—one of the banks he hated must be Desert Trust Bank. It could explain some things.

Or not. She parked in her usual space and grabbed her gym bag. Micah seemed a man of many moods—sometimes friendly and cooperative, other times surly and full of complaints—as if the world owed him something. She thought again of Sandy's comment that she didn't entirely believe Micah's story about the watch.

She shook off the idea. Solving this mystery might not be possible. It could come down to the fact that there were too many workers, volunteers, and residents milling about at the shelter. Things go missing; things get misplaced. Each little missing thing could have its own story, and they might never learn where the items ended up.

She needed a good workout. If no one was on the bags, she might just go inside and beat up one of them.

Chapter 25

Pen always enjoyed entertaining, and Benton Case was easy to cook for. They'd once been lovers for a brief spell. Now they were one of the rare couples who happily remained close after the passion had dwindled to an easy friendship. Tonight, she'd made his favorite pasta dish.

Her Christmas tree stood in the corner of the living room, beautifully decorated in her favorite shades of blue and lavender, and she had strung soft lights around the perimeter wall of the small yard. Beyond the wall, the view of Phoenix spread out below for miles in each direction, like a bonus spread of holiday lighting, just for the two of them. They stood outside in the mild breeze, enjoying a glass of wine while the Florentine pasta shells baked.

"So, what do you think?" Pen asked. She had told him about the two situations the Heist Ladies were working on.

"Both cases are intriguing but, truthfully, I doubt you'll ever know what happened to the missing items from the people at Heaven Sent. Shelters like that are not secure places. Sad as it is, I would imagine things disappear all the time." He sipped his merlot. "The other case sounds as if it may have merit—from a legal standpoint."

Pen heard the timer on the oven. "Let's go inside. I want to hear more, and dinner's ready."

He carried their wine glasses to the dining room. She dropped her light shawl over the back of the sofa and went into the kitchen. Filling plates with the piping hot pasta dish, garlic bread and salads, she carried them to the table. They toasted one another and resumed the conversation.

"Anyway, as you probably already know, prosecuting fraud can be tricky. First, you need evidence. And then you need witnesses who will come forward and admit they were cheated. It becomes especially difficult when the deception comes under the guise of some sort of religious activity. People tend to cling very strongly to their beliefs, for one thing, and they also don't like having it pointed out that they were caught in a gullible moment."

Pen nodded thoughtfully, remembering Anna who had sat next to her. The woman's trust in Orion and Sunshine had reached a fervor by the time the séance-like session ended that night.

"You mentioned evidence. What sort of evidence?"

"Catching them in the act is always good. That would mean law enforcement agents attending their services and documenting the claims."

"I can't think what, exactly, they are claiming. It's not as if an afterlife is something that can be proved or disproved. But that's not really what they seem to be about, even though there is talk about earning a place in heaven and other such rhetoric. The real push of the regular services is about raising money to build housing for the poor."

"Good," he said, taking a second slice of garlic bread. "That's a concrete claim, and one that should be provable. Or disprovable. If they take money and don't use it for what they claim they will, that's fraud."

"We're making a bit of progress there," Pen said, telling him of Gracie and Amber's efforts to establish the chain of real estate ownership.

He nodded. "That's good. But I'm not sure it's enough to take to the District Attorney or to the US Attorney if the properties are in more than one state. They'll want to see some kind of documentation before they organize a raid and search the couple's premises."

"Considering they are living in an old bus, I have a hard time picturing all their business enterprises actually being on the premises."

"You'd be surprised. An entire business can exist on a laptop computer these days."

"That's where the real evidence will be then." Her eyes lit up, but she couldn't exactly reveal to Benton, a former district attorney himself, that she'd just had a vision of stealing Orion's computer.

"What about the other routine they do, the sessions I think of as séances? Telling people Orion can communicate with their dead loved ones is cruel. And charging money for it—it's absolutely reprehensible."

He placed a hand on hers. "Pen, dear. Yes, you are right. Sadly, this will be the hardest of all your cases to prove. How does one prove that he didn't actually receive some message from the Great Beyond? There are bona fide psychics who receive messages the rest of us cannot understand."

"But not on cue, in front of an audience, revealing facts most anyone could either find online or can get the person to reveal with a few clever questions."

He laughed softly. "That's my girl. I know you'll figure out something." He reached for her empty plate and stacked it with his. "Now, what's for dessert?"

* * *

Pen was delighted when she received an invitation from the Fordyces to attend a second of their intimate gatherings "to communicate with our dear departed ones." She called Amber.

"Benton tells me we need proof—we'll get proof."

"Come by my place on your way to the séance. I'll get you all fixed up," Amber told her.

Pen touched the jeweled brooch on her lavender suit jacket as she approached the Moon Temple. Amber had said the tiny embedded chip behind the buttonhole camera would record an hour's worth of video. Pen thought it a good idea to record the entire process, from the greeting at the door to the 'show' inside. This time she planned on feeding out a few false details, just to see how her information would be used.

Sunshine seemed in an ebullient mood tonight, greeting each newcomer with a warm hand clasp and taking an interest as she asked their names. Pen barely spotted the little flesh-colored earbud, and she tried to aim the brooch toward Sunshine in hopes of catching a glimpse of it with her camera.

As luck would have it, Pen walked in just ahead of Anna, and the other woman suggested they sit together. Perfect.

This time, when Orion tested by calling out the name of Pen's mother, she tentatively raised a hand and stood.

"I believe you might be talking about me," she said, adding the right amount of hesitation to her voice.

When he heard her accent, he beamed. "I believe I am. I'm hearing the voice of a British woman. She was a war bride. You were born in the UK but have lived here much of your life."

Pen nodded. The information was almost verbatim from her author biography that was posted widely online.

"Your mother transitioned from this earthly realm to the other side, let's see … it's been two years ago now?"

Pen had planted that tidbit with Anna, standing near the entrance where Sunshine could overhear. In reality, her mother had been gone for decades.

"Twenty-seven months, oh gosh yes, that's right." She tried to put the right amount of enthusiasm into her voice without sounding as if she was mocking him.

"You miss her very much." His voice dropped into a sad register, and Pen felt Sunshine gently touch her arm. These two were good.

Pen nodded.

"Your mother is doing well. She's in a happy place. She wants you to know—" He squeezed his eyes closed, appearing to be concentrating very hard. "To know …" He let his breath out in a rush. "I'm sorry. I've lost contact. Maybe later. If I hear more from her I will write everything down. Please get in touch. I'll be happy to share whatever I learn."

He straightened his shoulders, took a deep breath, and turned toward someone at the other side of the room. The spiel began again.

Chapter 26

Amber had told Pen to stop by again after the séance, no matter how late. It was a little after nine o'clock when Pen texted to say she was on the way, and Amber had invited the other Ladies to come over and see the results. Only Gracie couldn't make it.

"I was able to record the live experience and also quiz one of the duo's avid followers. I just hope it turned out well enough," Pen said.

Carefully taking the brooch from Pen's lapel, Amber removed the backing and took out the small chip. She slipped it into a casing that allowed her to plug it into a USB port, and the video came up on her screen.

"This quality is amazing," Pen said. "The place is quite dimly lit and I was worried whether anything would actually show."

"Let's just turn up the audio a little …" Amber said, fiddling with controls.

They watched as Sunshine greeted newcomers. Pen had lingered near the entrance and had captured the arrivals of two more people, including Anna. The Ladies remained still, concentrating on the video as Orion came on stage and called on Pen.

"So, does he say anything truly new?" Amber asked, pausing the video when he turned to another victim. "Everyone knows this stuff about you. Anyone could find it."

"Exactly," Pen said. "He's found commonly available information to lead into the so-called *reading*. Other than the date of my mother's death—notice how he picked that up from what I told Anna before the show began. Watch this next bit. It's when Anna turns to me and talks. I hope this turned out well. It is, I believe, the sort of evidence Benton was referring to."

The video started again. On the screen, Anna tapped Pen's forearm. "The private sessions are really worth doing," she whispered. "I've had two of them with Orion in the past two days. He's marvelous."

Pen had turned toward her neighbor and caught the ecstatic look on Anna's face as she admitted the price she'd paid.

"Holy crap!" Mary burst out. "That's crazy."

"Yes, it seemed an astounding amount for a fifteen-minute session, to my way of thinking," Pen said.

Sandy spoke up. "How do Orion and Sunshine approach the money aspect?"

"You'll see at the end, there's an ever so slight reference to 'donations to our cause are always appreciated.'"

"They don't call it a fee?"

“Only a donation, and they make it sound as if it all goes to the housing cause.”

“Hmm. You’ll have to run this by Benton and see what he says. My guess is that as long as the money is given voluntarily it will be a difficult case to prove, legally speaking.”

“That’s my fear,” Pen admitted. “Although we have managed quite nicely in the past when law enforcement wanted nothing to do with our cases.”

Smiles all around. The video had ended with Orion and Sunshine on the stage, hands in prayer position, heads slightly bowed.

“One thing I can say for that pair,” said Mary, jutting her chin toward the screen. “They really are the ultimate DIY-ers. Melissa stages a good show, knows how to work a crowd, and apparently he handles the money and manages to keep the finances off the radar. They do it all.”

“Yes, they do,” said Sandy, “but we have a wide range of talents among us, too. We’ve caught their act. Now I think we just need to track the money and catch them *in* the act.”

Chapter 27

Melissa held a cardboard box on her lap as Foster steered the VW Beetle toward the center of the city.

"How come we're taking the money back to the resort with us this time?" she asked.

"I'll take care of it tomorrow. After we check out."

He'd been staring out at the road but didn't seem to be focused on driving. He could do the show in his sleep, as long as she prompted him through his earbud, but his mind was definitely elsewhere the last couple of days.

"Foster, I've been wanting to talk about that. Do we have to check out yet? I love staying at a nice place. I booked a facial and a spa day tomorrow."

He let her go on about how they didn't really need to stay in the bus. They had reset the draperies in the auditorium and rearranged the seating for the smaller groups and personal consultations, and it was a lot of work to change everything back for the big shows, she reminded.

"Can we stick with just the readings until Christmas?" she asked.

"Sure. It's kinda what I'd planned anyhow."

"And can we stay on at the resort? I *really* love it there …"

"What if they've booked our suite after tomorrow?"

"Well, I bet they'll have *something* available."

Her voice took on a sexy tone and he knew he was hooked. What Melissa wanted, Melissa got. Plus, as much as they were spending on meals and amenities in this place, management would be dumb to let them go if they wanted to stay forever. What the heck.

He gave her the smile she expected. "I'll bet you're right."

Forgetting about the routine of ordering an Uber to drive them to the resort, he'd steered the VW up to the guard gate and had to present his room key to prove they were guests. "The wife wanted this little cute retro ride today," he explained.

At least this way he would have his own car handy in the morning to take the package to FedEx. The first few deposits Richie had made for him showed up in the account just fine. Tonight in the room he would check again. The system seemed to be working.

Still, it felt as though things were closing in, and Foster hated that. With each passing day he became more antsy.

As predicted, the night manager was more than glad to extend their stay another five nights. Apparently, most people did family visits more than resort stays in the days leading up to Christmas. After that, he warned them, accommodations would become more scarce. New Year's

Eve was one of their most popular nights of the year, and all rooms were solidly booked.

All the more reason to get the heck out of here before year end. Foster feigned disappointment and thanked the man who had given him the perfect lead-in for the conversation with his wife.

"You heard the man, baby," Foster said once they were in their suite. "We have to be out by the twenty-eighth."

Her lower lip jutted out.

"But—I have a plan. We've talked about California. Now's the time to put that together."

She brightened a little. She did love southern California. "Come with me for a late-night swim. They keep the water real warm, and the stars are out …"

"You go ahead. I've got some banking to do."

* * *

"What the hell?" Richie grumbled when he answered the phone. "It's after one in the freaking morning."

"You answered. You must have recognized my number," Foster countered.

"Okay, yeah …" Richie's voice grew wary. "Everything's going okay, right?"

"You alone in the room?"

"Yeah. Girlfriend didn't stay over. What's up?"

"I'm watching the little transactions you've been doing. All's good. Now I need to send some international."

"Books—like the rest?"

"Yeah."

"A lot?"

"Uh, yeah, you could say that." His mind flashed to the various storage lockers loaded with boxes.

"Man, that's a different thing. Worries me. Stuff can disappear, people notice, they talk."

It was what Foster feared. He should have figured out ways to launder the money gradually, over time. Now he was stuck with a bunch of it.

"What do you want to do?" Richie asked.

Stuff can disappear. People talk.

"Let me think about it. I'm sending a FedEx tomorrow—handle it the same. I'll let you know about the rest."

Foster clicked off the call and paced the room a few times. Crypto currency might be an answer, but he'd done some reading on those, Bitcoin and the others. The consensus seemed to be that it left an electronic trail, was difficult to convert back to cash, and then became tricky to spend it in any large quantity. Like millions. Spending millions in good old greenbacks wasn't exactly easy either, he was discovering.

His head began to pound and he heard the sound of Melissa's keycard unlocking the door.

Chapter 28

Amber ignored the clock on her computer screen—she knew it was getting very late. Sunshine, Orion, and the Temple of the Rising Moon were nearly as elusive as ever. Even tracking their real identities, it seemed Foster and Melissa Fordyce owned nothing in their own names. So, okay, she supposed it was okay to run all their expenses through Moon Temple LLC.

People probably did that, although Sandy had hinted that *surely* a religious non-profit organization couldn't legitimately deduct *all* the expenses of the owners—board members, whatever they called themselves. At the very least, they must have bank accounts, the Ladies had all agreed. It became Amber's job to find them.

And she did—finally. The clock showed 3:06 a.m. when she located a Moon Temple account at a bank called

FEBG, a small Delaware entity. She marked the page and started to go further into the records, but exhaustion overtook her. With a yawn and a stretch, she closed her computer and stumbled to her futon to catch a few hours of sleep.

By five-thirty she was wide awake again and itching to figure out what was going on. Foster Fordyce had a law degree with a specialty in international banking. That had to be important.

She brushed her teeth, put her fluffy hair up into a wild ponytail, and made herself a green smoothie. The banking world was awakening in the US and would be in full swing in Europe by now. Any of her searches would likely blend in with the normal transactions, billions of them, which flowed through the banking system during each day. She liked the anonymity of it.

Back at the FEBG site, she dug deeply enough to get behind their firewalls and take a peek into the accounts. Moon Temple LLC had a standard business account, one with a few special perks for 501(c)3 non-profits. So far, that wasn't anything she wouldn't have already known. The balance in the account was in the high five figures. Puzzling, since Amber had personally witnessed an evening's take when the donation baskets came around. She'd felt fairly certain they took in nearly that much every night. They'd been working the Apache Junction location for at least three weeks—maybe longer—so wouldn't there be a lot more than this in the bank?

How naïve am I? Of course, most of the donations were in cash. How much of that actually made it into the bank account?

The page she was on showed merely a line-item listing for each of the bank's accounts, not details about any specific one. She highlighted the Moon Temple name on the list and entered a string of code that should have allowed her into the pages-behind-the-pages.

Nothing happened. Not even an Access Denied screen.

She chewed at a cuticle. Account holders themselves couldn't normally see the type of detail she knew existed. She should be able to tell not only how much of each deposit was cash and how many items were checks or money orders, but also the denominations of the currency and quite likely the serial numbers.

Not that she needed quite that much, but still. Nothing.

"Okay, there's more than one way at this."

She pulled out an alternate laptop computer she rarely used. Because it contained a little program—she hated to call it spyware, but it was close. Booting it up, she gave the machine a minute to update itself and then entered the complete address for FEBG and the Moon Temple account page. The software began performing its magic.

It broke through the bank's central server and came to a complete halt.

No further information exists for this search

"Oh, yes it does," she muttered, quickly typing a new command.

No further information exists for this search

"Come on, the guy's a lawyer, not a computer whiz." She entered a go-around command, thinking that an approach from a different direction would help.

Access denied

"Oh no you don't." She tried another backdoor method. She'd only used it once before, and it had been like saying "Open sesame." Not this time.

She needed to get off the spyware system quickly. The longer she stayed there, the more chance she would be discovered. She backed out of the program, erased her search history, and cleared the cache before shutting down the laptop.

"Well, rats."

Whoever was making the deposits was good. He was using hidden servers, specialized methods, and most likely multiple transfers to take the money from some other source.

"If it's Foster Fordyce, he really is a multi-talented guy," she said as she picked up her jacket and walked out the front door. Maybe burning off some steam with a run in the park would put some fresh ideas into her head.

Chapter 29

Sandy saw the cardboard sign before she put it together that the man carrying it was Ron from the shelter. She recognized the same dusty chinos and the oversized jacket he always seemed to have on. She had just passed a bus stop on Broadway, planning to pick up a few things at Fry's and grab a quick lunch before heading back to the bank. She slowed, wondering if it would be a nice idea to offer him a ride back to the shelter.

Before she had talked her way through all the reasons why, one, he might not be going back to Heaven Sent; two, he might not remember her and would be distrusting; or three, what the hell was she thinking to consider letting a grubby stranger into the car with her—he surprised her by cutting through the parking lot and approaching a car, which he unlocked with a key fob.

Same car, same scenario as before! She eased her Mazda into a parking slot and watched. He tossed the cardboard sign into the back seat, dusted off the seat of his pants, and got into the driver's seat. Sandy followed, sticking close this time.

It turned out to be a fairly short drive. At the next light he made a right turn into a nice residential neighborhood, then a left, a right at the next street. She dropped back to a half block away. He would surely spot her.

She saw him reach up for a moment, then a garage door opened at a home on the right side of the street. *What the hell!*

She sped up and stopped, blocking him from backing out. But he wasn't planning to back out, she saw. He pulled into the garage and got out of the car.

What to do? Thinking quickly, she got out of her car and called his name. He turned, and his face showed no sign of recognition.

"Ron? I'm Trini's friend at Heaven Sent."

A dozen thoughts flickered across his face. His eyes cut to the right, as if he debated running into the house and hiding out. He took a different tactic.

"Oh yeah," he said. "I saw you there."

"I'm confused," she said, looking pointedly at the house. "You've been staying at a homeless shelter."

He chuckled. "Oh, this? And the car? Not mine. This is my friend's house and he loaned me his car for the day. I was just returning it."

"Oh." Sandy felt a moment's acute embarrassment. "I just—"

"Hey, not a problem. An easy mistake."

"Can I offer you a ride back? Looks like you're kind of stuck here."

"Thanks, but no. Joe will be home soon and he'll take me, or I'll just walk to the bus stop. Like five minutes, ten tops, and he'll be here. I'm going to close up the garage and then sit on the porch to wait."

"If you're sure."

"Absolutely sure." He waved as she got back into her car, then he walked into the garage, pressed the closer button, and ducked out as it came down. He seemed fine as he settled on the edge of the porch.

Oh well, she thought as she drove away. Ron's explanation seemed reasonable enough, and she was secretly glad she hadn't needed to use the rest of her lunch hour to drive all the way out to Apache Junction. Maybe his friend even let him stay over some nights, which could explain why Ron didn't sleep at the shelter every night. Either that, or he'd found other shelters in this part of the city. Whatever the reason, he'd been polite and friendly.

She continued back to the nearest major street, where she pulled into a drive-thru and ordered herself a salad to take back to the bank.

Only later did she realize she should have asked him if he knew anything about the missing items from the shelter.

Chapter 30

Gracie's kids loved flipping channels on the TV, although they now zipped through programming like YouTube and Netflix. All morning she'd let them have at it while she cleaned the kitchen, made a shopping list, and ran to the store for everything she would need for Christmas dinner. When she got back home she laid down the law.

"Okay, outside with you both. Take a walk, go see some friends—anything to get out of the house awhile and away from that big screen. You're going to ruin your eyes and cause your brains to vegetate." The moment the words were out she realized she was speaking with her mother's voice. *You'll ruin your eyes, Grace Ann …*

"Sheesh," she whispered as the front door closed. She finished putting away the groceries before she realized they'd left the TV on. "YouTube. It's channel flipping gone berserk—and automated."

She reached for the remote but a face on the screen grabbed her attention.

"Praise the Lord!" said the man in a dark suit, white shirt, and narrow tie. His short hair was cut almost military-short. He held up one arm, palm outward toward what appeared to be a large audience in some kind of arena. A diamond ring flashed from his pinkie.

"Can Jimmy Joe get an Amen on that!" said the woman standing beside him.

The audience responded immediately. Gracie sat slowly on her couch.

The woman's face was alight with enthusiasm, a wide smile revealing perfect teeth and a model-pretty face. Her blonde hair was styled to the max, large and curly, and obviously sprayed with an iron touch.

"Thank you, Billie Lynn. Darlin' you're the very angel God wants to see doing his work." He had perfected the West Texas accent.

Gracie scrolled the screen upward so she could see the description for the video.

1999 Summer Revival for the Church of the Risen Savior, Amarillo, Texas. A congregation of more than 10,000 attend the inspirational message of famed evangelical preacher Jimmy Joe Johnson and his wife Billie Lynn.

"I don't believe this," Gracie whispered to the empty room. "Surely it can't be … but it really does look like them."

There was more. Fifteen other videos featuring the couple she knew as Orion and Sunshine. Only, back in the '90s they'd been doing an evangelical gig. And judging by the running footer at the bottom of the screen it had been about the money back then, too.

On a whim, she picked up her phone and dialed the 800 number on the screen, expecting it to be disconnected. It was answered on the third ring. "Heavenly Ministries. Bless you for calling."

Surprised, Gracie had to think fast. She tried to mimic the Texas accent. "Um, I just came across the videos of Jimmy Joe, and I uh …"

"You want to help, bless your heart."

"Uh, yeah. I want to help."

"And how much will your donation be today?"

"Well, I don't have much. Is five dollars okay?"

"We welcome each and every little bit that helps to further the Lord's work." The female at the other end was nearly as smooth as the pair on television. "And, of course, your help doesn't have to be one time only. We can set up a donation plan so your five dollars can be repeated each and every month."

"Um, no, I can't really manage that."

"So a one-time donation it is. If you'll just read off your credit card number. We take Mastercard, Visa, Discover and American Express."

Holy cow, what a spiel. Gracie excused herself to go get the card and immediately disconnected the call.

She scrolled the list of videos suggested because of her interest in this one. There they were, this time in wrinkled cotton clothing and unkempt hair. If they'd found Jesus in the '90s, by the early 2000s they had met a yogi. This time the cause was "save the environment" but there was still a toll-free number. She called that one.

"Namaste. Bless you for calling." Gracie would have bet it was the same woman who had answered a few minutes ago, minus the southern twang.

There was even a newly dated video with the current

program, the names Orion and Sunshine, and the outfits were the same that Amber had described. This time when she dialed the 800 number she donated five dollars. It would be interesting to see what name showed up as the seller on her credit card statement.

She leaned back into the sofa cushions, stunned. The Fordyces had been at this a long time and it was huge. She couldn't begin to imagine the amount of money they were bringing in.

Chapter 31

The blue Mazda turned the corner and disappeared. Ron's pulse gradually began to slow as he stood up from the porch step. He cursed himself for the fact that he'd reacted with a smile when that woman had pulled up and called him by name. Thank goodness he'd had the presence of mind to whip up a ready excuse for driving a nice car and coming to a middle-class neighborhood.

A low chuckle—he'd gotten away with it!

He let himself in the front door and went into the bedroom, reaching into the pockets of his oversized coat and pulling out handfuls of money. Lots of dollar bills, lots of miscellaneous coins, occasionally a fiver. He placed it all on the dresser, then carefully removed the jacket and draped it over a chair in the corner. He would wear it again this afternoon. The pockets of his grimy chinos yielded more cash, and he added those notes to the pile.

When he'd undressed, piling each item of the costume on top of the coat, he headed to the bathroom where he ran the shower until it was steaming hot. It used to bother him, putting on filthy clothing to go to work every day, but he loved what he did. The hours were good and the pay was fantastic. To Ron, most of all, it was the thrill of the game. The quick thinking—as he'd done just now when he came up with the perfect answer to the woman's inquiry and played it cool. She had no idea.

A lot of the losers on the street corners took their money and snorted it up their noses or drank it. Not Ron. He used to be one of the suckers who drove to an office job every day, stressed out, spending hours in traffic, watching men and women on street corners begging for a few coins. Then one day while stuck at an especially long red light he did a quick count. Roughly every fourth car would yield a handful of coins or a buck or two. The light came on.

Four million people lived in this damn valley, and at least half of them were on the road during rush hour. Pick an intersection, any intersection, and a couple thousand vehicles passed there every day. He did the math. The next morning he quit his day job and went shopping at the Goodwill store. He didn't buy anything inside. Instead, he went around back to the dumpster and picked out items of clothing that were too ratty to go on the racks.

He took everything home, laundered it to get the previous owner's filth out, then proceeded to add his own layer of grime to the ragged garments. A little motor oil and a good rub in garden soil achieved the look he wanted. After a couple of comments at the shelter—his hands were too clean—he began to keep a bucket of the dirt in the garage so he could make up his face and hands before he left each morning.

The shower was beginning to run tepid now. He stepped out, dressed in clean jeans and a pullover cable knit sweater. It only took a few minutes to count his cash. The coins went into a big jar, which he took to a Coinstar machine once a week or so; the bills were in his pants pockets.

He took a quick look out the front window; as usual during the week, no one in the neighborhood was home. This was an area of young working couples, and everybody was pretty much out the door around six in the morning and not back for at least twelve hours. Neighbors didn't socialize—there was no time—and the few who'd ever said hello to him wouldn't be able to name the company he supposedly worked for or even tell you what he did. He didn't know their details either, and really didn't care.

He went through the connecting door to the garage, got in his car, and drove to the nearest convenience store. Living a completely cash existence was a bit of an adventure, especially in the beginning when he'd wanted to pull out a credit card for everything, the way he used to. But he'd learned all the places to get money orders, so his bills were paid that way, and he didn't even keep a bank account any more. He'd cut ties to most sources the tax man would check. His rent got paid every month and the utility companies got theirs. He had streaming TV services that he prepaid by the year, and an internet connection in the landlord's name.

Inside the store, a new clerk asked what he wanted. He purchased money orders in specific amounts. The clerk didn't know or care that one was for the electric company and one for the water bill. Ron sealed them into their envelopes and dropped them in a mailbox. It was shortly after noon; he had enough time to catch a movie or go bowling before doing his evening rush hour shift.

He laughed out loud when he got into his car. Who else had life figured out as well as he did? Work two or three hours in the morning, a couple more in the evening, do it when you feel like it, skip work when you want. Go anywhere, do anything in the off hours. By living simply and finding every bargain available, he'd be able to stash away enough cash to buy a house or take a world cruise, or move to Belize. Life was good.

He debated whether to spend the night at Heaven Sent again. It was always interesting to check out the scene, see what was going on. Most of all, he felt a thrill from getting away with it, fitting in well enough to get a free night's stay and a couple of meals. And there was that weirdo temple place next door. Palming a twenty had been fun. What if next time he got away with a couple more? He nearly salivated.

A psychologist would have a field day with him, Ron thought as he drove toward the cine-plex. They'd want to analyze why he felt this need to deceive, and most would want to delve into his childhood to find out what had been missing. The truth was much simpler—he did it because getting away with stuff was fun.

Chapter 32

December twenty-third, the evening of Pen's little party. Although the guests would mostly be the Heist Ladies, others were welcomed too. It was their annual gift exchange, along with mulled wine and light hors d' oeuvres since it was the evening preceding two or more days of sheer indulgence in the food department.

Benton was first to arrive and he presented Pen with a lovely necklace, a pendant with a tiny gold butterfly, and a book about how the law catches criminals. She kissed him when she saw the necklace, gave an exuberant hug over the book.

"It's perfect research material for my novels," she exclaimed.

"I thought it would be." He beamed with pleasure at her delight in the gifts. "I also brought wine, for those who might not want theirs spiced and served warm."

Through the beveled glass front door, Pen caught sight of Gracie, who was balancing a huge tray of homemade cookies. Her husband stood behind, holding a stack of empty boxes the guests could use to fill with their own selections of goodies. Benton rushed to the door to let them in while Pen put her new book on her desk.

Sandy and Mary followed along behind the others, carrying gift bags with their Secret Santa gifts. And Amber bustled in five minutes later, holding a large stewpot of something very fragrant. "Posole," she said, "my mother's traditional New Mexico recipe." She carried it to the kitchen, explaining hers would be an eat-and-run visit because she had a flight to Santa Fe at nine-thirty.

"Mom and Dad are so excited that I'm coming home for Christmas this year," she told everyone. "Not sure why, since I go nearly every year. Maybe they've got something up their little Santa Claus sleeves."

Benton served drinks and Pen steered them toward a table laden with canapes. For a 'light' meal, she had gone all out with new recipes.

"Enjoy them while you can," she teased. "This just happens to be a year when I'm not under a book deadline. Next year it could be frozen things from the warehouse club, warmed up."

"Hey, those are good, too," Sandy said. "Putting sprigs of parsley on the serving trays makes all the difference."

Benton and Scott, as the only males present, had drifted toward the deck where Benton lit his pipe and Scott asked questions about the landscaping.

"So, not to talk shop at a holiday party," Gracie said, "but since the men aren't here and it's just us girls … I have a bit of a bombshell."

She went into the details about how she'd come across Foster and Melissa Fordyce performing variations of their routine.

"They've got every audience type nailed, from the evangelicals to the hippies. In one of the videos, Foster's even wearing a long gray beard and has some kind of yogi turban on, and she's wearing the simplest of gauzy clothing. In their deep South routine, they're the next Jim and Tammy Faye Bakker, complete with all the right words to get the audiences to melt in their seats. I couldn't believe the variety of roles they assume."

Amber clicked her tongue. "Not surprised."

"And …" Gracie continued, "they're still raking in cash from the series of videos. I called the toll-free numbers and the lines are being answered. I pled poverty and still got talked into making a small donation."

"Oh, no. Really?" Sandy said.

"All the in the name of research. Because … look at this." Gracie pulled out her phone and brought up her credit card bill. "Amber, can you take some data from this? Maybe it'll help toward your research into where the money goes."

"It can't hurt," Amber said, stuffing the last bite of a mushroom cap into her mouth. "I'm hitting a blank wall. Total frustration. Somebody is hiding the cash deposits behind a ton of encryption methods, some of which I've never come up against."

Pen nudged her. "Benton," she whispered. The men were coming back inside.

Mary picked up two cheese puffs and handed one to Sandy. "I'm volunteering to help serve Christmas dinner at the shelter. Wanna come? They'll be doing one tomorrow night and another midday on the twenty-fifth, and they can use extra helpers each time. The Food Bank got a bunch of turkeys and other foods donated, so it'll be a lot more than just the residents. Could end up being a line out the door."

"Sure. I was going out with some other single employees at the bank Christmas Day, but—"

"Where's that posole?" Scott asked.

"Follow me," Pen told him. "We'll serve it up directly from the pot."

"—the Christmas Eve meal would work out great for me," Sandy finished, with a wink at Mary. "I wonder if that guy Ron will be back. Did I tell you I saw him yesterday, driving around again?"

Mary started to respond but Amber had brought her a bowl of the pork, chile, and hominy stew. "You gotta try this if you've never had it before," she said.

The men were already raving about the dish, having found seats on the sofa. Scott immediately reached for the remote and found a football game. While the men were immersed in the sport, the Ladies finished their stew and then went to the tree to get their gifts.

Mary received a warm-up jacket in her favorite hot pink. A wink from Sandy reminded her they'd been shopping together one day when Mary exclaimed over it. Amber's gift was a pair of warm gloves—"For your visit to Santa Fe," Pen said. Gracie got cake decorating supplies for the new hobby she swore she was going to begin after the first of the year.

Sandy gushed over the silver and turquoise pendant she suspected had been mailed from a certain couple in Santa Fe from their daughter's description of Sandy's tastes, and Pen loved her new writing journal. "One can never have too many places to jot down plot ideas as they come. I shall keep this one in my bag with me at all times."

Amber glanced at her phone screen. "Looks like it's snowing in Santa Fe already. I'm in for a white Christmas, if my flight doesn't get delayed. Right now it's showing to be on time."

"So, I suppose that's your cue," Pen said. "But first, we shall get into those fabulous cookies. You mustn't go off and leave them all with me."

They filled the boxes, then Amber picked up her coat and purse. "Don't you go solving this valley-wide crime spree without me."

The Ladies gathered around her for hugs. "I'm certain we won't, sweetie," said Gracie.

"Everyone have a wonderful Christmas!" she called as she walked out the door.

Chapter 33

From the king-sized bed, Foster watched the bathroom mirror as Melissa did some elaborate little twists with her hair, somehow making the strands come out in long curls, but his mind wasn't focused on his wife. His thoughts were bouncing around, a zillion miles a minute.

They had two more days at the resort before they would lose the room. That manager had been adamant about the place being fully booked from the day after Christmas through New Year's Day, and even though Melissa was racking up enough room charges to make any hotelier drool, it looked pretty certain they'd be back living in the bus in a very short time.

While her concern was to create perfect hair and makeup and choose an ideal restaurant for their Christmas dinner tomorrow, his focus had to be on an escape plan.

It was time to go—the edgy feeling in his gut told him so.

Richie Templeton had finished depositing the cash Foster had sent, and he'd been nervous as a cat, worried someone was prowling around in the bank records and could trace the transactions back through him. Well, screw him. Foster could figure out something else.

He had already looked into converting the money to cyber currency and dismissed that idea. It looked as though real estate was going to be the answer, but it had to be in a certain place. Many countries now had 'know your client' laws in place, which required purchasers to give all kinds of personal details and proof of their identities. A cash deal somewhere like that would instantly be reported back to the US and therefore accessible to the IRS. It was a move specifically designed to catch money launderers. As if a religious organization was into that stuff.

So, Melissa's grand idea of a villa anywhere in Europe was likely off the table. But he'd located a few jurisdictions where a purchase could work, and one of them had some private islands. Now *that* would surely appeal to her sense of a grand and glorious life.

When he first met Missy, he was tired of living in poverty and she was the girl with the big plans and the workable schemes for getting what they wanted. Now, they had plenty. She thrived on working a con, constantly being 'on' in front of others, but he was getting tired of it.

He indulged in a vision of a tropical island with a simple grass shack. Or not so simple—an elaborate home with wide views of the ocean, cool verandas, and palm frond roofs. A place where he would fish all day or lie out in the sun while a staff cared for the place and he never had to plan anything more elaborate than what he would order for breakfast.

But that was a ways off. First, he had to get them there—with all the money they'd worked so hard for.

"Hey, sweetie, you're not dressed." Melissa interrupted his thoughts. She had finished her elaborate pile of curls and put on trim black slacks and a pink sweater that looked like it was made from baby duck feathers.

He pulled his thoughts back from the tropics but his expression must have been blank.

"Christmas shopping? Lunch out and then we're going to that musical program …" Her mouth went into a little knot. "We talked about this last night."

He set his laptop and papers aside. "Sorry. I forgot. I need to stop by the bus and check some things."

"Not today … please … Honey, I'll have to change back into my hippie clothes if we go out there. I'm so sick of that outfit …"

What Melissa wanted, Melissa got. He knew better than to present any logical argument for the fact that the day would be better spent making ready for a departure rather than listening to Christmas music sung by some bunch of angel-faced kids.

"Okay, give me ten minutes." He headed into the bathroom and turned on the shower before she could say anything more.

Chapter 34

Trini was at her best when she was doing for others, Mary decided. And Heaven Sent gave her that opportunity. Her friend positively beamed at each newcomer who walked through the door. She had organized multiple serving tables so the line could move more quickly, and had set up additional dining chairs in the new, still unoccupied dorm room. Even so, they had a crowd that lined up out the front door.

Sandy had been on the serving line, adding portions of mashed potatoes to the trays, when Mary arrived.

"Anything *unusual* that you've noticed?" Mary whispered to her friend.

Sandy shook her head. "I've been right here every minute since I walked in. You might ask Trini. She's bustling around all over the place."

Mary spotted the director coming from the reception area and pulled her aside into the women's restroom.

"Have any other items gone missing?" she asked after checking to be sure they were alone. She hated to admit they still had no clues as to who was stealing the residents' keepsakes.

Trini shook her head. "No one's reported anything. But as a precaution, since we have so many strangers here for the meals, I've put a volunteer in each of the dorm rooms, someone to just hang out casually and keep an eye to be sure no one comes in and starts going through our residents' belongings while we're busy."

"Good idea. I can take a turn at that, if you'd like. Or if more help is needed in the kitchen or dining room, just let me know."

Trini thought for a moment. "If you could check the trash receptacles in the dining room? These folks don't throw away much—even the plastic forks are valued—but it's been more than an hour since I looked. We may need some garbage hauled outside to the dumpster on the east side of the building."

"I can handle that," said Mary with a little salute. "I'll check back when I'm done."

Outside, it was already nearly dark. Twilight fell quickly in the desert. She carried two large black bags to the dumpster and heaved them into it. Next door, the Temple of the Rising Moon seemed to be earning its name, as a full moon rose behind the Superstition Mountains, almost directly over the neighboring building. She smiled at the synchronicity of the naming, then glanced at the property.

The building and school bus were dark. Orion and Sunshine's VW didn't seem to be around, either. Trini had commented yesterday how the couple was either keeping very late hours or perhaps staying somewhere else. They'd most certainly been around for each of their 'shows' and the private readings Pen had mentioned.

A man in dark clothing appeared at one corner of the building, most likely one of the ones Amber had called 'the goons'. Seemed they did double duty as ushers and security. Well, that was probably a good thing, Mary thought. It couldn't hurt to have someone keeping an eye on things; it could be the neighbors felt nervous about all the homeless hanging around the shelter, especially tonight.

She took a deep breath of the cool desert air and turned to go inside. Sandy could probably use a break in the mashed-potato department. She was about to open the side door into the kitchen when she saw someone cross between the shelter and the other building. His figure seemed familiar and she realized it was the homeless man, Ron.

At the same time, she heard the distinctive sound of the VW bug pulling off the street. Headlights grazed the chain link fencing and lit the back of the property. Looked like Orion and Sunshine were home. Well, if Ron needed something over there, at least there were people around to answer his questions.

Mary walked inside and immediately got recruited to wash dishes.

Chapter 35

Ron took a look at the line of people waiting for the turkey dinner at the shelter. Okay, it would have been simpler and quicker to grab something at a fast food place. It wasn't as if his pockets weren't filled with plenty of money.

He remembered a snide comment made once by a coworker, back when he had a stupid office job. "You'll do anything for a freebie, won't you, Ron?" the guy had said. "You'd probably take a free meal from a hungry person if you got there first."

The remark had stung at the time, but the more he thought about it he'd decided. *Yeah, so what? I get there first and the other guy's moving too slow—then yeah, I deserve the food every bit as much as he does.*

The one thing he didn't like about getting freebies was

having to wait around. His time was valuable—more than a hundred dollars an hour, he'd calculated, based on his take at the street corners. This food line was moving too slowly for his taste. He glanced over toward that hippie place. Maybe they were having one of their *services* tonight. The idea of getting away with a fistful of that cash was pretty appealing.

He walked across the open space between the shelter and the Moon Temple, laughing a little at the sight of the real moon rising above it. Pretty sky. One of these days he might take some time off, choose a good lounge chair somewhere, and do things like stare at sunsets and the rising moon. But not yet.

His best month on the corners was right now, and the take would continue to be good until after New Year's Day. People would get all those gifts tomorrow, and the next day they would rush right out to exchange everything, or to spend gift cards, or whatever else they thought they had to do after a couple days of family closeness started getting old.

Ron approached the front door of the temple place and tried to read the sign telling about the hours of their programs, but it was too dark to see very well. The building looked closed, but he reached out and tried the front door anyway. Locked.

"Hey! What are you doing?" called a graveled male voice.

Ron jumped back and turned. "Nothing. Nothing at all." Thirty feet away stood one of those goons who dressed in white and passed the money basket around during the services. Ron dipped his head so the guy wouldn't get a good look at him, but it was too late.

"Hey, you're that guy—" The man's growl was

interrupted by a yellow VW Beetle pulling into the driveway.

The moment the man turned toward the car, Ron sprinted away.

Chapter 36

"That's the guy!" shouted the man Melissa always called Mack. One of several Macks.

Foster rolled down his window and stuck his head out. "What guy?"

"Guy that stole from the collection a couple weeks ago."

"So why you hanging around? *Get him!*" Foster stared after the fleeing figure. He had no clear idea what he planned to do with the man once they caught him, but some primeval surge of anger said that the man needed to be taught you don't steal from Foster Fordyce.

He jammed the VW back in gear. Its tires spun on the dirt driveway as he pulled around the back and parked it beside the bus.

A few minutes later, the security guard came back,

barely able to breathe. "Guy got away," he huffed. "Outran me."

Foster stared pointedly at the guard's jiggling midsection. *No wonder, you tub of lard.* "Keep an eye out. If he comes back around here, I don't want him getting away. And tell the other guards too. A lesson needs to be taught here. Nobody rips off the money we're collecting for a good cause."

"Right, boss. I'll tell Joe and we'll both be watching the rest of the night."

Foster stared after the man as he walked away, limping slightly. Whether they caught the thief or not, it didn't matter. There had been just enough light from the street lamps, and Foster never forgot a face.

"I feel like cruising the area, see if I can spot the jerk," Foster said as he and Melissa got out of the car.

"Honey, it's Christmas Eve. And it's our last night at the resort … Come *on* …"

He should have told her to screw Christmas Eve. He'd already endured a shopping trip that was basically an excuse for him to buy her a diamond bracelet she'd already picked out for herself, lunch at some chichi place where the waiters stared down their noses, and an ungodly two hours of listening to a kids' choir—the kind with the high voices that made him grind his teeth.

Instead, he ushered her politely into the bus and asked her to tally up the boxes of cash to make sure nothing had disappeared while he made a call and added two more security guys back on the job for the night. No one groused about having to work Christmas Eve—Foster paid them well.

"I'm going outside to check some stuff," he told Melissa. "You can wait in here where it's warm and then we'll go."

He wanted to be sure none of the exterior compartments on the bus had been breached. While he was out, he went around the building to check the doors there, as well. Everything seemed just as he'd left it. Maybe the Macks were doing their job after all.

The reinforcements arrived and he collected his wife for the drive back to spend their final night in luxury. It would be the last such night for a while, if his plans worked out. But she didn't know that yet.

Although Foster hoped they would spend Christmas Eve in their suite with Melissa wearing the lacy red little outfit he was going to present to her, it seemed she had more of a Currier and Ives ideal in mind. She pointed him in the direction of downtown Scottsdale where the holiday light display was said to be fantastic.

Bundled in scarves and gloves and puffy jackets—although the temperature was well above fifty—she took his arm and they walked up and down the streets. Shop windows held elaborate displays and fake snow drifted through the air, dispensed from some unseen mechanism at the rooftops. Vendors sold hot chocolate and she insisted they each get one. He griped about there not being any schnapps to add to his.

"Get into the spirit, honey," she said.

"Is this how you spent your holidays as a kid, doing stuff like this?" He imagined an adorable little blonde girl putting extra marshmallows in her cocoa, and he felt a surge of love for her.

"Well, kind of," she said with a grin. "My daddy would be working the crowd in a place like this, picking pockets while they stared at the lights."

"Seriously?" Living with two drunks, he'd never spent a Christmas Eve out in a public place as a kid. The parents were usually passed out on the sofa by eight, and if he wanted a Christmas tree he put it up himself.

"I could show you Daddy's techniques," she said, "but I don't want to work tonight. It's Christmas."

They rounded a corner and saw people heading toward a church with open doors.

"Oh, Foster, let's go there," she said.

He gave her a long stare. Seriously? Then he shrugged. Okay, might be interesting to see someone else put on the show for a change.

They took seats near the back and watched as the congregation stood, sat, or knelt on cue. Since almost all of it was in Latin, he quickly grew bored and let his mind wander back to the details of his plan for leaving Arizona. He hadn't told Melissa much of it yet. At the moment she seemed transfixed by the ceremony taking place up front.

"I never knew you were raised Catholic," he said, as they walked back to the car afterward.

"Oh, I wasn't."

"But you understood what was going on in there tonight?"

"The words? Heck no. But I liked some of that priest's moves. You know, the hand gestures, benedicting everyone or whatever you call it, waving the incense around. We could add something like that to our routine. The candles were a nice touch. People really lapped it up."

"So you really *were* working on Christmas Eve," he teased.

"More like research. A person can always learn something new."

They had reached the car and he unlocked her door. "Speaking of new things—" He almost said something about hitting the road in the bus, but thought better of it.

"Well, it's Christmas and I have a nice sexy little surprise for you back at the room."

She made a purring sound and teased him with suggestive ideas as they headed back to their suite.

Chapter 37

Sandy walked in the door and knew at once she'd made a mistake. The Christmas Eve potluck dinner was being held at the home of a coworker. The house was beautifully decorated, the dishes set out on the buffet table looked lovely. She set down the cranberry salad she'd made and circled the room, saying her obligatory hellos.

But her heart and mind were with Mary at Heaven Sent. Here, she would spend hours making small talk with people she saw every day; there, she might be making a difference. She thanked the hostess and pled a migraine as her reason for leaving right away.

"I'll bring your serving bowl to the bank on Monday," said the worried woman. "You'd better get some rest. Are you okay to drive?"

"It's not far. I'll be fine," Sandy assured her.

I'll be more than fine, she thought as she drove away. A thought had come to her on the way to the dinner, and she planned to act on it now. She pulled into the near-empty parking lot of the first Walmart she came to.

Inside, she raided the accessories department and bought every remaining pair of warm socks and gloves, no matter the sizes. Someone could use them. Knitted caps too. The clerk told her these were all due to go on half-price sale at midnight, but when she found out where the items were going, she got the manager to authorize the discount now. The purchases filled two large bags.

"Throw in those boxes of chocolate Santas," the man said. "And the candy canes. The homeless deserve some fun at Christmas too."

When she walked into Heaven Sent, she felt like Santa, and when Trini plopped a red and white hat on her head, Sandy really got into the role.

"Ho-ho-ho," she bellowed when she walked into the dining room. She couldn't remember having more fun, ever, when she saw everyone trying on their gifts.

From the food service line, Mary looked up and grinned at her friend. Once her bags were empty, Sandy joined her, the jaunty red Santa hat still on her head.

"I thought you couldn't make it tonight," she said, as Sandy took up a position and added dinner rolls to the plates.

"Change of plans. This sounded like more fun."

* * *

Three hours later, exhausted, the two women joined Trini in her quarters. The residents had mostly gathered in the dining hall for a movie; some had gone to bed already.

"I'm totally pooped, but it was a good holiday," Trini said, massaging her stiff neck. "The gifts and candy were a complete hit. Thanks, Sandy."

Mary seconded her comments.

A crease formed between Trini's eyebrows. "Only one little thing marred the weekend."

"What was that?" Sandy asked.

"Lizzie left her cart outside while we were serving the dinner," Trini said. "And something went missing from it. I feel like it's partly my fault—I got a little insistent with her that there was no room indoors, with the crowd we had. But I could have let her park it in the women's dorm. Should have done that."

"What was missing?" Mary wondered.

"I don't know if you noticed a necklace she usually wears. Probably not, since she normally has a scarf tied around her neck, especially on the chillier days. I guess the chain had broken so she put it with her shiny objects. The whole little box of them was gone, even though the cart was parked around the side of the building, inside the chain link fence. But the gate wasn't closed, so I suppose anyone could have had access."

"And yet it's exactly the type of thing the thief has been taking for the past few weeks," Mary said. "Doesn't that seem coincidental? And if it wasn't someone who's been here before, how did they know Lizzie kept her treasures in that particular little box?"

Sandy began to get an uneasy feeling. "What time was this?" she asked.

"After dark. Lizzie arrived around six, right when the crowd was thickest. She was upset about leaving her cart so I let her go to the head of the food line. She must have been finished eating by six-thirty. It was dark when she went out, and when she reported the loss I went out with a flashlight to help her look through her things.

"Ron," Mary said. "I saw him as I was taking out the trash. I actually saw him in front of the place next door, and one of their men shouted at him. He ran and the security guard took off after him. I just thought he was chasing Ron away because they didn't like a homeless guy hanging around there. But what if …?"

"What if he's the thief who took the other keepsakes as well …?" Sandy said. "He was one of those from Amber's spreadsheet, one who stayed here all the times something was stolen."

"And we never got to question him about that, did we?" Trini asked.

Sandy shook her head. "We didn't. Plus, there's more."

She told them about the times she'd seen Ron panhandling on street corners. "And twice he's walked over to a parked car, gotten in it, and driven away. The second time I was able to follow. He drove up to a nice house in a middle-class neighborhood and pulled into the garage."

"He lives there?" Mary's eyes were huge.

"He said it was a friend's house. I believed him."

Trini looked thoughtful. "Ron can be something of a charmer, all right. He just seems … different from a lot of the homeless. He's got a certain confidence, and he … okay, this will sound weird. He smells better."

The others laughed.

"I don't mean to be cruel. Please don't take that wrong. But you can tell when a person doesn't bathe often or when they use the basic, plain old soap and shampoo we provide here, versus the person who uses a quality brand of body wash, a guy who doesn't have ground-in dirt in his skin, has soft hands and feet."

"You think Ron's a fake?"

"Or very recently homeless. It could be the deep-down grime hasn't really settled in yet. He hasn't been on the streets long, I'd bet on that," Trini said.

"Maybe the friend with the house lets him stay over sometimes. Could be why he's not a regular here," Mary suggested.

"You're right," Sandy said. "There could be a dozen explanations. But it's still bugging me that he was one of only six who were here every single time there was a theft. I think we should keep an eye on him."

"Agreed," Mary said. "Now, how do we go about doing that?"

"I wish I'd thought to jot down the address of the house where he went. We could see if he turns up there again. Or, we could wait for the friend, assuming there is one, and ask some questions."

"Could you find the place again?" Mary asked.

"I'll try. He'll be watching out for me, though. We'd better get the rest of the Ladies in on it if we plan surveillance."

Trini smiled. "Wow, you guys talk like pros."

"Well, we have a little experience," Mary told her with a grin.

Chapter 38

They'd spent a wonderful final night at the resort, complete with amazing sex, but the next day dawned with Melissa in a stormy mood. She dropped two massive shopping bags of new clothes on the bed and gave her surroundings a disdainful look. Gone were the days of the spa, the concierge, and having six fluffy pillows on her side of the king-sized bed. They were back to being Orion and Sunshine, living in a damn bus.

Foster caught the pout and decided this was the time to play his ace. "Let's get out of here," he said.

Her eyes lit up. "A different resort—why didn't I think of that?"

He shook his head. "Better. We leave Arizona."

"I'm ready. California, here we come!"

He reached into an upper cupboard, moved aside a

cardboard box of money, and found a bottle of wine. So what if it was early afternoon? He scrounged for the only two wine glasses and made sure they were clean.

"So, here's what I'm thinking," he said, planning his words carefully. He'd learned long ago that if you must give Melissa news she didn't want to hear, you had to deliver it alongside something she would love. Good news – bad news – more good news. The classic crap sandwich.

He poured the wine and handed one to her, inviting her to sit beside him at the dinette. He turned on his tablet and brought up a picture he'd bookmarked. With a visionary wave of his palm, he painted a picture. "Private island."

"Private island? What about the villa in Greece?" She raised her glass to meet his, a look of skepticism on her face.

"Greece is old news. Literally old, as in crumbling to pieces—but, hell, anybody with some money to spend has already gone there. I'm thinking … tropical. The warm, beautiful waters of the south Pacific and a whole island, not just a house."

The corners of her mouth turned up. "A whole island. It's, wow—"

He could tell her imagination was churning.

"Think about it—soft breezes, warm water, fresh fruit and all the fish we want to catch, fresh for dinner every night. It's a retirement lifestyle a lot of people would kill for."

"Retirement? Wait a second, Foster. You mean we'd be out there all alone?"

"We can hire all the natives we want to keep the place in top shape and to cook for us and do our laundry …"

"You want to live somewhere with no one other than servants around."

"Well, yeah, baby. It'll be just us. You can run around in your bikini all day—or nothing at all. You *know* I'd love that." He didn't mention the fact that Richie Templeton thought someone was snooping around in their electronic bank records—quite likely the IRS.

"But what about our work? Raising money for our charitable work is our *life*—it's what we do."

"*What* charitable work?" Had she gone off her rocker? "How many of those freebie houses for the poor do you think we've actually built? You know as well as I do—the answer is zero."

She waved off the comment. "But I would miss the crowds. Our audiences give back a lot of positive energy. You know how much I thrive on that, sweetie. I feed off their energy."

And their *money*.

"We'll find some place that's near enough to a city where you can get your fix of crowds and noise. There are airplanes that can take us anywhere in the world." But that wasn't the whole solution. The con was everything to her. She absolutely sparkled every night when they counted the take.

She drained her wine glass and held it out for a refill. He could tell she wasn't completely happy with his answer. He topped up her glass and slipped an arm around her shoulders.

"Baby … it's just that I'm getting concerned about all this money laying around. We can't put any more of it in the bank without raising a lot of flags, and I'm losing sleep over the fact that it's sitting around in those self-storage units all over the place."

"Who's going to break into a self storage unit and haul away a bunch of boxes of books?"

That was not the point. "Anyone could. There's probably ten million in each of those places. Maybe more. Plus, I'm ready to start enjoying the money. We've worked hard for it. We deserve a few luxuries, and I'm as sick of this bus as you are."

At last, he had struck the right chord.

"Oh, honey, you're so right," she said. "Let's dump this thing and get first class tickets to somewhere exotic where we can shop for an island."

"Well, see, that's the thing …" He poured more wine in her glass.

Chapter 39

Ron felt like a prisoner. Yesterday, he'd pulled into the garage and gone inside for a shower, intending to head out to his favorite sushi place immediately after. And then *she* showed up—the slightly heavyset blonde woman from the shelter, the one who'd shocked the hell out of him by appearing at the driveway before Christmas.

When he picked up his keys to go to Zushi, he'd spotted her blue Mazda cruising slowly down the street. As if a jolt of electricity had shot through him, he backed away from the windows and saw that she stopped in front of a house three doors to the west. She'd sat there several hours. And, damn the luck, Zushi didn't offer delivery. He'd dined on cold cereal and kept to the back bedroom where he pulled the drapes and only turned on the TV set and one small lamp. He thought she'd believed his story about the house and car belonging to a friend but, if so, why was she watching?

Now, since six o'clock this morning, there was a compact Ford in the same spot. He could tell the driver was a woman, but not much beyond that.

What the hell?

He was missing some of the best traffic days of the year. Somebody else would start working his corners, especially the one near Superstition Mall. *Damn!* It was one of his best locations, especially when all those mooches headed out to exchange their Christmas gifts for whatever they really wanted. People always felt generous at the holidays. Plus, they somehow thought giving away some cash would help them on their taxes. He knew better, but he wasn't about to set them straight.

He really needed to get out there by noon, work the lunch hour crowds, and then again in the early evening. He paced from room to room, deciding what to do.

"Oh, come on," he said to the four walls. "Just do it. Get out there and lose the bitch in traffic."

He went into the bedroom where his grubby clothes lay across the back of a chair. Slipping on the grimy chinos, stained shirt, and filthy jacket always took a force of will. He chose to think of it as if he were an actor putting on his costume. His role was to be a homeless street person, and it was a part he played well. Dirty white socks and ratty boots completed the outfit.

Then he went to the bathroom mirror and pulled out his 'makeup' which consisted of an oily lotion he rubbed over his face and hands and a bucket of greasy soil he had scraped from the back lot of an oil-change shop. He ran dirty hands over his face to create the look. Trying not to flinch, he rubbed some of the mixture into his hair, making sure it stood out in clumps. The final touch was to pull on a tattered watch cap.

He turned away from the mirror for this. The one thing he admired about himself was his luxuriant hair. Even worn longish, when clean his hair was a source of pride. But he had to put that aside when he went out in costume.

With a final peek through his window blinds, he saw that the Ford was still there. Okay, this was it. He hoped knowing the neighborhood would give him an advantage.

Jamming a few essentials into the jacket pockets he went through the kitchen and into the garage. He started the car and pressed the garage door opener, putting the vehicle in gear as soon as the door raised high enough to clear. He backed out and swung the car to face his stalker, although he was careful not to make eye contact with the woman in the driver's seat. The moment he passed her, he sped up and took the turn at the corner pretty fast. She would have to start her car and turn around in order to follow.

He wove through the residential streets, frustrated because so many people were still off work and way too many kids were playing with the big plastic toys they'd received yesterday. But his chaser would have the same obstacles to negotiate. He caught a glimpse of her two blocks behind, and lost her again when he turned right onto Power Road.

It was a thoroughfare where no one obeyed the forty-five speed limit; he was able to get up to sixty without attracting attention. But apparently the Ford driver was willing to do the same. She was only a block behind as he raced toward the light at University. It turned yellow and he blasted through the intersection. She didn't.

Free at last. Just to be sure, he took a series of turns

through some parking lots and then a couple of residential areas. She never showed up.

At his favorite supermarket parking lot, he chose a crowded section and watched until no one was walking nearby before he got out of the car and walked away. Three blocks later, Ron was settled at a corner, cardboard sign in hand.

He murmured the appropriate "God bless you" to each person who dropped money in his coffee can, but his mind was elsewhere. Who the hell *were* these women?

Chapter 40

"We can't just hire a moving company to go around to each place and gather all the packing boxes, sweetheart." Foster thought he'd been over all this, but she didn't seem to comprehend. "You and I need to go there personally. It's millions of dollars."

"Yeah, yeah. All neatly stacked in boxes labeled as books or towels or pots and pans. Movers handle that stuff all day long and they don't open the boxes to see what's inside."

"How do you know they don't?"

"Because they're not interested in books or towels ..."

"Until they open one box and see that under a layer of books there's a whole bunch more paper, and it's green and has old presidents' faces printed on it." He bundled up a blanket and stuffed it into an upper cabinet to keep the glassware from rattling and breaking once the bus was underway.

"Okay, so it's a road trip instead of first-class tickets," Melissa grumbled.

"I've got it all planned out," he said. "We hitch up the trailer and head for Amarillo tomorrow."

"Tomorrow! That's not much time to pack up our stage gear, especially since none of the Macks seem to be around."

"I let 'em all go. And we're not taking the stage gear. Let the landlord clear it all out. He's getting some great sound equipment and all the curtains and stuff."

"Foster, we need our things. The show …"

He stopped in mid-stride and faced her, taking her chin in his hand. "When we get ready to do the show again we'll buy new equipment."

He was sick of the stage and the shows and the crowds, but he had no intention of telling her. Maybe later. Or maybe not. His life goal was to be a millionaire—from the childhood days of deprivation, it was all he could think of. Now he was there and he wanted to savor it. Why couldn't she be happy with the same thing?

He took a gentle tone. "We need the utility trailer empty so we can fill it with all the boxes we're going to collect. Amarillo, Albuquerque, El Paso—then we're on our way to San Diego." Where he was negotiating for a container and passage for themselves to the South Pacific.

Melissa stepped out of the bus, and he saw her wander toward the auditorium. He brought up a map on his computer screen and started plotting their trip. Amarillo and Albuquerque were both along the I-40 corridor, so that seemed simple enough, although the old bus wasn't exactly a contender with the big rigs at freeway speeds. He looked at alternate routes and came up with a plan.

* * *

They drove out of Apache Junction the next morning, headed toward Show Low. The one thing Foster had failed to plan on was the weather. The rain's steady drizzle turned to huge, wet snowflakes as they climbed above five thousand feet in elevation, and it began sticking to the road when they were still miles from the nearest town.

"I hate driving in snow," Melissa whined.

You're not driving. "Don't worry, baby. I got it." His gut clenched and he eased off the gas a bit. What did a kid from Houston know about snowy roads anyway? But it was the manly thing to be brave in front of his woman, right?

"Look, we're only twenty miles from Show Low. We'll stop there and wait it out, grab coffee or something. Hey, do you know how Show Low got its name?"

Her eyes were still focused outside, where two faint tracks in the snow provided their only clue as to where the road was.

"The way I heard it was these two guys owned a big ranch out here, but they started not getting along real well and one of them wanted to move off to Fort Apache. This is, like, in the 1870s or something. When the two guys decide to part ways, they sit down to play a game of cards over it, winner take all. So, the game's going on pretty late and finally one guy says to the other, 'Show low and you take the ranch.' The one named Cooley turned over the lowest card—got himself, like, 100,000 acres, all the cattle, the crops and the ranch buildings. Probably the first time the low card won anything that big." He glanced over at her. "Interesting, huh?"

"I suppose."

An eighteen-wheeler came toward them and Foster instinctively steered to the right to give it plenty of clearance. Bad move. Behind the bus their empty trailer bounced when it touched the edge of the pavement and began to swerve sideways.

As the big rig passed them, Foster overcorrected and the trailer jackknifed. The front of it smacked a back corner of the bus with a startling *bang*, and he gripped the wheel to stay in control.

Too late. The bus began to skid and went off the road, into a sea of pure white.

Chapter 41

Mary remembered an episode of *Magnum PI*, where someone said the worst part of an investigation is surveillance. After two days of staring at the house, which might or might not belong to Ron, where he might or might not actually be present, she was about ready to chew her nails.

The only validating evidence they had so far was yesterday. Someone—male, possibly Ron—had backed out of the garage at this address and had taken off. In his rapidly moving car, his unkempt hair and dark knitted watch cap were the only clues. Mary swore he'd deliberately tried to evade her, but when she described the sequence of moves to Sandy, they'd both had to admit it could have been anyone leaving for an ordinary day out. Sandy had tried to make Mary feel better about losing him; she wasn't certain she could have done any better.

Right now, either of them would give anything just to spot the man and positively identify him as their suspect. Sandy still wasn't a hundred percent sure of the address, with these little subdivisions full of cookie-cutter houses. The one where she'd stopped and actually spoken to Ron had a brightly blooming bougainvillea on the right-hand side of the garage door, as did this one, their most substantial clue so far.

Not for the first time, Mary wished one of the other Ladies had been with her for the chase.

She opened her Thermos and poured herself another cup of tea, wondering how long at this rate before she would become desperate for a bathroom. She'd taken her first sip when her phone rang.

"Hey, Amber. How would you like to spend a glorious afternoon out in Mesa, waiting for a man to come home?"

"Um, on a scale of one to ten … that would be a zero." Amber laughed. "However, I do have some news for you, something I had to be at home to accomplish."

"Okay, you're given a pass for not sitting out here in your car. Although I'm not saying I still won't call on you at some point."

"Fair enough. So, I've been prowling around in the property tax records. For that address you gave, where you're sitting right now, I assume, I've got the owner's name."

"Tell me it's Ron-somebody?"

"Sorry, no."

Mary felt her spirits sag.

"It's a William P. Duckly."

"Do we know who that is?"

"Not from the property records, but I did some

scrounging around on social media. There's a William Duckly on Facebook who's sixty-seven, gray haired, thick glasses. From his recent posts, it looks like he and the wife had a houseful of kids and grandkids visiting for Christmas."

Mary looked up the street at the forlorn house.

"Well, that's definitely not Ron. And it doesn't seem to mesh with the 'friend' story he gave Sandy either. He said he stays *with* this friend. We've only spotted one car and one person here."

"William's hobbies are gardening, building wooden toys, and travel. Looks like he and the wife do a fair number of RV road trips." Amber was apparently scanning through the man's posted pictures.

Builds wooden toys … Mary remembered Sandy's description of the day she'd spoken to Ron. He'd parked the car directly in the center of the garage, and there was no mention of any woodworking tools inside.

"Could you search property records to see if Ron owns a property near here?" Maybe they had the wrong house after all.

"Tried that. Remember, we don't have his last name. It wouldn't be a far stretch to guess that *someone*, somewhere in that subdivision is named Ron or Ronald, but I'd have no way to narrow it down without more info."

"Sorry—I suppose I knew that." Mary heard the discouragement in her own voice. "It's all this sitting around. Guess I'm burning out."

Sandy had already run out of vacation days, which is how Mary ended up taking most of the surveillance shifts. How many of her nights and weekends was she willing to give up just to find a few missing trinkets?

"If I think of something else, you can bet I'll search it."

"I know. You're the best, Amber." She'd no sooner clicked off the call when her phone rang again.

"Hey, Mary, it's Trini. I don't know if this is important or not, but it looks like that guru couple next door has pulled out."

"Left?"

"This time with the bus and a trailer that holds all their stage gear. I saw him hitching up the trailer yesterday, and this morning they drove away."

"What about their little car?"

"It's still here. Maybe they're coming back and I'm reporting a great big nothing."

"No, I'm glad you called. Not sure what it means, but I'll get back to you," Mary said.

Her mind whirled. This couldn't be good. Just when they'd discovered the Fordyces were definitely scamming people with their claims of building houses for the poor, the couple took off. And now it looked as if Ron was also suspicious. She needed to get with the rest of the team, and quickly!

Chapter 42

Melissa screamed as the bus jounced on uneven ground. Every muscle in Foster's body tensed as he fought for control of the unwieldy rig. Sky blended with land in an unbroken expanse of white. After an eternity the bus and trailer came to a stop. At least they were upright.

Foster's hands trembled as he reached down to be sure his pants were dry. Holy crap, that had been close!

"Did that truck just run us off the road?" Melissa was practically shouting.

He'd been about to ask whether she was injured—clearly, she wasn't. He shook his head. "I don't think so. Just hit an icy patch."

He turned in his seat and looked back. The coffee maker lay on the floor. Cardboard boxes had slid from under the table, now blocking the narrow aisle down the center of the bus. One upper cabinet had come unlatched, and a stack of plates had slid halfway out.

"Put all that stuff back in place," he told her. "I'm going outside to check the trailer."

His feet sank into six inches of snow, and the white stuff filled the tops of his low-cut boots. The good news was the trailer also sat upright. The bad news—the tow bar had bent at an impossible angle. No way could they tow it, even as far as the next town. He let out a string of curses, as much for his expensive boots as for the trailer.

An old blue pickup truck came out of the whiteness, a durable-looking thing that surely worked on a ranch, not some fancy city vehicle. The driver slowed. Foster saw two gnarled hands on the wheel and a Stetson atop a head with gray close-cut hair. The elderly man gawked at the trailer's signage "Temple of the Rising Moon," took one look at the bus with its vividly painted rainbows and flowers, and kept going. Great.

Foster yelled a few choice words that were immediately lost to the wind. Visibility was down to nothing, and he realized they were in a bad spot. If someone came along and rear-ended the skewed trailer he'd be trapped against the back of the bus. If the oncoming vehicle happened to be a big truck, his body would have to be scraped off it.

He gripped the trailer's latch, wishing he'd thought to put on a heavy coat and gloves. Minutes of wrestling the thing wrenched his back and strained every muscle, but eventually his icy hands got the hitch detached from the bus. He shoved it out of the way. The trailer rolled a few feet down the slight incline before it became stuck in the snow. At least it was completely off the road.

He circled the bus, ears intent on listening for

oncoming vehicles, checking for further damage. If the old boat would start, all he had to do was guide it back onto the road. Show Low couldn't be that much farther.

Inside, Melissa had secured the kitchen gear and made certain to set appliances and knickknacks where they couldn't slide. He suppressed irritation that she hadn't done that in the first place. This wasn't the time for the two of them to start bickering.

"Okay, let's pray this baby starts," he said.

She gave a smartass grin and held her hands together, as she had done so many times for their audiences.

The tires slid on the embankment—a long anxious moment for Foster—before the bus got traction and slowly lumbered onto the roadway again. After twenty more minutes Show Low emerged out of the whiteness, with tall pines laden in the heavy snowfall. They eased along the highway, which changed to Deuce of Clubs Drive in the center of town. A gray stucco building with pitched roof had a sign out front: Bluebird Café Breakfast All Day.

Foster steered the bus to the side of the parking area and turned off the engine. He hadn't realized how tense he'd really been until he slid out of his seat and felt the cramping in all his lower regions.

"Let's get some breakfast," he said, helping Melissa into her fluffy faux-fur jacket.

"It's midafternoon," she reminded.

"I don't care. All I can think about is a couple eggs, a slab of ham, and pretending I'm starting this whole day over."

She looked as though she could start the day over, as well. Beneath her perfectly done makeup her face was pale, her mouth trembling, and strands of hair had slipped across her eyes.

The Bluebird Café could have been plopped into any small town in the Southwest and felt right at home. In this version, the interior walls were a dingy cream color, the leatherette booths done in dark brown, and the Formica tabletops were shiny red. A waitress with a tray full of coffee mugs told them to sit anywhere they liked, and since there was only one empty table the choice was simple. Apparently all of Show Low had decided the cozy little spot was the place to be on a snowy day.

Menus were propped against the wall, held in place by a metal contraption that held salt and pepper shakers, sugar and creamer packets, tiny tubs of jelly, a ketchup bottle, and a sticky-looking little jug of maple-flavored syrup. Melissa looked skeptical—this whole place was a far cry from the resort where she'd spent the past week being pampered.

Foster didn't care. At this moment all he wanted was to warm up and get some food before tackling the rest of the route to Albuquerque. When the waitress—a woman whose face seemed far harder than her years—delivered their meals, he asked about the best route.

"Well, you sure don't want to drive all the way up to Snowflake and try to connect with I-40. We heard it's shut down. Happens at least once every year when it snows real hard, and there ain't enough motel rooms in Holbrook to handle everybody that gets stranded." She topped their coffee mugs while she talked. "And I-25 wasn't much better as of an hour ago. One of the truckers said there was a big pileup. Wind, low visibility. I'd wait it out a couple days, if I was you."

Foster's mind raced through the itinerary he'd planned. There was no spare time for delays.

Melissa piped up. "We should just find a room here, honey."

"My cousin owns the Full House Inn, just down the way. But I'd get there early. Come dark, everybody who's on the road is gonna want to get to shelter. This is supposed to be a bad one."

According to his careful itinerary, the next couple of days were planned for Albuquerque and Amarillo, and both cities were directly in the path of the storm. Well, crap, he thought as the waitress walked away.

Chapter 43

Sandy shooed Heckle and Jeckle, her two black cats, off the sofa and removed the cover she used to shield guests from cat hair. A quick dusting of the coffee table, a pot of tea to go with the last of the Christmas cookies, and she was ready for the Heist Ladies to arrive. She needed backup right now.

The news from Amber that Ron did not own the house she'd pinpointed, capped by Trini's revelation about the guru couple getting away, had thrown her off balance. She wanted Pen's steady good sense and Amber's quick access to all types of records, not to mention Gracie's humor and Mary's muscle. Somehow, it felt as if they needed complete teamwork right now.

"I'm glad you called this meeting," Pen said, once they were all seated in Sandy's living room. "Thank goodness for texting. You must fill us in now."

She deferred to Mary, who told them about Trini's call first.

"So, they've just pulled up stakes and left?" Gracie questioned, her mouth practically hanging open.

"Apparently. She said they hitched their trailer to the bus yesterday and drove out this morning."

Even Amber seemed surprised. "I thought they'd scheduled a whole bunch of their 'readings' and practically had people begging for appointments."

Sandy shrugged. "Something must have happened to change their plans. I just wish we knew what."

"They've gotten away with all that money," Pen said, leaning back and looking somewhat stunned.

"We don't know that yet. I'll just do some …" Amber murmured. She already had her laptop out and was typing furiously.

"Do you suppose the money was in the trailer?" Mary asked.

Sandy shook her head slowly. "I don't know … Trini said they used it to haul all their stage gear, sound system equipment, and such."

"That's one thing we could check," suggested Pen. "Trini probably knows the owner of the rented building. Perhaps he could let us in and we would know if they completely cleared out. It could be they're taking a break and will return."

"Great idea." Mary picked up her phone and called Trini. Minutes later she had a name and number and was phoning the landlord. "He's agreed to meet us there any time. Said their lease was up the last day of the month, so he wasn't surprised they've left."

"I bet he'll be surprised when he sees they left a Volkswagen behind." Gracie laughed out loud.

"Um, I don't think they're just taking a break," Amber said. "I've found that credit card I had traced to their business awhile back. It was used at a gas station in Globe and the purchase was nearly two hundred dollars."

"That would fill the tank on a bus, I'd guess," said Sandy.

"Yeah. Most likely."

"And they wouldn't run all the way out to Globe if they were using the gas here in the Phoenix area." Gracie said it and the others all nodded.

"So. They're on the road," Mary said. "Any other charges to let us know which way they went? Roads head off in about five different directions from Globe."

Amber shook her head. "Sorry."

"Has there been any more movement of the money?" Pen asked.

Again, a negative. "Nothing substantial going into or out of the account."

The only sound for a full two minutes was the ticking of the grandfather clock in the foyer.

"Well," said Pen, setting her teacup on the table. "I suppose a couple of us could go out and meet with the landlord at the Temple. They may have left behind some clues as to their plans. And I've completely forgotten to ask you, Mary, how is the surveillance going?"

Mary groaned. "That's coming up a big goose egg, too. I'm beginning to wonder if we've been spotted. Ron is certainly keeping his distance from the house."

Sandy was fidgeting. "Either that or I've made a big mistake and put us on the wrong location. I don't know. This is really discouraging."

"Let me take a turn," Gracie offered. "Maybe he's recognized both of your vehicles, but couldn't have seen my minivan yet, and it'll fit right in with the neighborhood."

Mary gladly ceded the position. "Go for it."

"All right, then," Pen said. "Mary, would you come with me to the Temple building and we'll check this with the landlord? Gracie takes the watch for our mysterious Ron, and Sandy should get some rest before returning to the office in the morning. Amber, please report anything new you find out about the Fordyces and their finances."

"Once we know for sure Ron lives in that particular house, and know he's not home, I think we need to get inside," Gracie said. "The whole point is to retrieve the items stolen from the homeless people."

"You're right," Sandy said. "I should have considered that and done something about it right away."

"Use caution," Pen said. "It wouldn't do to have one of us arrested for breaking and entering unless we're quite certain of catching him red-handed."

A silent look passed among them. Time to get moving!

Chapter 44

Ron felt drawn to Apache Junction again, something about the proximity of the shelter there and that temple place where the cash flowed like a steady river. He got off the bus and ambled toward it, doing nothing to draw attention to himself. He kept his pace slow, his head down, but his eyes were watchful.

The pudgy woman in the blue car and the other one—the one who looked like she could take down a wrestler—had been hanging around his home neighborhood way too much recently. They had the look of federal agents, and that bothered him. Their hanging around Heaven Sent could just be part of their undercover operation. He'd decided to take precautions.

As soon as he checked out the hippie couple at the temple—the lure of all that cash was simply too great to ignore—he would take the next bus back toward Tempe where he knew of another shelter. He could hang out there until the nosy women went away. If they didn't get the chance to question him, they couldn't nail him for anything.

"Well, if it ain't the little guy with the sticky fingers," said a male voice. A man with a vicious scar on his chin had stepped onto the sidewalk in front of him.

Ron's gut went watery. He looked up and recognized two of the security men from the temple. Shaved heads, hard faces, muscles like baseballs under their jackets. Oh hell.

"Yeah," said the second one, who had closed in behind him. "He's the one."

They positioned themselves ahead of and behind him, blocking the sidewalk.

"You know, our boss was real unhappy about that money you took." Each of them took a step closer.

"What money?" Ron raised his chin, hoping for an air of defiance. "I don't know nothin' about that."

"Oh yeah, you do. I bet if I went through your pockets right now, I'd find the cash you took from our boss."

His gut churned some more. They would find cash, all right, and even if it didn't come from their stupid quasi-religious boss they wouldn't hesitate to take it and leave him lying in an alley.

"Okay, okay," Ron said, weighing his options. "You're right. I've got the twenty, right here in my pocket. I'll just give it back—no harm, no foul." He couldn't take his eyes off that nasty scar and wonder about it.

"Well, see, that's not how it works," said the second goon. "Our boss, he didn't tell us to go after the money. See, he told us to teach the weasel a lesson."

"Yeah," said Scarface, "so that's what we gotta do."

By stepping closer they had edged him toward a thick cluster of oleander. Two more steps and the three of them would be screened from the street view and they could do whatever they wanted. Ron felt panic rising. He'd never been good in a fistfight; he was more suited to quick thinking, to outsmarting his enemies. A picture of Emilio Fernandez, the schoolyard bully, came to mind—it had been the one time little Ronnie got beat to a pulp, and he'd vowed it would never happen again.

"Maybe we could work out some kind of a settlement," Ron said. "You know, something your boss never needs to know about. How about you go back and say you taught me real good, but you take the money instead?"

"How about we *do* teach you real good *and* we take the money?" said the second goon, giving an evil laugh.

"Yeah, that sounds good to me," said Scarface.

Oh boy. The thick shrubbery brushed against his back. Ron glanced from one of the muscled creeps to the other. He was about to be toast. Without a second thought he did the only thing he could do—he shoved between them and ran out into traffic.

Chapter 45

Pen watched the clouds race eastward across the sky. The storm was on its way out, and she would miss the rainy, gray days. Arizona, known for clear skies and hot sunshine, sometimes wore her down. Days like these past few reminded her of her childhood in England. She glanced up to see a little Ford pulling into the parking lot.

Mary parked outside Heaven Sent and walked over to the Temple of the Rising Moon, while Pen lowered her window to say hello.

"Looks pretty quiet around here," Mary said.

"They aren't exactly lining them up at the door, are they?" Pen joked.

"I'm going to walk around back and take a look. Stay warm in the car." Mary set a brisk pace as she ducked between the tall palm tree and a big oleander near the base of it.

She returned less than two minutes later. "Just as Trini said—the bus and trailer are gone; the VW is sitting there. Back door is locked up tight, and I don't see any sign of those security guards."

"I believe Amber named them the goons."

A late-model red pickup truck pulled into the lot and stopped at the front door of the building. A forty-something man, with the build of a Marine, got out and looked toward the ladies. Pen got out of her car and joined Mary.

"Royce Williams," the man said. "Did I talk to one of you on the phone?"

Mary shook his hand and introduced herself and Pen.

"So, my tenants moved out a little early?" he asked.

"We think so. But they've left a car out back. They're wanted for questioning, and we're curious as to whether they may come back," Pen said. The 'wanted for questioning' was a brilliant bit on her part, she thought.

"I always do a walk-through—usually accompanied by the tenant," Royce said. "Need to know whether I owe their security deposit back to them. Looks like I'd better go ahead with it now. Come along, if you want."

Pen was glad they hadn't needed to ask for the privilege. The women followed as Royce unlocked the front door. Immediately, she noticed the purple curtains which had sectioned off the room for the séance groups. Chairs for the audiences sat in rows, although slightly more disheveled than she'd last seen them. She spotted a sticker for Acme Party Rentals on one of them.

"Okay," he said, pushing between the draperies. "Looks like I've got a cleanup job here."

In the larger portion of the warehouse-like space, the risers and chairs were still in place. The big stage where

Orion had stood, bestowing blessings upon the crowd, and the backdrop curtains were all there.

"Dammit—they didn't clean out anything," he said. "What the hell were they doing here anyway?" He glanced at Pen. "Sorry for the language, ma'am."

She waved off the apology and pointed out the sticker. "It appears the chairs and risers may have been rented. Certainly, Acme would come to retrieve their part of it all."

Mary had meandered to the area behind the audience seating and was studying a large table. "But this stuff looks like theirs. There's some pretty expensive sound equipment here, and a lighting control panel." She slid two of the levers, and spotlights shone on the center of the stage.

"It's quite a lot of gear," Pen murmured. "Surprising they would abandon it."

Royce strode past the rows of seating, bypassed the stage, and walked behind it. The women could hear metallic clanking, then the sound of a door opening.

"Do you suppose the Fordyces plan to come back?" Mary whispered to Pen.

She gave it some thought and shook her head. "I doubt it. But the purpose of—" The answer hit her just as Royce reappeared.

"No deposit back for these guys. This is a massive job," he said. "Gonna take me days to get rid of this stuff. That, or hire a crew. And technically I can't start until after the thirty-first."

He removed his ball cap and ran fingers through his dark hair, looking as though he'd like to kick something. "You ladies done here?" He started for the front door.

"Yes," said Pen. "Thank you for letting us take a look."

"Hey, you come across that couple, you let me know. I didn't charge them near enough as a cleaning deposit."

He ushered them out and locked the door, still muttering. "I knew it! Between their religious patter and her batting those baby-blues at me, I was stupid to believe a thing they said."

Mary smiled and thanked him again. Pen only wanted to agree with what he'd just said. They watched him drive away, throwing dirt as the pickup spun out of the parking area.

"What do you make of it?" Mary asked. "I saw your face in there. A lightbulb came on, didn't it?"

"Quite possibly. Think about it a moment. The trailer arrived here filled with all that gear—lights, sound equipment, draperies, large screen monitors—and it left here empty?"

"Seemingly …"

"I have this dreadfully titillating feeling it was filled with money."

"Oh my god, Pen. You're right. All the time we've wondered what they did with the bulk of the cash, all the searches Amber has been doing for their banks … and the money was right here under our noses, sitting in that trailer."

"It would be so terribly risky," Pen said. "Can you imagine—if someone had taken a fancy to the trailer and hauled it away while the Fordyces were not looking?"

"It's probably why they lived in the bus, so they could keep an eye on everything."

Pen stood beside her car, staring toward the distant mountains. "And yet … something does not feel exactly right about this theory either. I only wish I knew what that *something* is."

Chapter 46

The bus might as well have been a freezer. Foster was beginning to wish he would simply freeze to death—it would be easier than listening to Melissa's complaints.

"There's a foot of snow outside the door," she whined. "How will we get out of here? And why isn't the heater working?"

Because I totally forgot about propane. Why couldn't the damn generator run off gasoline, like the engine? Why couldn't just one *motel have a vacancy last night?* "Sweetie, just stay in bed and add another blanket. I'll go check it out."

It was all he could do to keep a civil tone and, for the first time in their marriage, he thought—for one brief flash of a moment—of just walking away.

Walk away? Yeah, right. He stepped off the bus and his trainers filled with snow. The legs of his jeans were instantly coated in white. *Why don't I own a pair of snow boots? Because you grew up in the South and this is the first deep snow you've ever seen except on TV.*

They were in this together. Hell or high water—either of which would be more welcome than this white crap—he and Missy had to get through it as a team.

He walked across the parking lot where they'd spent the night and into the café, stomping snow off his feet and swatting at his pants, feeling like a fool in front of the locals who'd actually dressed properly for the weather. While a young waitress (who probably owned the perfect coat and boots) poured coffee into two Styrofoam cups and placed four donuts into a white bag, Foster checked his phone. Still no signal.

"Does this happen often here?" he asked, holding up the phone. "No phone, no internet?"

"Pretty much every storm," she replied. He was fascinated by the way the ring in her nose wiggled when she spoke.

"So, what do I do to get a signal?" he asked.

"Nothin. It'll come back when it comes back."

"Crap. What'll I do until then?"

"I know, right? You know what my mom says? 'Read a book.' Like that solves everything. Makes me want to scream. I tell you, the minute I save up enough I'm moving to Phoenix where they never have these problems."

He thought of the traffic, the pollution, and the summer heat. "Sure. No problems. And the skies are not cloudy all day."

She gave him a funny look, along with his change. He stuck the pastry bag inside his inadequate jacket and picked up the two coffees.

"Have a good one," she said.

As if. He trudged back to the bus and nearly lost one of the coffee cups as he struggled with the door. Inside, Melissa was sitting up in bed, pillows and blankets piled all around her, scowling at her phone.

"I can't seem to get a signal," she said.

"It's out all over," he said, handing her one of the cups, then taking the donut bag out of his jacket. "Maybe this'll warm us up a little. If you feel like getting dressed, at least there's heat over at the café, and we can get some eggs or something. They have a TV up on the wall, so maybe we can hear a weather report and find out how long this storm's going to last."

But a weather report wasn't going to solve his main problem. The ship on which he'd reserved a container was sailing in a week, and he still had to get the two of them and the bus around to four cities in three states. The weatherman couldn't solve his problems, but at least an internet connection could put him in touch with the coast.

Chapter 47

Ron huddled behind an alley dumpster and massaged his foot. His heart rate hadn't yet returned to normal, but at least the car had only grazed him. He'd run on adrenaline for six or eight blocks, until he was sure the two men weren't following. One leg of his chinos was ripped and a gash on the calf was still bleeding pretty good. The foot hurt like hell but he didn't think it was broken.

In real life he would have probably seen a doctor, but that would require getting home first to clean up and then making up a plausible story. And *that* whole scenario would mean avoiding those two women agents who were spying on his place, not to mention staying clear of the goons who wanted to teach him a lesson. *Okay, already—lesson learned. Just leave me alone.*

He used the sleeve of his shirt to stem the bleeding

on his leg, then realized his foot had swollen too big to get back into his shoe. *Well, hell.* He leaned back and rested the injured limb on a cinder block that was lying beside the dumpster. The sun was overhead now, shining down into the alley, and it wasn't too unpleasant out. Might as well settle in for a little while and think about his options.

He pulled a quart-sized plastic zip baggie from the inner pocket of his roomy jacket, ridiculously happy that the goons hadn't frisked him and discovered his treasure stash. When he thought the feds were watching him, knowing he might not go back home for days or weeks, he'd dumped the contents of his metal tin into the bag so he could keep everything safe and with him.

Now, poking through them with a grimy finger brought back fond memories. There was the gold-toned locket he'd realized wasn't real gold when he looked closely at it. But still, it was cute. The pocket watch might actually be real gold. He could try taking it by a pawnshop to see if someone would authenticate it, but that would lead to questions. Hell, it might even be on a watch list of some kind. Or not. Homeless people didn't exactly call the police or their insurance companies. The latest thing, a thin gold chain, probably wasn't worth much but the tiny tab near the broken clasp did confirm it was 18 karat.

He heard footsteps, dropped the chain bag into his baggie and shoved it back into his coat.

"Hey, buddy, you need some help?" asked a kindly male voice.

Ron looked up to see a man, casually dressed in jeans and sweater, staring at him from across the alley. Then he noticed the clerical collar.

"What kind of help?"

"Well, whatever. It looks like you're injured."

Quick thinking. Don't let anyone, even if it is under some kind of confessional-privilege status, know the real situation. "Well, I did hurt my leg and foot. If I could just get where I could lie down and rest it awhile …"

"Maybe I should get you to the ER."

"Oh no, it's not that serious." Ron was glad he'd covered the open wound. "I'm staying at this place over on 103rd Street. Could you give me a ride there?"

The priest helped him to his feet. It was all Ron could do to put weight on the hurt limb, but he managed it without crying out. He hobbled to a white car parked in front of a Panda Express, wondering what the priest had been doing walking down the alley if he'd been eating at the fast food place. But he couldn't question the gift of the ride. His entire left side was throbbing in pain now.

"So, where to?" the stranger asked once he'd seen Ron buckled into the passenger seat.

"It's called Casa de … something or other. It's near the corner of 103rd and Sagebrush."

"I know the place. Friend of mine is the manager."

Bless him for not dwelling on the fact that it was a homeless shelter. Ron's appearance probably said it all, and priests were trained in discretion, weren't they? The ride took fifteen minutes, during which Ron listened to the priest's small talk while hoping he didn't look as though he was about to pass out.

He managed to limp into the men's section of the home before his legs gave way and he collapsed onto the bed he'd been assigned last night. The priest and the shelter manager stood in the corner mumbling, no doubt about him, but he no longer cared. When the manager came back with warm water, antibiotic ointment, and bandages Ron thanked him and insisted he could take care of the wound himself.

While he cleaned and treated his injury the man went away, coming back with a pair of worn but clean pajamas and an extra blanket. He extended his hand and held out a bottle of aspirin. "Better have a couple of these and then get some rest."

Five minutes later he was sound asleep.

Chapter 48

"This has been one of the worst winter storms in recent history," the weathercaster was saying. "The northern part of the state, particularly above the Mogollon rim, has been especially hard hit, and travel is not advised on I-40, I-17 or any of the secondary roads, shown at the bottom of your screen. I-40 remains closed near Flagstaff, but other places are equally troublesome."

Mary slowed the treadmill, nearing the end of her workout, and gazed at the television screen on the wall ahead of her.

"Here's just one of many small incidents, this one out near Show Low," the too-cute young woman said, "where apparently a trailer became detached from the vehicle towing it."

The video cut to a snowy highway scene. An enclosed

trailer sat at a steep angle to the roadway, tail end up, the hitch apparently buried in a snowbank. A familiar logo grabbed Mary's attention. She jumped off the back of the treadmill and shut it down.

As the camera switched back to the news anchor, who quipped about somebody not having a good trip, Mary reached for her towel and phone, which she'd left on a nearby chair.

"I know where they're going," she blurted the moment Pen answered. "Well, I should say, it's the direction they headed. They didn't make it far because of the storm."

She explained what she'd seen on the news. "I'm going up there."

"Mary, no! The roads are terrible."

"Okay, not this minute. But I'll keep an eye on the reports and once I can, I'm heading out. If I can get to that trailer before they haul it away, I'll call the police. I'm betting that thing is stuffed full of cash. I need to be the first person to get to it—anyone else will just take it and vanish."

"Well, you're probably correct about that. But you shouldn't go alone. I shall come along."

"Pen, are you sure?"

"I will raid the closet for all my snow gear and remain at the ready. Phone me when it's time. I can be out the door on ten minutes' notice."

The call came at noon.

"I remembered one of my ex's customers lives up in that direction," Mary told Pen when she arrived at her friend's Scottsdale home. "I called him and he said the plows were out early this morning. There are clear tracks in all directions, although the last he heard Interstate 40 had not yet been officially opened."

"We'll drive my Land Rover," Pen said. "No argument. It's gassed up and ready to go, and we don't know whether we will need its four-wheel-drive capabilities for this little excursion of ours."

Mary looked at her small Ford sedan, compared to the beefier vehicle sitting in its garage bay. Common sense told her Pen was right. They loaded her gear into the back of the Rover alongside Pen's duffle bag, a rolled-up snowmobile suit, and two pairs of snowshoes. She'd also thought to add a tool kit and pry bar.

"Seems weird, bringing all this stuff, when we're standing here at seventy degrees with a sunny sky," Mary said. "But that's probably what the Fordyces said when they drove right into the blizzard."

"Precisely." Pen gave her a warm smile as she climbed behind the wheel.

The beauty of getting out on the highway soon after the media has broadcast a dire-sounding situation is that traffic is nearly nonexistent. They made great time through Globe and the long stretch north. As they approached Show Low, they began watching for the abandoned trailer.

For an excruciating few minutes Mary was afraid someone else, possibly the gurus, had beat them to it. But just before a sign announced the Heber turnoff in twenty miles, there it was, mired in more than two feet of the white stuff and nearly hidden. Pen found a slightly wide spot and pulled over, setting her emergency flashers, despite the fact they hadn't seen another vehicle in twenty minutes.

"Whoa. It won't be easy to get this baby dislodged, will it?' Mary said. The trailer hitch was completely buried and barely visible behind the muddy snowbank the plow had thrown off to the sides.

"The good news is that the Fordyces most likely cannot

pull it out with their school bus. A large tow truck will be in order for this task."

Mary listened intently. The silence was complete. "No other vehicles anywhere near. I'd say this is our chance."

Pen slipped her snow suit over her clothing, strapped on a pair of the snowshoes, and grabbed the pry bar. Mary did the same, and they approached the back of the trailer. A sturdy hasp and padlock held it shut. She took the pry bar from Pen and inserted the end of it behind the lock.

On the first pull it slipped, sending her backward, where she landed on her butt in the snow.

"Okay, gotta get a better grip." She approached the lock again, a glare of determination on her face.

This time, the hasp began to pull away from the metal door. She repositioned the tool and braced herself with both legs. In minute increments the space widened, until at last the screws came free. Hasp and lock fell aside.

"Success!" Pen cheered.

"All right. Now to find the bounty." Mary wrestled the closure mechanism, hacking at the iced-over places with the pry bar, until finally it slid aside and the door began to edge outward against the heavy snow.

When Mary had a space large enough to get her head in position, Pen handed her a small flashlight and she peered inside. The trailer was empty.

Chapter 49

Following the snowplow was a messy business. Foster saw the machine come through Show Low in the early morning hours and made a quick decision. Now or never. He'd cranked up the bus and steered out of the café's parking lot, leaving Melissa to grab loose items and stow them. After about ten miles of dealing with the coating of road grime that coated his windshield every few moments, he allowed the bus to fall back to about a half-mile behind the plow.

Logistics had never been his friend. The endless details of getting from Point A to Point B, setting up a new show, planning the costumes and having them made—Melissa was much better at those duties. Now, he was preparing for one of their biggest moves of all, and he had kept her in the dark about a lot of it.

During the night he'd been able to receive internet on his phone for a few precious minutes. The company he was renting the container from had responded with an invoice and a note. Send payment now. Ship sails December 31.

He had four days to hit four cities and load a container. He wanted to follow his character Orion's advice and adopt a peaceful and calm attitude, to live in the moment and not stress over future events. But, hell, that just wasn't him. Never had been. He kept the radio tuned to a channel with weather reports and said the closest thing he'd ever uttered to a real prayer.

Melissa appeared at the seat beside him, handing over an insulated mug of coffee. "Sun's barely lighting the sky," she said. "I didn't know we were getting such an early start."

"Had to. It's the calm between storms, according to the news. We've gotta hit Albuquerque, Amarillo and El Paso, then get ourselves to San Diego." He took a swig of the coffee, and even though it was instant, he was glad she'd had the presence of mind to boil some water on the little two-burner.

"I've got good news and better news," he said. "Before we get to San Diego I want you to go shopping for furniture. Anything you want for the new island house. We've got a container that'll only be a third full with the boxes. We need to fill it up with stuff that really makes it look like we're moving all our household goods."

"Sounds like fun." She beamed her angelic smile at him.

"And the better news is that I've found some great choices of islands for sale. I just need you to narrow it down to your favorite." This last bit definitely fudged the truth, but it was better to keep her upbeat and happy for his next request.

"We'll need to take turns with the driving," he told her. "All those stops I told you about—we have four days to do the whole trip."

She made a face. She hated driving the huge old bus.

"San Diego … shopping for all those fun things …" he reminded.

"Eyes on the goal," she said. "Okay, we got this thing."

She got up and went to the tiny refrigerator. "I saved some pastries from that café in Show Low. Want something to go with your coffee?"

"Sure."

She brought him a cheese Danish on a paper napkin. "I just remembered … did we ever give the Macks their final pay?"

"Yeah, baby. I took care of them." Something made him think of that guy who'd taken money from the collection baskets then run away, the one he had ordered his men to chase down and 'teach him a lesson.' Foster had paid the Macks their salary, but had he remembered to call them off? He took a big bite of the pastry. Oh well, surely they had quit by now. He finished off the cheese Danish and asked if there were any cherry ones.

Melissa took the wheel an hour later and they passed into New Mexico without incident. When they reached Socorro she stopped, declaring it was time for lunch. But Foster didn't want to take the time at the restaurant where she'd parked the bus. He hopped out and walked to the McDonald's next door.

"Decision time," he said when he returned and set the bag of burgers on the table. "Interstate 25 is right here and we need to either head north to Albuquerque or south to El Paso."

"Isn't there still snow up north?" she asked.

He consulted his phone and tapped a few links. "Looks like we're between storms. This last one is hitting Oklahoma now, but another one's coming. We got a day, maybe two, before it hits."

He wavered for only a minute, then picked up a Quarter Pounder and a sleeve of fries and carried them to the front. As he took the driver's seat he turned back to his wife. "Get some rest. The next long stretch will be yours, and it'll be dark by then."

Chapter 50

"What do spies call it when they've been discovered?" Sandy asked Gracie. "We've been *made*, or something like that?"

Gracie shrugged. The two were standing at the end of Ron's street, doing their best to look like two neighbors out for a walk who had paused to visit.

"You and Mary gave it a lot of hours, we all did, but he must have spotted us. The one time she caught a glimpse, he took off and got away. I don't think he's even here anymore. We haven't seen a light on in the house, haven't seen a curtain move for more than two days."

Gracie pulled her phone from her pocket. "Let's see if Amber had any luck reaching the homeowner. If he's Ron's friend, maybe he knows something."

Amber sounded a little distracted when she picked up

the call. "Sorry, I'm running late for a dental appointment, but I can tell you what little I found out. Since I discovered a William Duckly owns the house, I did a little more checking on him. He doesn't live there, so I'm thinking it's a rental. I found a phone number for him … hang on a second."

The connection went fuzzy and Gracie thought she'd lost Amber, but in a moment her voice came back.

"Sorry, I was parking. God, I hate the dentist."

"Duckly. Phone number."

"Right." She read off the digits, which Gracie repeated so Sandy could enter them on her own phone.

"We'll check him out. Good luck at the dentist. Can we bring you anything afterward?"

"Nah, it's just a cleaning. I know, I'm such a weenie."

Duckly's phone was ringing. Sandy held up an index finger as he answered. She and Gracie had walked back to the minivan and got inside for the quieter surroundings.

"Mr. Duckly, this is Sandra Werner with Desert Trust Bank. I'm calling about a home you own at 1490 Rabbit Run Trail."

"Uh-oh, there's not a water leak or something, is there? Cause this is not a good time."

When *was* a good time for a water leak, she wondered. "Oh no, nothing like that. I'm running a … credit check … and it's about your tenant."

"Yeah, Ron Smith. What about him?"

"He um … does he pay his rent on time?" She knew it sounded lame but it was the quickest excuse she could think of.

"He's been a good tenant. Only been in the house five or six months, I guess. I'm not where I can get to the records right now."

"And he's always been on time with the rent?"

"Brings me cash on the first, every— Um, look, I gotta go. Whatever you're checking about him, he's fine."

Sandy stared at the dead phone in her hand. "That was odd. He seemed talkative and then bam—cut me off."

"Probably thinks you're from some legal office, trying to find out if he's obeying all the laws."

"So, I guess the only thing I learned is that Ron *Smith* pays his rent in cash each month."

"That's great—I mean, it's definitely him. We know he panhandles for cash all the time. It makes sense he would pay his bills with it."

"But what a rat! He's staying at the shelter, getting free meals, convincing people to give him cash, then he comes home to a pretty decent house."

Gracie nodded. "I agree. He's a rat and a cheat and he knows how to work the system." She had pulled a little notebook from beside her seat and was scribbling furiously. "So, I've got his name, address, the landlord's name and phone number. We can turn it all over to … I don't know. There must be some agency that will come after him."

Sandy looked at her. "We don't even know if he's breaking any laws. Moral ones, sure. But is there any law on the books about panhandling but living in a nice neighborhood?"

"You're right. There probably isn't." Gracie dropped her pen and leaned back in her seat. A moment later, she sat up straight again. "Okay, so it's not our job to figure out the man's lifestyle. What we came for was to see if he's been stealing from the homeless at the shelter. So, I say we get inside that house and we find their stuff. Steal it back."

Sandy's mouth opened. "But—"

"But what? He's not here. You've been staring at this

house for days. Let's just tippy-toe around back, pry open a window or something ... It's a rental, for Pete's sake, it won't have a deluxe security system or anything."

The break-in proved easier than either would have guessed when they found the side door to the garage unlocked. Ron's car was gone.

"Wear your gloves," Sandy whispered as they walked through the empty garage. "We don't want to leave prints."

"Seriously? You think he'll call the cops?"

Okay, maybe not. But there had been several children playing across the street. What if one of them mentioned the two women. Gracie assured her they would come up with a reasonable explanation if it came to that.

Inside, the kitchen felt cold and unused. A peek inside the fridge revealed three cans of Bud Light, a bottle of ketchup, and a loaf of white bread. The freezer contained only a bin of shrunken ice cubes and the ice maker was set not to make more.

"Darn. I was hoping for one of those notorious foil-wrapped packets like you see in the movies. Bad guys wrap drugs in them. We could have found all the missing items right here," Gracie said.

"Let's not hang around too long." Sandy glanced nervously across the kitchen counter into a sparsely furnished living room.

"Okay, you take the bedrooms and bathroom. I'll finish the kitchen and living room." Gracie tapped her index finger against her chin. "You don't suppose he would have buried the stuff in the yard out back?"

"One thing at a time." Sandy was on her way to the short hallway which led to two bedrooms and a bath.

The front bedroom was empty except for a full-sized bed, bare mattress, and a bureau which proved to be empty.

The bedroom at the back was obviously the one Ron used. There was a queen-sized bed with cheap discount-store linens, hastily made. A chair in the corner held a dirty pair of chinos—she recognized Ron's style. On top of a chest of drawers was a small flat-screen TV.

She went through both nightstands and came up with nothing more interesting than a pocket knife. The man didn't even keep a box of tissues or condoms. A drawer in the chest held a basic assortment of men's underwear and socks, all clean and neatly folded. Another contained a half-dozen T-shirts in dark colors. Through the open closet door she saw jeans, polo shirts, and a few button-down shirts on hangers. Everything was clean, fairly new, and definitely middle class.

Ron, the beggar and supposedly homeless man, had a secret life as an ordinary guy.

Gracie appeared in the doorway. "Have to say, this is one of the neatest men I've ever seen. No sign of hobbies, collections of junk, or the 'it might be useful someday' pile of wires and strings every guy hangs onto."

"Same here," Sandy said. "If you're done in there, give me a hand. If you can go through those boxes on the closet shelf, I'll peek in the bathroom."

"Did you check under the bed?"

Sandy knelt on the small rug beside the bed and raised the edge of the spread. Immediately, she sneezed, but she only spotted a lone sock near the foot of the bed. There were some tracks in the dust where something, probably the little rug, must have slipped partway under and been pulled out again.

"Nothing here," she said with another huge sneeze.

Gracie had pulled two shoeboxes from the closet shelf. "Woo, money!" she said as she opened the first one to reveal handfuls of wadded bills.

"Guess we know where all those donations end up."

"Should we take it?"

"And do what? We can't exactly return it to the owners. But take a picture. There might be some way this can be used as evidence."

"Yeah, evidence that we broke into the man's house."

"Good point. Don't take a picture. Just keep looking for those stolen items." Sandy headed toward the bathroom. "Check the pockets in all the clothing," she called back.

Five minutes later, Gracie appeared at the bathroom door. "Other than an empty cookie tin and a shoebox that actually held a pair of shoes, I found nothing," she admitted.

"Nothing here either." Sandy rinsed her hands and wiped them on the single towel on the rack. "We should get out of here."

Back in Gracie's minivan, both women felt the weight of discouragement. "Could we have been wrong about Ron being the thief?" Sandy mused. "It seemed a logical conclusion, but we haven't found anything at all to tie the thefts to him."

"We'd better talk to Pen and the others. I just don't know what to do next."

Chapter 51

"We've never had a case with so few leads," Pen admitted when they spoke later that afternoon.

She and Mary had cruised the main streets of Show Low, a task of ten minutes, but there was no sign of the hippies' school bus.

"I know," Sandy said on the phone. "We felt so sure Ron was our thief from the shelter, but there was nothing in his house that implicates him. Panhandling, sure. We found some grimy clothing and a couple boxes of cash—maybe a few hundred dollars total, although it was so grungy neither of us wanted to touch it."

"We located the Rising Moon's trailer, but it was empty. Mary wasn't happy. Actually, both of us had been so certain it would contain the money. It was a huge letdown when it didn't."

"I think we're all feeling disheartened," Sandy said, catching Gracie's eye. "At this end, we just aren't sure what to do next."

"I know. Our quarry has disappeared, as well, and there are simply too many roads to follow. Mary and I have decided to get some lunch and consider the options. Unless we get a solid lead, we may be driving back home this afternoon."

"At least Amber is still working on the Moon Temple banking angle," Gracie reminded.

"Indeed. Perhaps she will come up with something to prove their dishonest intentions, and we could still turn this over to the authorities," Pen said. "In the meantime, why don't you two take a break? Sandy, you have put in long hours. Go do something fun for a change."

"Wish I could. I'm so far behind at work, I really need to go in, lock myself in my office for the rest of the day, and catch up."

"All right. Whatever eases your mind. Meanwhile, we shall press on and will share the results, if any." Pen tapped the button to end the call, turning in her driver's seat to face Mary. "Lunch was somewhat of a spur of the moment idea, but what do you think? Sustenance may give us some ideas."

Mary agreed. "Plus, we can use our time to ask around, see if any of the locals remember a brightly painted bus coming through here. I'm guessing it's not something they see every day."

"I recall a small café at the other end of town. Let's gas up the Rover at that station across the street, and then we can eat."

Pen walked inside the station's convenience store and inquired about the bus.

"Oh, heck yeah, I remember seeing that thing. Looked like the old hippie buses we used to see in the seventies, 'cept this one had a guy in sissy boots and a woman who looked like she spends her whole day in a beauty shop," said the female clerk who rang up Pen's purchase of a lip balm.

"Did they stay in town?"

"Ha—everybody stayed in town last night," said the woman, revealing a perfectly even set of dentures. "Wasn't no way to get out after about four o'clock yesterday afternoon. Town's only got one snowplow, and he couldn't very well get to all five highways at once."

"Do you know which road he would have cleared first?"

"Prob'ly the one over to Payson. It gets the most traffic."

Pen nodded and thanked her. The highway to Payson led back toward the Phoenix area, and she doubted the Fordyces would have done that. But knowing they'd been in town was at least something of a lead.

The Bluebird Café was warm inside and smelled of bacon. Both women ordered BLT sandwiches. When the waitress delivered them, Pen asked about their quarry.

"Old bus painted blue with all these rainbows and silly pictures on the sides—and some kind of words about the moon? Oh yeah, they was here. The guy was *some* kind of grumpy, kept coming in every five minutes to see if our internet was working. The lady didn't say much to me; she seemed kind of ticked off at him."

"Do you know where they stayed the night?" Mary asked.

"Yeah. In their bus. Right out there." The woman pointed toward a side window that overlooked a muddy parking lot.

"Do you know what time they left, or what direction they were going?"

"Well, yesterday afternoon they come in, all wired up and hot to get to Albuquerque. Wanted to know the quickest way, and I told 'em not only was there no quick way, there most likely was no way at all. I mean, the roads was getting snow-packed real fast."

Albuquerque. At last, a solid clue.

"And this morning? Once the roads opened up, did they say what direction they would take?"

"They didn't say nothin' to me. The bus was here when I came to work, but they lit out while I was still prepping in the kitchen."

A man at the counter pushed his empty plate aside and looked at them. "I might know."

"This is Harvey, the snowplow driver," the waitress added.

Pen asked him to go on.

"Bus like you described followed me out of town, east on 60. Wasn't really safe out yet, but he was in some kind of all-fired hurry. Practically tailgated me, even though the plow's got that sign on the back, 'Stay Back Thirty Feet.' There's all kinds of splatter and little rocks and stuff. Guess he finally figured that out cause he dropped back a ways."

"Highway 60, that goes toward the New Mexico border, right?" Mary asked.

"Yep. I think he stayed behind me as far as Springerville, but that's when I turn around. Bus musta gone on."

They thanked him for the information and quickly finished their lunch. Out in the Land Rover again, Mary laughed. "No secret conversations in a town this size, are there?"

"In our case it worked out well. We know a lot more

than we did an hour ago."

"So, what do you want to do? Albuquerque's a pretty big city, really spread out. How can we hope to catch them?"

Pen started her engine and turned up the heat. "I honestly don't know. But we've come this far. With luck, our vehicle is faster and we may catch up."

Chapter 52

His foot sported a rainbow of purples and blues, Ron discovered when he unwrapped the elastic bandage. The swelling had not gone down, but at least it was no worse. The cut on his calf had scabbed over decently, but the surrounding skin was still an angry red. He looked around at the roomful of beds. Except for one man sleeping it off and another who was in the process of putting on his clothes, the others must have gone to eat breakfast. Ron groaned. He needed to get out of here.

Thoughts of the outside world jumbled around in his head—his car, his house. He'd left the car at Fry's—was it two days ago now? And while the 24-hour store always had cars in the lot, there was a good chance security cameras or a roving guard had spotted the white sedan and noticed it hadn't moved. If they'd had it towed, it was a whole new set of problems to deal with.

And what about those women who'd been watching his house? Living life off the grid didn't mean some stupid government agency couldn't have an eye on you. What if the IRS had put it together that he hadn't filed a tax return in more than ten years? That blonde woman, in particular—she had the look about her. Just because she helped out at Heaven Sent didn't mean she wasn't an agent.

He sat on the edge of his bed and reached down for his shoes. Every muscle in his body screamed, and he nearly fell back to the pillow. But he gritted his teeth and persisted. He managed to get out of the pajamas and into his own pants and shirt without having to stand and put weight on the foot. Now would come the real challenge. He stood, bearing most of his weight on his good foot, and zipped his pants.

He refused to think about the pain as he tested a shoe on the injured foot. Thank goodness he'd worn his old Nikes the other day, instead of his usual heavy leather boots. The flexible trainers stretched a little, allowing him to ease the shoe around the swollen places. The laces would never tie, but he secured the ends of them in a loose knot so they didn't drag the ground.

He nearly toppled over as he took the first few steps, but he managed to gather his coat with the bag of treasures inside and his watch cap. By the time he got to the front door he was sweating.

He peered out through the glass door, scoping out the street beyond. He was miles from where he'd left his car and it was at least fifty yards to the corner bus stop. He felt way too exposed. If those goons knew he was here, there was no way he could outrun them this time. He'd be dead meat.

Suddenly he was a little kid again, a kid who wanted to cry out for mommy to make it all better, to have someone else take charge and fix all his problems and make him some hot soup. *Too bad, Ronnie, that ain't happening.*

"Hey, you're up," came the voice of the manager, startling him. "Can I do something to help you?"

Ron nearly blurted out the part about wanting hot soup but caught himself. What came out was, "I need to get to my girlfriend's house."

"Want me to call her for you?"

"Um, she doesn't have a phone right now. But I've got a little money …" He reached into a pocket and came up with twenty dollars in rumpled ones and fives. "If you could call me a taxi, I'm sure I have enough for that."

The manager looked as though he wanted to offer a ride, which would force Ron to come up with some reason why that wouldn't work, but apparently he thought better of it.

"Sure," he said. "I can do that."

The meter ticked $19.25 as the cab pulled into the Fry's parking lot. Ron spotted his car and breathed a huge sigh of relief. He handed the driver the twenty dollars in his fist and magnanimously said, "Keep the change."

The guy sent a scowl his way, but Ron ignored it and concentrated on getting to his feet again. The left one throbbed, but he kept going through the excruciating pain by reminding himself that once home he could dose himself with some drugs and really start taking care of the wounds.

If those agents weren't hanging around.

And *if* those thugs from the temple didn't somehow spot him and give chase.

He got into his car and locked the doors, eyes peeled

for the goons, even though logic told him there was no way they could know he would come to this place and get into this car. Still. Better to be cautious after all the drama of the past few days.

When Ron reached his neighborhood he cruised past without turning in, staring down the length of his street, looking for either of the vehicles the women had used. Nothing. It was past the hour when the neighbors would have left for work and all seemed clear. On the next pass he turned in, raised his garage door and drove inside, closing it immediately.

Whew. He'd made it before the government spies got here.

It felt good to be back. He suddenly wished he'd made more of a home of the place, kept more food and small creature comforts here. He got the jar of instant coffee from the cupboard and drew tap water into a pan. While it heated, he hobbled to the bathroom and rummaged through the supplies. Not much in the way of wound care, but he found alcohol and some antibiotic cream. He showered off the street grime and tossed his dirty clothes in the corner.

He should have taken the borrowed pajamas from the shelter—they would have been most comfortable while he sat around with his injured foot elevated. Instead, he settled for a pair of sweats and a baggy sweater he'd almost tossed out a month ago.

By the time he returned to the kitchen the pan had nearly boiled dry. He cursed his forgetfulness, added more water, and set it on the burner again. The throbbing foot got his attention and he decided to make an ice pack with a plastic zip-top bag. But somehow the ice maker had shut off and the cubes were nearly all gone, shrunken to little knobs coated in white dust. He dumped the entire bin into the baggie and set the ice maker to come back on.

When had his life changed to this? His idea of carefree living out of society, remaining unnoticed by the government, doing what he wanted when he wanted … How had he come to the point where he was being followed and beaten by thugs, hiding out in his own home. Where was the adventurous travel he had envisioned? Why hadn't he spent some of his cash income on making a more comfortable home for himself?

He poured boiling water over the instant coffee granules in his mug and made his way to the living room. He set his coffee on the table and stretched out on the sofa. *See? I could have at least bought myself a recliner.*

A flash of light from the front window caught his attention as he picked up the TV remote. A car passed by.

"Crap." Should have closed the blinds. He hauled himself off the couch and over to the window, peering up and down the street. No sign of either agent's car. Where were they?

He moved away from the window. What was going on? The government doesn't watch for awhile and then quit. For that matter did they actually sit in cars, watching a place and spying on a person? Wouldn't the agents just come to the door and insist that he talk to them?

His gut churned and he realized he'd not eaten any breakfast. But the thought of food made it churn worse. Television would be a good distraction, he decided as he settled back on the sofa and set his ice pack in place.

The morning shows were all a bunch of drivel—perky women blathering on about stupid book clubs and relationships. He flipped channels until he came to one with an old black-and-white gangster show. There. That was more like it. Al Capone was being chased by the Feds. Then he remembered—it wasn't murder charges that brought down Scarface Capone. It was tax evasion.

He switched to another channel but couldn't stop the wave of despair he felt rolling over him.

Chapter 53

The sun had come out at some point while Foster slept, and by midafternoon when they reached Albuquerque the major roads weren't too bad. He remembered the location of the self storage unit he had rented on a street called San Mateo. Two years ago it had been when he took the unit and paid in advance. He didn't recognize the manager at the gate, but there were no questions and he drove directly to unit 127.

The footing was a little icy in the shady patches, but they would make the best of it. He dusted off the padlock and opened it, heaving the garage-sized door upward.

"Whew-*ee*, that's a lot of boxes!" Melissa said, staring into the space which was lined floor-to-ceiling with them. "How much we got here?"

"Shh. Voices down," he whispered. "I coded them so

we don't have to open them up to find out."

He gazed around the room, judging. Would they be able to fit all this into the bus? Well, they had no choice at the moment, but before the next stop they would need to rent a trailer.

"Let's get started. It'll be dark soon." He picked up a box and stacked another on top, carrying them to the door of the bus. "I'll start finding places for these inside. You just keep 'em coming."

He set the first two boxes on the dinette table and took out his phone calculator. Quickly translating his handwritten codes into dollar amounts, he entered the sums and then carried the boxes to the back, where he began packing them under the queen-sized bed in the corner. By the time he came back, Melissa had three more boxes waiting for him.

Enter the dollar value, stash the box, get another. Repeat, repeat, repeat. They weren't a fraction of the way through the storage building before the under-bed space and top of the bed were full. He stacked boxes to the ceiling, and started on the tiny lavatory space. Next, he filled the passageway, then added to what was already under the dinette. Soon, the dinette's bench seats were full.

"How we doing?" he called out to Melissa.

She had removed her jacket and was breathing hard when she dropped two more boxes on the step. "Take a look."

The locker was barely half cleared.

"Okay, hold off a minute." He did some quick calculations. They couldn't wait until Amarillo to get a trailer. They needed one now, and a simple little U-Haul wouldn't cut it. "Let's lock up and come back."

"Food would be good," she said as she watched him

double-check the padlock.

When she climbed into the bus her eyes went wide. "Holy cow! What—how? Honey, how are we going to sleep or take a potty break?"

"Sleep sitting up, take advantage of restrooms at the gas stations," he said.

An hour later, they drove away from the sales lot, a brand new 'toy hauler' trailer hitched to the bus. The salesman had assured them it would easily carry six ATVs or two side-by-side vehicles in its enclosed space. Given the fact that they were paying in cash, he probably would have promised them anything.

When Melissa whined about not taking the time to enjoy a good restaurant dinner, Foster simply gave her a look. No way was he leaving the bus in a parking lot. The three million dollars already inside was not going to make some petty crook's day.

It took them until nearly ten p.m., lock-up time for the storage facility's main gate, to finish emptying Unit 127. Foster checked the map, debating. They were already more than a day behind schedule. That ship wasn't going to wait.

They could skip Amarillo and easily make it to El Paso and then on to San Diego. But this was a now-or-never operation. There would be no coming back to get the cash later. Once they left the States for their island, there wouldn't be another cargo container. The arrangements and rigmarole to make this happen—it was too much to contemplate doing it all over.

He pulled the bus and trailer out of the storage place and followed the route to I-40, eastbound.

Chapter 54

Amber called Pen's phone, but Mary answered. "We're on the road toward Albuquerque," she said. "Got some solid leads about their plan, but once we get there we're not sure where to go."

"You're heading in the right direction," Amber said. "I've gotten back into that Rising Moon Temple … whatever they call it … back into the banking information and I can see their credit card transactions. So far, there's the gas they bought in Globe when they left, but I just got a hit for a gas station in Albuquerque."

She gave the address and Mary wrote it down. "I'll check it on the map and we'll head toward that part of the city. With luck maybe they'll stay at a hotel nearby. Be sure to call again if you catch them checking in somewhere."

"They might stay at some camping site," Pen said, after

Mary ended the call.

"True. Hopefully it'll be one where you have to pay by credit card." She sighed. "I don't know … I'm getting worried. This is a lot of driving and a lot of miles, and we don't even know that we'll spot them."

Pen nodded, keeping her eyes on traffic. Dusk was closing in fast and it felt as if they'd been on the road forever. If Amber's lead didn't turn into something concrete, Pen was tempted to find a decent hotel and get a good night's sleep before continuing.

"I can take a turn at driving," Mary offered. "Most likely that's what Foster and Melissa are doing and it's the way they've gotten so far ahead of us."

"Let's see what Albuquerque brings. It's only a couple more hours."

By ten p.m. both women were nearing exhaustion. They had been lucky to miss most of the evening rush hour traffic. With icy patches on the streets in some places most people, it seemed, had gone straight home by six or seven o'clock. Their first stop was the gas station at the address Amber had given.

A quick chat with the attendant told them nothing. The twenty-something young woman, with her hair in dreadlocks and three silver hoops in her left eyebrow, had come to work at five p.m. and hadn't seen any brightly painted school bus.

"She's as communicative as most at her age," Mary reported when she came back to the Rover. "Couldn't take her eyes off her phone long enough to actually pay attention to my questions."

"It's all right," Pen said. "They are obviously long gone now. I've been looking for nearby campgrounds and hotels. It's not a part of the city with much camping, I must say.

The nearest is twenty miles farther north. But there are hotels galore, many of them clustered around what must be a sort of business park. Shall we check?"

Making the rounds of hotel parking lots netted no sign of the familiar bus. They had stopped for a quick dinner at a fast food place and continued. Now, the hour late and the searchers tired, they checked into a nearby Marriott.

"I'll give Amber one more call before declaring this day at an end," Pen said, picking up her phone.

Mary yawned and rummaged in her small bag for her nightshirt. "Whatever she tells us, I'm not leaving this room before morning."

"I was going to call you," Amber said immediately. "But I was worried it's getting kind of late."

Pen reported their lack of findings.

"Well, I have better news than that. I've been able to get into Foster Fordyce's browsing history. He's been searching for private islands for sale."

"What!"

"Yes, and all of them far outside US jurisdiction."

"This isn't good news," said Pen.

Mary emerged from the bathroom in time to hear that part, so Pen put her phone on speaker.

"His searches seem to be concentrated in the South Pacific, specifically around Indonesia, Bali, places like that." Amber paused. "And I know what you're going to ask next—how are they getting to Bali in an old school bus?"

Even in her tired state, Pen found the energy to laugh. "I guess I would have come to that question soon."

"He's booked passage on a ship called *Corinthian*, and it sails from San Diego two days from now."

"They're going by ship? That seems odd."

"Not when you take into account that they've also reserved a container to be placed aboard that same ship."

The penny dropped.

Mary's words came out in a rush. "The container will be full of cash."

"And if you can be in San Diego you can catch them before they board."

Chapter 55

The sun appeared over the horizon as the bus hit the outskirts of Amarillo. Foster grew up in Texas but didn't think he'd ever seen anyplace as flat as this. He reached over and nudged Melissa in the front passenger seat where she had dozed uneasily half the night. Before they left for El Paso later today, they really did need to rearrange boxes so they could use the bed and access the toilet. He was about to bust, he had to piss so bad.

"Hey, baby," he said as she roused, her hair in tangles and a drop of drool glistening on her lower lip. "How about I treat you to a big old breakfast at Cracker Barrel?"

He could see the debate going on in her head. She was always watching her weight, but she did love those biscuits and gravy. Finally, she smiled.

"It's right up here at the next exit. We'll freshen up a

little and get some food before we go to the next storage place."

Her smile went limp. He didn't blame her. His muscles were sore too. He parked the bus where they would be able to see it from the restaurant windows. Forty minutes later, bladders emptied, stomachs filled, they drove on.

Amarillo was the first place they'd ever stashed a bunch of cash, once it became evident they couldn't tote all that money along everywhere they went, and they had fond memories here. It was also the culmination of what he'd called their Tour of the South—Georgia, Alabama, Mississippi, Lou'siana, and Texas—the early days when their success had really taken off.

He found the address of the storage facility and felt a twinge of concern. The neighborhood had certainly gone downhill. He hoped their boxes were safe. The lock on the garage-sized locker was fairly rusted, and he had to find some spray lubricant in the tool kit and work it some to get the thing open.

But there they were—stacked mostly against the back wall—boxes labeled as Books, Kitchen Stuff, Towels … they'd thought of nearly everything a person would logically store away. Melissa immediately spotted one labelled Costumes and she'd peeled off the tape. On top of a layer of cash there really were costumes.

"It was so much fun to dress like Dolly," she said, holding up a spangled dress, which he remembered had fit her like a glove.

"Yeah. Big hair, big clothes … unfortunately not the big boobs."

She punched his arm. "Hey! We looked good up there on stage. We could have been Dolly and Porter if we knew anything about singing."

"I'm glad we knew more about religion. It pays better." He pushed the sequined dress back into the box. "Come on, we gotta get moving. We need to get these out to the trailer and be on the road before noon. And we've still got eight hours of driving after that."

She gave him a pained look. He should have kept that little detail to himself.

"We'll get us a real Texas barbeque dinner tonight," he promised.

"And we'll go online and look at our island, right?" Her face was eager.

"Soon as we have a little time to stop." He hadn't actually located a specific island, but he figured he'd have lots of time aboard the ship.

Damn sea voyage was going to take three weeks, and there would be nothing to do—other than having a hot time in their cabin. This wasn't one of those cruise ships with endless activities planned for the passengers. In fact, they would likely be the *only* passengers among a minimal crew of one or two dozen men. At least they would surely have satellite communication and he'd be able to tap into the internet when he needed to.

He had positioned the back of the trailer precisely outside the garage door. He opened it and she began bringing the boxes for him to stack. Stoked on her high-carb breakfast she kept up an endless chatter.

"I can't wait to finish buying my furniture," she said. "I've chosen the best mattress money can buy. And I have in mind just what I want for the living room … Oh, and I'm getting all new kitchen gear—gourmet cookware and some really great cutlery."

The trailer was already half full, now that they had added boxes from inside the bus. Plus, they still had another stop to make.

"Take it easy with the shopping, baby. What you've already picked out—that's probably enough for now. We'll have to see how much actually fits into a container. Plus, you'll want to add some local things, right?"

"Of course. We'll decorate with local art and colorful fabrics and … oh, my goodness, I'm just really seeing the place come together already!"

Fine. Keep up the bubbly voice and cheerful attitude. He would need to feed this enthusiasm back to her when she was bored out of her head on the utilitarian cargo vessel.

A chill breeze swept between the rows of storage units, and Foster looked up to see the sky had become overcast. The garage wasn't even close to empty. He jumped out of the trailer and helped Melissa double-time it with the boxes.

They were nearly finished when a pickup truck drove into the alleyway between the storage units. A burly guy in a down jacket and ball cap got out. He eyed the painted school bus and trailer. "Gonna start snowin' in a little bit."

Foster looked over the top of the two boxes in his arms. "Yeah, we heard about that." Maybe he hadn't taken the weather report seriously enough. He stacked the boxes in the trailer and looked toward the unit. They should be finished in another fifteen minutes or so.

"Fine. Just sayin'." The other man glanced toward their open garage door, gave Melissa's tight jeans the once-over, and unlocked the door to the unit across from theirs. He set up a ramp from the tailgate of his truck and wheeled a motorcycle down it, apparently planning to fit it into an already crowded space.

Foster signaled to Melissa to ignore the guy and bring the last few boxes, which he secured with the tie-down straps that had come with the trailer. Garage door closed, trailer securely locked, they climbed into the bus and waited for pickup dude to finish and move out of their way.

"Looks like the storm will pass through here, west to east, and hopefully will stay north of us," Foster said, staring at the weather app on his phone. "We need to get to Lubbock and then make our way south and west to El Paso."

"Uh-huh," Melissa murmured. Her eyes were intent on the pictures of couches on her own device.

"Baby, you'd better sleep while I drive this afternoon," he cautioned. "We gotta load more when we get to El Paso, then we'll be on the road all night again."

"Uh-huh, I will."

He bit back his impatience—it wasn't only with his wife. The guy in the pickup was taking forever to get out of their way, a storm was moving in, and they had less than twenty-four hours to be in San Diego.

Chapter 56

Ron was hungry and he was mad. Dammit—why hadn't he thought to stock the house with more food? He'd eaten so much delivery pizza he ought to be speaking Italian by now. And why had he run from those goons, straight into the traffic?

From his semi-permanent position on the sofa, he bent his left leg and gingerly pulled off his sock to have a look. The foot was dark purple, nearly black in places—that couldn't be good. And there were red streaks radiating from the cut on his calf. He should have taken the priest up on his offer to go to the ER, but those kinds of things always got tricky. They wanted his insurance card—he didn't have any—or they would take a Medicaid card. Didn't have that either. Life off the grid was great, until it wasn't.

From the way the entire limb was throbbing, though,

he knew he'd better see somebody. There was an urgent care center a few miles away. He could manage to drive himself there, get some antibiotics, and pay in cash.

With a plan in mind, he pulled on a pair of jeans. Even his loosest pair of shoes wouldn't go on over the swollen left foot now, so he bundled it in extra socks. From his cash stash in the closet he pulled out enough to cover the doctor visit, stuffing bills into his pockets.

The car took a couple of minutes to warm up. He rubbed his hands together briskly; it felt like more weather was on the way. When he raised the garage door, he felt a momentary stab of fear that one of those female agents would be out there, somehow knowing he was about to show his face again. But a glance in each direction told him their vehicles were not nearby.

The urgent care center he'd planned to visit was closed. He cursed his luck, but he knew of another one a bit farther away. He imagined going back home and then having to talk himself into going back out. With more rain on the way, he might as well get this over with, grab a bucket of chicken to last awhile, and get back home where at least he could be warm and comfortable.

The Superstition Creek Urgent Care looked jammed. The entire front parking lot was full; he even cruised through it twice in hopes that someone would vacate a space. No such luck. The lot behind the building had a few empties and he took one. The walk to the front door would be agony, but he told himself to buck up.

"I've been through more pain than this," he muttered, although he couldn't honestly think of an example. He opened his door and swung the tortured leg out.

A shadow fell across the open door. "Thought that looked like you," said one of the goons. "You clean up real good, homeless guy." He had a grip on Ron's car door and looked as though he was contemplating slamming it against Ron's leg. The mere thought made Ron want to throw up.

"Let's take a little walk," said the second man. "We got something to discuss." He grabbed Ron's left arm and yanked him to stand up.

When Ron nearly collapsed, the guy who had him by the arm chuckled. "Boss said to teach him a lesson. Think he's learned it yet, Pete?"

Pete shook his head. "He's a slow learner." He looked toward the clinic and saw a couple coming out to the parking lot. He stared hard at Ron. "Not doin' so good walking, huh? Well, we'll take a little ride then."

Like two helpful buddies, they each took one of Ron's arms and guided him toward the car they'd left sitting a few feet away. They shoved Ron into the back seat, and Pete got behind the wheel while the other one climbed in beside their prisoner. Pete began to drive.

"Boss don't like people helping theirselves to his money," said the guy beside him, his voice low and almost seductive. "We're supposed to share that message and make sure you don't do it again."

With that, he grabbed Ron's right hand and wrenched violently at the fingers, twisting them until the bones crackled.

"You gonna promise not to take money that ain't yours now?"

"I promise! I promised last time."

"Yeah, but we wasn't sure you got the message."

"I got it, already! I got it!"

Pete was eying him in the rearview mirror as he drove. "Promises come cheap. We gotta make sure you remember."

Ron never saw the uppercut coming. Pain shot through his jaw and felt as if it were coming out his eyeballs. He gasped and tears ran down his cheeks.

"Just let me out," he begged. "I'll never go near that place again."

"Damn right you won't," said the one beside him.

From the front seat, Pete was smirking. "Bet you will."

"No! I swear I won't! Never!"

"Oh, like not even now?"

Ron looked out the window and saw they were arriving at the Temple of the Rising Moon. Shit! What would their boss do to him?

"I think we performed our duties, don't you, Kurt? I say we hand deliver him and see if this ain't worth a little extra bonus."

Kurt gave an evil chuckle. Pete pulled the car around the side of the building and came to an abrupt stop.

"What the fu—! The bus is gone."

"And the trailer." Kurt looked a little pale.

"Oh, man, we're screwed. Quick! Dump him and let's get the hell out." Pete was already out of his seat. He yanked open the back door and grabbed Ron's left arm, twisting it up behind his back as he landed on his bad foot.

"We can't give him the chance to talk," Kurt said, joining in and dragging their victim toward a clump of cactus.

His arm swung back, preparing for another of those uppercut punches. Ron's last thought was that he'd probably just wet himself, right before everything went black.

Chapter 57

Pen carefully noted Amber's information—the dock number and sailing time for the cargo vessel *Corinthian*. It would sail day after tomorrow from the port of San Diego to Jakarta, Indonesia.

"I'm also seeing a whole bunch of online shopping on their credit card," Amber told her. "Furniture places. Doesn't that seem funny, since it looks like they're leaving the country?"

"Perhaps they aren't leaving but are shipping the money to an offshore bank. Maybe they plan on staying in California," Pen said.

But the moment she suggested it, the idea didn't seem right. Trusting that much cash to the hands of a cargo crew? Still, the duo had surprised them more than once, and it didn't always seem logic was their guide. She and

Mary had spent a restful night in Albuquerque awaiting further news of their targets, and now it was time to make plans. They would simply have to follow along and see what happened.

She turned to Mary when the call ended. "It appears we must get ourselves to California."

"I'm on it," Mary said, showing Pen her phone screen. "Southwest Airlines can do a combination of air, hotel, and a rental car …"

"Sounds perfect. There's no time to go home first. We should just fly from here. How quickly can we get a flight?"

Mary scrolled through the choices. "Next direct flight is in two hours."

"If the Fordyces left directly from here yesterday, they would have had to drive straight through the night and could be arriving by now. We'd best get moving."

They were at the departure gate when Amber's next call came. "I don't know how this affects your plans … Another charge just came through on their card. It looks like they gassed up the bus in Amarillo yesterday afternoon."

"What? Texas!" Pen looked at the line of passengers moving toward the jetway for the San Diego flight.

"I'm sorry. It just came through. It's from a Pilot Truck Stop and it's enough money to be a full tank of gas for the bus."

Pen filled Mary in on the new development. "Are we flying off in the wrong direction? If they're in Texas and we head to the west coast …"

The gate agent called their boarding group.

Mary took a deep breath. "I think the container is the key. The Fordyces have clearly made plans to leave the country. Wherever they are driving now, I still believe they're on the way to that ship."

Most of the people were in line, moving to board the plane.

"All right," Pen said. "I trust your instinct on this."

"We'll be in San Diego in less than two hours, rested and refreshed," Mary said as they stepped to the back of the boarding line. "Foster and Melissa will have driven through the night—they'll be tired. We can arrive before they do and we'll watch the dock area. That bus of theirs isn't exactly a blend-in type of vehicle."

"I spoke with Benton early this morning, and he gave me names of a couple of contacts in southern California. As soon as I have use of my phone, I'll reach out and see what can be done. We need the authorities in on it when we catch these con artists with the evidence." *If they have the cash with them,* Pen reminded herself.

The flight was a full one, and the two women weren't able to get seats together. But that was fine. As the flight attendants went through the standard pre-flight spiel, Pen began sending texts: Benton Case suggests I reach out to you regarding a couple planning to flee the country with a container of illicit cash. Would like to touch base when my flight lands at SAN.

Before she received any responses, the order was given to shut off cell phones.

Chapter 58

The bus reached El Paso around ten p.m. Every part of the journey annoyed Foster. Melissa's non-stop chatter about décor didn't abate (do you like this fabric better or that one, honey?), in spite of his reminders that the furniture was only there to fill in around the boxes and make this *appear* to be a household move. They were not actually furnishing a house, not yet.

During the entire trip, a strong wind buffeted the vehicle and made it hard to hold on the road. That was another irritating thing. If you looked up the word 'boring' in the dictionary, Foster would bet the definition described the long road through west Texas. In the lumbering vehicle with the heavy trailer, nothing moved at the speed he would have liked.

At least they'd not encountered snow. He reminded

himself to be thankful about that. It worked until, after winding their way through El Paso's seedier back streets, they arrived at the storage facility to find the high chain-link gates locked. Razor wire topped the surrounding fencing, and the manager's office was dark. A sign said the hours were six a.m. to eight p.m.

What had he been thinking, leaving so much cash in a place like this? As he recalled, it had been nearly five years ago, and the neighborhood hadn't been quite so downtrodden. He had diligently renewed the rental each year, but now he wondered how secure the facility was. Would their boxes still be here?

Melissa had finally crashed on the bed at the back. He parked the bus on the street outside the storage facility and decided to join her. But his eyes refused to close and his mind wouldn't relax. They were carrying nearly thirty million dollars already, and he couldn't help feeling like a prime target. It was foolish to sit here in this neighborhood.

He got up, pulled his pants back on, and went to the front. No sign of anyone on the street, but it wasn't worth the risk. He started the bus, circled the block, and headed back the way they'd come.

After giving up on finding a campground open, he settled for a superstore parking lot where he made certain there were lights and security cameras on all sides of the rig. He settled on the bed beside his wife and she cuddled into his side. His eyes stayed open for a long time.

When his alarm buzzed at five-thirty the sun hadn't yet cleared the horizon, but Foster was already awake. He walked across the street to the first fast-food joint with lights on, came back to the bus with two coffees and breakfast sandwiches, and prodded Melissa.

"Hey, sleepyhead. Up and at 'em. We got a busy day."

She grumbled but complied. He had to give her credit for being a trouper.

They got to the storage facility in time to see a half-asleep manager arrive. The man didn't seem to notice the bus and trailer across the street, until he unlocked the wide chain-link gates and wheeled them aside. Through his open window, Foster gave his unit number and the man waved them through. He looked as if he didn't really care where they went as long as he could get inside the warm office and have his first coffee.

Loading and stacking the boxes had become routine and they worked quickly. When the trailer became too full to hold anything more, they again piled boxes on the bed in the bus. The tally was nearing fifty million now. They could have built a decent-sized housing community if all this cash had actually gone where Orion and Sunshine promised it would.

Foster tamped down that thought right away. He hadn't worked this hard for all these years just to cater to people with their hands out. He'd grown up in poverty and figured his own way out of it. Let them do the same.

He and Melissa were set for life. All he had to do now was protect what was theirs. He triple-checked the locks on the trailer and bus before climbing into the driver's seat and heading toward Las Cruces and on to Interstate 10.

Chapter 59

Sandy's cell phone buzzed down inside her desk drawer. She took a peek. Trini. What could she want?

"Hey Sandy, is this a bad time? I tried to call Mary but didn't get an answer."

"I've got an employee review in five minutes, but this is fine. What's up?"

"Remember the homeless guy, Ron? You were thinking he could be the thief …"

"Right."

"I found him this morning outside the building next door. He looks like he's been beaten pretty badly. I called an ambulance and they took him to Memorial."

"What—oh my gosh. Um, let me think … I want to question him before he gets released."

"I don't know how soon that will be. He was unconscious and bleeding."

"Thanks, Trini. We'll check it out." Sandy hung up, wondering if the police would get there first. Would hospital personnel call the law if they felt Ron's injuries were the result of a crime? If so, they needed to hear about the bigger picture.

She called Gracie and passed along Trini's news, then sent a memo postponing the employee review. This would not go over well if upper management learned she had put off one of her official duties to run off on a crime-solving errand.

Gracie met her at the ER waiting room. "Have you seen him yet?" Sandy asked.

"No. They tripped me up with the first question, which was the patient's full name."

"I'll give it a try. He told his landlord he was Ron Smith."

Sandy approached the glass window with a circular metal microphone built into it. "I understand my cousin has been brought here after some kind of incident. He was beaten and found unconscious."

"His name?"

"Ron Smith." She said it with as much confidence as she could muster.

The woman at the desk behind the glass reached for a manila file in a stand-up rack. Interesting that they still used those. She flipped it open; it appeared to Sandy the file contained only one sheet of paper.

"Ron Smith?"

She nodded and gave her best worried look.

"Good to know. He was brought in here with no ID and only the name Ron, apparently given by someone at the scene when the ambulance arrived. I'll buzz you back there. It's exam room 12."

Sandy waved Gracie toward her and they walked through a heavy wooden door when the buzzer sounded. Exam room 12 turned out to be a curtained off section of a much larger space. An impossibly young nurse stood at the bedside, adjusting an IV line that led to the arm of a man lying under a sheet. At the head of the wheeled bed stood a monitor with about a dozen red, green, and blue blinking numbers. The nurse gazed up at them and turned to leave.

"Oh! I didn't hear you come in. Relatives?"

"His cousin. I just got word he was here. What on earth happened to him?"

"In plain terms, he's got lots of broken stuff." The young nurse looked apologetic. "Sorry—that was a little inside hospital humor."

The 'broken stuff' was evident when Sandy and Gracie got close enough to see the man in the bed. One eye was completely swollen shut, the surrounding skin a deep burgundy, and the other eye was closed. His nose was twisted at an odd angle, and his lips were puffy with cuts in several places. His hair color was Ron's only recognizable feature. His clothing had been removed and replaced by a flimsy hospital gown with snaps along the shoulders.

"The doctor will explain everything when she gets here. We had a cardiac emergency down the hall a few minutes ago."

"Is it okay if we wait with him?" Sandy asked.

"Sure. Here's a chair, and you can drag another one over from 11 if you'd like. No one's in there." She waved vaguely toward a corner filled with crutches and cast-building supplies. A stiff metal chair sat next to a portable x-ray unit on wheels.

Gracie watched until the nurse disappeared down the corridor.

"Well. You've got yourself in a fine mess here, Mr. Ron," Sandy said.

No response from the unconscious patient. He seemed to be breathing all right, although a little raggedly, and none of the indicators on the monitor were screeching or anything alarming.

"I wonder what's with the foot," Gracie said. She pointed to Ron's left leg, which had been left uncovered by the sheet. "Seems weird someone would beat the heck out of his face and then, oh yeah, let's trounce his foot, too."

Sandy was poking around the room. "I wonder what they've done with his personal effects. This might be our one and only chance to conduct our own search."

Gracie spotted a large plastic bag with clothing in it. She pointed. "I'll keep an eye on the hall."

Sandy pounced on the bag. A quick pat-down revealed a set of keys, no wallet. She pulled the garments from the bag, one by one. Relatively new jeans, stained with some blood and plenty of dirt. Except for the fact the EMTs had cut them off the patient, they would have been in good shape after laundering. Same for a long-sleeved button-down shirt. One sock was clean, the other had some bloodstains and was stretched out of shape.

"Looks like he wore this sock over the injured foot. And there's only one shoe. I'm thinking the foot injury happened before today."

"Makes sense." Gracie turned to look at the items Sandy had set on the bed.

"The jacket interests me most," Sandy said. "It's certainly not the big, filthy thing I've seen him wear on the street corners."

She reached into the pockets, one by one, pulling out a pair of decent quality leather gloves and an empty silver money clip.

"No ID and no credit cards. Fits with the guy in the rented house who pays his rent in cash. Looks like a believer in living under the radar."

"Kind of sad, really," Gracie said. "What did he think would happen if, like today, he had an accident or something. There's no family to call."

"Maybe he had a wallet and it was taken by whoever beat him up. There's also no watch or other jewelry." Sandy held up the jacket and noticed the roomy inner pockets. "Oh ho, what's this?"

Gracie glanced back through the opening in the curtain toward the corridor. "Hurry up!" she stage-whispered. "Here comes the doctor!"

From the inner pocket, Sandy grabbed the top of a large plastic zip-top bag. Inside, she got a quick glimpse of a small locket and a gold pocket watch. As Gracie greeted the doctor, Sandy had no choice but to drop Ron's jacket and the plastic baggie back into the personal-effects sack.

Chapter 60

Pen's phone pinged with a message the moment she turned it on after their flight landed. "Amber says the most recent gas purchase was made in Tucson."

She and Mary breathed a sigh of relief. At least the Fordyces were headed west again, so the trip to San Diego wasn't a false lead. While Mary handled the rental car paperwork, Pen called to check in with Amber.

"Based on the time they purchased fuel and the distance they have yet to travel, they'll probably arrive in San Diego between eight and nine tonight," Amber told her.

Pen quickly thought about what they needed to accomplish first.

"Oh, another bit of interesting news," Amber said. "It looks like our suspect for the thefts at the shelter is out of commission, some kind of accident, I guess. Gracie and

Sandy are at the hospital now."

"Oh gosh. Well, do keep us posted. I hope they can recover the stolen items."

Mary stepped away from the rental desk and held up a key. "We're ready." She took the wheel and, with the address of their hotel programmed into the GPS, headed off the airport property. The route took them along the edge of San Diego Bay and they noted the commercial shipping docks.

As they drove, Pen placed a call to Charlie Blue, Benton's longtime colleague.

"I understand you have a pretty amazing story and evidence to back it up," Charlie said when Pen introduced herself. "When can we meet?"

"We're on the way to the Hyatt, a friend and I. How about if we meet in the lobby in thirty minutes?"

Mary made the turn at the hotel entrance and pulled the car under the porte-cochère, where a bellman greeted them and took their bags. By the time they checked in, rode to their sixth-floor room, and freshened up it was time to go back down.

Charlie Blue proved to be exactly as Benton had described him—late fifties, gray hair, fit and trim. He introduced his younger colleague, Josh Framingham, who could have been a center for the Lakers.

"Shall we talk in the business center?" Charlie suggested, glancing around the busy lobby. "I think we'll have more privacy."

They settled at a table in the unoccupied room and Pen brought out her laptop. She quickly located the video file Amber had created from the button cam footage the Ladies had taken.

"This is one of their *shows*, as I call them," she told the agents. "It all has a very spiritual tone, and they play their parts very well. Amber took this on her second visit to the Temple of the Rising Moon." She clicked a link and let the video do the talking.

"That looks like a lot of money," Josh commented at the end when Amber had turned to follow the collection basket down the row where she was sitting.

"And it's not going toward building homes for poor people, as they claim. We checked out some of the addresses where these houses were supposedly built," Mary said. "The claims are completely bogus."

"I also have footage of a séance-like performance I attended," Pen said, "if you'd like to view that. They don't take up a collection, but the fee for future readings runs into the thousands of dollars per session. And they have many little ploys for enticing people to sign up for multiple sessions."

"We'll need all this as evidence," Charlie said. "Send me the files. What else have you got?"

Mary brought up the photos she'd taken inside the couple's bus, showing the boxes of money, the passports and earbuds, and the closet full of costumes.

"We have reason to believe some of the money is deposited to their religious non-profit banking account, but we think there is far more cash that goes unreported." Pen prayed the men wouldn't ask just how she happened to have this information. She would have to come up with something that would not reveal Amber's hacking expertise.

Mary spoke up quickly. "The routine has been going on a lot longer than these past few weeks in Arizona. One of our friends saw video on You Tube where the Fordyces were playing the same scam in different guises in different cities. In Nashville, for instance, they were Christian evangelists named Jimmy Joe and Billie Lynn. We think their routine goes back years."

The agents looked at each other. "I'll get on that," said Josh. "Get copies of those other videos."

"They left Apache Junction in a rush, and most of their stage gear is still there. If you hurry, you may be able to confiscate it before the landlord clears the place, and you might find more clues," Pen suggested.

Charlie shifted in his chair. "Now, getting to the present day, what's the reason all this is landing in California? You mentioned you have reason to think they're heading this way … are they starting up the show again?"

"Everything we've given so far is just the background," Pen said. "We have reason to believe the Fordyces have made their way through New Mexico, Texas, and now to California." Again, she sidestepped exactly how Amber knew what charges were on their credit card. "We think they're planning to escape the country, possibly with a great deal of the cash they've accumulated."

"This is grand theft, fraud, embezzlement, and obtaining money under false pretenses—in multiple states," Charlie said. "And if we can catch them leaving the country …"

"I should think they can be locked away for a very long time," Pen said.

Thoughtful nods from both agents. Josh was already reaching for his phone.

"Catching them will be the trick, especially if they leave US soil." Charlie looked worried, as though this would be harder than the ladies could guess.

But Pen had more. "There's a ship called *Corinthian*. And they've arranged a container." She gave the name of the moving company Amber had located.

"*Corinthian* sails first thing in the morning," Josh said, staring at his phone screen. "They'll be loading cargo during the night."

"Can you prosecute them?" was Mary's only question.

"If we can catch them, yes. They'll try the old 'everyone gave money willingly' defense, but that doesn't fly. They obtained the money under false pretenses. Plus, it's going to be real interesting to see how much of it was actually declared through this nonprofit of theirs. If the principals have skimmed for personal use, that's embezzling. Oh, yeah. We *can* get them."

"Get warrants in process," Charlie told Josh as they rose from their chairs.

"We ought to contact Treasury as well. IRS will be interested in all that cash." The men turned back to the ladies and thanked them.

Pen and Mary looked at each other as the agents bustled out. Both had a sinking feeling this whole thing could become entangled in government red tape while the Fordyces sailed away.

Chapter 61

Foster could barely keep his eyes open. When the bus drifted onto the rumble strip at the side of the highway for the second time he pulled over. It was mid-afternoon and they were still east of Yuma.

"Take the wheel for a while, baby," he told Melissa. "I gotta grab a quick nap."

Then he looked at the bed in the back, partially covered in boxes of money once again. Great. He found a pillow and traded seats with his wife, trying to prop himself comfortably against the side window.

"Be extra careful," he said. "You got a really heavy load here and the bus handles different now."

"When we get to Yuma we should stop for some food," she said. "It's only a couple of hours. Maybe a real restaurant this time?"

"No restaurants. One of us has to always be with the bus."

Her lower lip stuck out, but she took the wheel. He dozed fitfully until he felt the bus slow down and stop.

"Feel better now?" she asked in her perky little voice.

"A little. Where are we?"

"Yuma. I pulled off at this exit because there's a lot of fast food places. Could I get a salad at that Burger King over there?"

He scrubbed at his face with both hands. "Sure. Here's some money. Grab me a Whopper."

While she was gone he edged down the narrow clear space to the back, used the head, and came back to make enough space for them to sit at the dinette for their meal. Five-thirty p.m. and the sun was disappearing in the distance. They'd be doing well to reach San Diego by eight, and it would be a scramble to get the container loaded. He phoned the moving company to update them on their arrival time.

"No problem. We got three containers going on the *Corinthian*. We'll getcha." The call ended abruptly.

Don't stress over it, Foster told himself. *You're tired and hungry, but we're almost there.*

He spotted Melissa walking across the wide parking area from the Burger King, and he opened the door for her. The smell of his favorite cheeseburger perked him up. He tore into the wrapper the moment they sat down and began wolfing it down.

"I'm so excited about this, honey," she said, poking around in her salad, rearranging the greens and the chicken. "Can you believe how cool this is? We made all this money basically just touring the South and the West. I'm thinking once we've been on this tropical island for awhile, when we're ready for a break from it … we should come back and do our tour in the Midwest, maybe even go up into New England. I'll bet we can bring in big audiences there, too."

"Missy! Stop it! Isn't it *ever* enough for you? We've got close to sixty mil here and we're about to go live the life of our dreams. Can't you just enjoy it?"

"But—"

"Geez—once a con, always a con, I guess." He finished the last two bites of his burger and wadded up the wrapper. "Sit here and finish your salad. I'm getting us back on the road. We're running late."

He ignored the tear running down her cheek. But once the bus was on the interstate again he began to feel badly about his tone of voice. Despite everything else, they'd never fought much. They'd always been a solid couple who were on the same wavelength about nearly everything.

It's the trip, the stress. Make it up to her once we get aboard the ship.

She stayed at the table until they crossed the California state line and passed the exit for the Imperial Sand Dunes. Then he heard her drop her salad bowl into the trash. When she returned to her seat she didn't say a word. Even when he tried an apology, her eyes stayed on the road straight ahead.

Chapter 62

Why don't we just go?" Gracie muttered. "It's been *hours.*"

"I feel rotten, leaving him alone." Sandy looked at the sad figure on the bed.

Ron had been in and out of consciousness, moaning when he did rouse but mostly just lying there. The doctor had come in once, assessed that the injured foot would need surgery. The nurse came in every half hour or so, usually cranking up the amount of morphine feeding through the IV line into Ron's arm.

"Look," said Gracie. "We got what we came for."

She nodded toward Sandy's tote, which now held the zipper bag of stolen treasures. "When they get finished with the life-and-death emergencies, they'll come get him. He'll be in surgery a while and then put into a room somewhere. We really can't do anything for him, but I've got a husband and kids at home who'll be wanting some dinner pretty soon."

"You're right. You go ahead. I want to run out to the shelter and return these things. I have a feeling that's going to be the only happy ending about this story."

"That's the right thing to do," Gracie agreed. "The police would have to enter them into evidence or some such thing, and the value is so little I doubt Ron would ever get prosecuted for taking the things. At least we can get them back to their real owners."

"Exactly." Sandy stood and looked down at Ron. "What was he thinking, I wonder."

She arrived at Heaven Sent just as the evening meal was being served, a meaty chicken soup that smelled wonderful. Trini's eyes became moist when she saw the recovered bag of items.

"You got them back."

Sandy nodded. "Maybe you can help me identify each piece and make sure we're handing them over to the rightful owners."

"Sure. Come on back to the dining hall. We've got something special planned and I want to see what you think." Trini led the way.

When they arrived she pointed toward the new addition where a huge WELCOME banner was stretched across the doorway.

"New Year's Day, we're officially open for occupancy," she announced. "Of course we did fudge it a little when that cold snap came through and I allowed people to fit in there. What a few bureaucrats don't know won't hurt them."

Sandy squeezed her arm. "That's great news, Trini. You

do so much for this community."

Trini smiled. "Everyone pitches in, including you and Mary. And that reminds me, you are both invited to our ribbon-cutting ceremony and a special dinner we're hosting that day. Turner Farms donated several really nice hams, so we're doing the whole tradition with black-eyed peas and the works."

"It sounds really nice. I'll let Mary know." She held up the plastic bag she'd taken from Ron's possessions. "Shall we?"

Trini studied the contents and pulled out a tin Altoids box. Inside was a thin gold chain with a broken clasp. "I felt so guilty about this one. I'm really relieved it turned up."

She carried the tin over to Lizzie, who sat at one end of a table, alone. Her cart full of possessions sat against the west wall, and the old woman wasn't letting it out of her sight. Sandy hung back, watching the woman's reaction as she recognized the box. Eyes full of wonder, she opened it and lifted the chain out. And she actually beamed when she realized all her shiny foil papers and other bits were still inside. Trini patted her shoulder and they walked on to find the little girl who had wept over her missing locket with the pink stone.

"I think that's everyone who is here right now," Trini said, with a grateful smile. "Oh—did I tell you the news about Micah? He got a job. He told me this morning. He doesn't start until January third, but he's so thrilled. He'll be here tonight and I will see to it he gets his grandfather's watch."

Sandy told Trini to pass along her good wishes. She hoped Micah's luck truly was changing for him. She left the rest of the items with Trini and headed home.

Later that evening she called Gracie to report. "It was such a thrill to see them get their things back. Remind me never again to underestimate the sentimental value of a small item."

"Or the power of a kind deed," Gracie said. "It's just too bad that guy Ron didn't have to do some jail time for stealing those things. What a creep, taking advantage of the homeless like that."

Sandy sighed. "I know. I've thought about all this, and I wonder who beat him up. Maybe he ultimately did pay a price."

"Maybe. I really want to ask him. What do you think of paying him another visit at the hospital tomorrow?"

Chapter 63

Pen and Mary rode the elevator in silence, until Mary broke the quiet with a question. "How did you feel about that meeting?"

Pen made a face. "Worried. The minute the agents began talking about warrants and bringing in other agencies … I must admit, I have my doubts they'll be organized in time."

"Me too."

The doors slid open and the women walked the length of the corridor to their room.

"Pen, I can't just sit here and stare out over the harbor and hope some government types get there in time to stop Foster and Melissa from getting away with their crimes."

"To spirit away all that cash."

"Well, exactly! It's a crime that they made such false

claims and roped donors into their scheme, but what really chills me is that they are simply going to sail off into the sunset and consider themselves the winners in their evil game."

"We'll never be able to stop the ship from sailing … will we?"

"Not if we don't try." Mary faced the harbor, only a few blocks from their hotel. "I say we go for it."

Pen's face lit up. "We'll need a plan," she said, enthusiasm growing in her voice.

Mary turned and picked up her bag, tossing it on one of the beds. "We could be the federal agents, ordering a search. Let me see if I brought anything vaguely resembling a business suit."

Pen switched her favored pastel lavender blouse for a dark blue one, and Mary came up with dark slacks and a white shirt to go with her black blazer.

"We have nothing resembling official ID," Mary said. "I could call Amber. Maybe she could email me a design and we print it out at the business center downstairs."

Pen stopped in mid stride. "Wait. Impersonating federal agents could get us into even more trouble than our suspects are already in."

Mary had one arm in her blazer's sleeve. "Oh gosh, you're right. So …?"

"I'm not saying we cannot give them the *impression* we are here on official business," Pen said with a grin.

"I like it." Mary slipped into her jacket and picked up her phone. "Let me get the address of the company where the Fordyces reserved their container."

As they rode the elevator down and had the valet bring their rental, she programmed the address into her phone's GPS. "Thank goodness for technology. The whole dock area is a maze of buildings and I would never find it otherwise."

As it turned out, the offices of Seafarer Shipping were closing. A secretary walked out, locked the front door, and got into her car as Pen and Mary drove up. They waved her down and asked about a couple who were supposed to be shipping out a container tonight.

"Oh, it'll happen," the woman said. "Clint's back there and the whole crew. They move cargo all night. But it's the end of my work day, and I'm in a bit of a hurry …"

They thanked her and waited until she drove away. The chain link gate beside the building was wide enough for an 18-wheeler to pass through, but it only stood open about a foot. Mary and Pen edged through and went in search of this Clint.

An oversized forklift rounded the corner of the building, a metal cargo container on its forks, the driver leaning sideways to peer around it. "Hey, you can't be back here," he called out. "Customer service is closed for the day."

Mary approached the slow-moving machine. Squaring her shoulders and flashing a small leather folder which actually contained her business cards, she performed her best imitation of someone official. "We're looking for Clint."

The driver tilted his head toward the loading dock at the back of the building, where a man with a clipboard seemed to be giving orders to four burly guys. The women walked toward them; Mary flashed the card holder again from a distance where details couldn't be seen. Clipboard-guy turned out to be Clint.

"Yeah?" he said, eyeing them with a squint.

"We're investigating a couple named Fordyce, and we

understand they have booked a container to be shipped aboard the *Corinthian*?"

Clint shrugged.

"Can you verify that for us?" Mary asked, giving a pointed stare toward the clipboard in his hand.

He gave the top page on the stack a quick glance. "They're on the list."

"Is their container already loaded?"

"Don't think so. Look, lady, I'm busy here. Without a warrant, you're not getting me to call everything to a halt and start checking these big old metal boxes. We got a dozen ships sailing in the next couple days."

"You can't simply verify whether the Fordyces and their container have been here and whether that container is already aboard the *Corinthian*?" Pen asked.

"Show me your warrant." He started to turn away.

"Look, mister, at this point we're just asking questions informally. You want a warrant, we'll get the whole detail down here and take this place apart." Mary prayed the real feds would be along shortly.

"I want a warrant." Clint turned and shouted to one of the men who was wheeling a pallet on a portable lift.

Pen and Mary exchanged a glance and walked away.

"Nice man," Pen said as they neared their car.

"There's more than one way to catch a thief. So, if we can't take a look in the container, we can at least keep an eye out for the Fordyces. That hippie bus of theirs won't be exactly invisible in a setting like this."

Pen looked at her watch. It was earlier than she'd imagined. "I'm beginning to wish I'd taken a short nap when we arrived at the hotel."

Mary laughed. "We were both so keyed up about meeting with the US Attorney's people, you couldn't have slept if you had tried."

The evening air down by the water was becoming chilly. Mary started the car and turned on the heater.

"According to Amber's estimate, the Fordyces probably won't arrive for another hour or two. Perhaps I shall grab a quick nap here and now," Pen said, stretching and tilting her seat back a bit farther.

Mary watched for fifteen minutes and noticed Pen never really settled to sleep. "I don't know if I should bring this up, but I'm hungry. We haven't eaten in more than twelve hours. If it's true we have at least another hour to wait, how about if we go grab something?"

"Agreed. And it should include coffee. I feel the need."

Three blocks away they found a diner that fairly well fit the description 'greasy spoon' but the sandwiches were hearty and the coffee strong. They ate quickly, wrapped half of each sandwich for later, and ordered coffees to go.

Chapter 64

Melissa still hadn't spoken a word to him by the time they reached the outskirts of San Diego. Was it his nixing the idea of another tour anytime soon, or the remark he'd made at the end of his rope, when he said "once a con, always a con"? Maybe she'd taken offense at that. Or maybe she'd been stunned that he didn't go along with her desires. The woman *was* accustomed to getting her own way.

He would have to think about all this later. Right now he had his hands full, steering the loaded bus and trailer through heavy traffic. As they got nearer to the bay, he struggled to locate a sign or something identifying Seafarer Shipping in the myriad of office-industrial buildings near the harbor. Programming the address into the GPS was something he'd asked Melissa to do, and which she had ignored. Apparently her hearing had gone, along with her speech.

Finally, he pulled to the side of a street to check the map. He'd no sooner picked up his phone than a text came through. It was from the captain of the *Corinthian*. Change of departure. Pier 17, 2300 hours. Your container is here. Your cargo is not. The message had been sent two hours ago and he'd missed it.

Holy crap! Instead of having eight hours to load their belongings, they now had three. He frantically checked for the location of Pier 17 and programmed the GPS to guide him through the labyrinth of streets.

"Well, our furniture may not be there," he muttered, as much to himself as to Melissa.

It was the first thing he'd said in hours that got a reaction. She sent a startled look in his direction, then got on her phone with a call to, presumably, the decorator at the high-end furniture store where she'd done all this online shopping. Foster didn't care—he just needed to get the bus to the correct pier and prepare himself to scramble like crazy to transfer all the boxes.

He pulled away from the curb and began following the GPS's verbal directions, going past the office of Seafarer Shipping and out to some kind of arterial street that seemed to service all the various businesses and docks. Melissa's conversation barely registered, other than the occasional "okay" and "uh-huh."

Meanwhile, he put his phone on speaker and called the *Corinthian*'s captain. "I've just now received your text," he said by way of apology. "We are fairly close, heading your way."

"Whatever, sir. I'm only telling you that the harbor master has set our sailing time forward and there's nothing

I can do about that. If your cargo is aboard, fine. If not, we sail anyway."

"We'll be there."

"Good. No refunds if you aren't."

A trickle of sweat ran down Foster's spine. This was too important to screw up. The edgy feeling that had dogged him ever since Apache Junction closed in on him. They we *so* close to their dream—it *couldn't* be snatched away from them now.

Okay, one thing at a time, he told himself. Find the pier, load the boxes into the container, pray the furniture caught up with them. Get themselves to their cabin and watch the coast of California vanish in the distance. He repeated it like a mantra, and the voice in his head nearly made him miss one of the GPS instructions. He made a sudden turn to bring the bus onto the frontage road.

Ahead, he saw a sign indicating their pier. And there sat *Corinthian*, a cargo ship with a five-story tower at one end. The bridge, crew quarters, and presumably their passenger cabin would be in there. The rest of the entire ship was nothing but a flat surface, stacked high with metal containers. A massive metal rig spanned the width of the ship and containers were being hoisted by a crane and pulleys, which set them in place with the precision of a kid building a Lego castle.

Foster brought the bus to a halt, having no clue what to do next. A man in a hardhat waved him forward.

"You lost, buddy?" he asked.

"We're sailing tonight," Foster said with a nod toward the ship.

"And what—we supposed to hoist this bus up there?" He laughed derisively at his own joke.

Foster tried to shoot him a scathing look, but he felt

hopelessly out of his depth. "Our trailer and bus are filled with our household goods. Seafarer Shipping arranged a container for us—it's supposed to be here already."

Hardhat guy looked at a clipboard he was carrying. "Yep, okay. I see that. There was some furniture company here earlier. Thought they already loaded all your stuff."

Foster smiled. "Yes, we were expecting them. They brought the larger items. What we have are boxes of, um, books and bedding and other stuff."

"Yeah, okay. It's that green unit over there, number 25740. Pull up beside it and we'll take it from there."

Foster put the bus in gear and drove up beside the green container. What had that last bit been about?

Two burly men stepped forward, wheeling hand trucks, and one started to open the back of the trailer.

"That's okay, guys," Foster said, as he unlocked the trailer. "I got this. I've loaded these boxes so many times I could do it in my sleep."

One of the men, who was built like a solid block wall, looked up and met Foster's eyes. "Not on our dock, you can't."

"What? No, seriously, I don't mind. And I'm quick. I won't make the ship late or anything."

"It's a union dock. Nobody touches nothing here but members of ILWU local 15."

Hardhat guy walked over. "Problems?"

"Nope," said the stevedore. "Just explainin' the rules. Guy wanted to load his own cargo."

The supervisor chuckled. "Sorry, that won't happen. These guys get union scale and you're paying it either way. Except that there ain't any other way. They'll do the work."

The two had already begun reaching for boxes and

stacking them on the dollies. Foster took the supervisor aside.

"Look, it's just that we have some valuable things."

"Books?"

"Exactly. My wife is a collector, and there are some rare first editions. And she's very picky about how her dishes and glassware are handled."

The man patted Foster's shoulder. "Don't worry. We handle delicate cargo all the time, as long as the boxes are marked. Plus, we're bonded and insured. Your stuff will be safe or it gets replaced by our insurance. Now why don't you go on over to the gangway, and a steward will show you to your cabin."

Foster felt his gut clench. One peek inside a box, and his whole story was blown.

Chapter 65

"That's the bus!" Mary shouted. She startled Pen out of a doze. "It just passed us, back there!"

She was pointing behind them as she cranked the car's engine, stalled, and had to try again.

Pen turned in her seat. "I don't see anything—there's no vehicle."

"He must have come out of the back lot at Seafarer. I had looked down for just a minute, I swear." Mary's voice was a little frantic. "The headlights were coming straight toward me and I shaded my eyes. Then when I looked up I realized it was that damn hippie bus. Do you think they spotted us?"

She maneuvered the car into a tight turn in the middle of the narrow street and hit the gas. No sign of the bus ahead.

"He must have turned on one of these side streets," Mary said, her head swiveling in each direction. "Keep a close watch. He's towing a big white trailer. They surely can't move that fast."

They covered three blocks, but the bus had disappeared somewhere into the maze of small streets, alleys, and buildings.

"You said they came out of the back lot at the moving company?" Pen asked, picking up her phone. "Maybe they'll know where the Fordyces went."

In the dim light she studied their notes, coming up with the number. But when she dialed it, a recording came on: "You've reached the offices of Seafarer Shipping. Our offices are closed right now. Please call back—"

"We should go back. That Clint wasn't super friendly but maybe he can tell us something," Mary said. She dreaded facing him again but there seemed no choice.

A pale gray car was parked at the curb in front of the shipping company now, and Pen spotted the tall figure of Josh Framingham at the wheel.

"Mary, stop here!" Pen lowered her window and got the agent's attention. "The Fordyce's were here but they left, no more than three minutes ago."

From the passenger seat, Charlie Blue leaned forward and looked at her. "We just got some new intel on it. The *Corinthian* is at a different pier."

"Where? Let's go there!" Pen said.

"Huh-uh, not so fast. I'm still waiting for our warrant to come through," Charlie said. "The rest of our team will bring it as soon as the judge signs it."

Mary let out a low growl.

"How long is that going to take?" Pen asked.

"Should come through within the hour," Charlie

replied. "Don't worry."

Easier said than done, Mary thought. We've chased these guys all over the West and they're about to become untouchable.

The agent's phone chimed and he took the call. A vehicle with bright lights came up behind Mary, so she drove forward and pulled to the curb.

"I have an idea," she said, tapping Amber's number on her phone. "The ship, *Corinthian*," she said. "Can you get updated information about which pier it's sailing from. We were told Pier 17 but that's changed."

"Let me see …" Amber's voice trailed off as she worked quickly at her keyboard. "Try Pier 23. Departure at 2300 hours."

"What! It was supposed to be around six o'clock tomorrow morning."

"That's what it shows here on the Harbor Master's schedule."

"Okay." Mary turned to Pen. "I'm not waiting around for the bozo feds to get their warrants together. Let's head over there. We may not be able to legally search the cargo, but we'll think of something."

"If nothing else, we could alert the captain to the fact that he's transporting contraband," Pen suggested. "That should put things on hold for awhile."

They located signage pointing them toward Pier 23 and followed it until they came to a tall, reinforced gate. A guard stepped out of a small booth.

"Which ship, please?"

"*Corinthian*," Mary said, sending him her best smile.

"That's not a passenger vessel, ma'am. You probably want the cruise ship terminal, but I doubt they're boarding this late in the evening."

"No, we definitely want the *Corinthian*."

"I'll need to see your boarding documents."

Uh-oh. "Um, well, we aren't actually boarding the ship. We have to catch some friends of ours who are sailing on it. Tonight. It's very important—a family emergency." She felt her composure cracking.

"These are friends? Or family?" The guard's polite demeanor was also showing cracks.

"Friends," Pen said decisively. "One of our friends has a family emergency."

"And their names?"

"Fordyce. Foster Fordyce."

He consulted a list. "Don't see 'em."

"They may have booked passage under their business name—Temple of the Rising Moon."

He grinned. "Okay, I get it now. I bet my girlfriend set me up with this. She's into all that moon and stars stuff."

Pen sat up straighter. "Young man, I am old enough to be your grandmother and I assure you I am not *into* practical jokes. We are quite serious about needing to reach Mr. and Mrs. Fordyce."

He quit laughing. "Sorry, ma'am. But I'm still not allowed to pass anyone through without valid documents. This is a secure area of the harbor."

Mary looked at Pen. Maybe they *would* have to wait for Framingham and Blue and their stupid warrants.

Chapter 66

Foster paced beside the bus, his gut in a twist, his eyes trying to watch everywhere. Sure enough, the green container was about a third full with the furniture Melissa had ordered. If he could get her to speak to him again, he would compliment her on a job well planned and executed. She'd handed her travel bag to a *Corinthian* crew member and stalked up the gangway thirty minutes ago.

Meanwhile, it was killing him to see the stevedores handling the boxes of cash. A dread hung over him—what if the tape didn't hold? What if they dropped a box and twenty-dollar bills went flying through the air? If he'd thought being poor was hard, having this much money and knowing he could lose it all was worse.

He'd convinced the men to pull a heavy china cabinet and dining set out and place the boxes nearer the back of the container. They did it without comment—they were probably getting time-and-a-half wages for working this late at night anyway. To keep himself busy, he'd gone through the bus and pulled out all the boxes from their hidey holes, stacking them on the ground near the trailer. One of the union men started to say something but Foster sent him a look. No way were they trooping through the bus.

He kept an eye on the ship. The massive crane had backed away. Apparently, Foster's container was the only one not loaded. He glanced at his watch every ten minutes as the trailer emptied and the container filled.

Ten o'clock came and went. The dock workers seemed to be moving slower than ever.

At ten twenty-five the last of the boxes left the trailer, and Foster locked it.

"You'll need to get that bus off the property," said one of the union men.

He hadn't foreseen that. How far away was considered 'off the property' and how long would it take to get back? No point in arguing now, though. He watched as the men secured the container with heavy metal hasps and a large lock. He insisted they hand him the key, right on the spot.

Then he climbed into the bus and drove it down the long pier. It was ten thirty-five.

He drove to a section where containers were piled four high, rows and rows of them, and he pulled the bus behind a stack that should be out of sight of the offices and the men he'd just left. Hopping down, he bade the old machine a permanent, if not fond, goodbye as he took off at a trot to get back to the *Corinthian.*

As he rounded the final row of stacked containers he nearly bumped into a woman. There were two of them and something about them seemed familiar. Arizona. Behind the ladies were two men in suits. This wasn't good.

He politely excused himself and turned away. Surely, they were here for some other reason? No, he knew better. Ignoring the men's shouts, he ran.

The ship's whistle gave a long blast and he could see dock workers untying the lines to the gangway. Foster's long legs gave him an advantage and he sprinted toward the metal ramp, leaping at the last second and clearing the railing by inches.

Another long blast of the whistle and *Corinthian* began to move away from Pier 23.

Chapter 67

Sandy walked into Room 328 and looked at the prone figure on the bed. From a side chair Gracie stood and walked over to her.

"Kind of looks like a badly put-together version of Frankenstein's monster, don't you think?" she commented.

Ron's damaged foot was encased in something reminiscent of a medieval torture device, a metal cage-like thing with screws and bars, all suspended in a sling on pulleys above the bed. The blood had been washed off his face, but the swelling was still extensive, the bruises very much purple, and a track of stitches ran across his forehead near the hairline.

"Ha-ha," said the man in bed. "If you're here to cheer me up, that's not the way to do it."

"You don't remember us, do you?" asked Sandy.

His forehead wrinkled in concentration and he winced from the movement. "It's kind of a blur."

"I volunteer at Heaven Sent," Sandy told him. "Trini's the one who most likely saved your life by calling the ambulance."

"I don't remember any ambulance."

"You were in bad shape. Even in the ER yesterday, you weren't exactly up and chatting."

He tried to nod but apparently even that motion brought pain. "So, the homeless shelter sends people now to visit the sick and downtrodden in the hospitals?"

Gracie reached out, as if to pat his shoulder, and he winced. "Well, at least he hasn't lost his sense of humor."

"We found the things you stole from the homeless people at the shelter," Sandy said. "I took it all back to them. Really created some smiles when they saw their things again. Ron, why would you do such a thing?"

He turned his palms upward. "Cause I can?"

"Seriously? That's your answer. We know you bring in a lot of money panhandling on the streets. Why take a little girl's necklace? Or a man's watch from his grandfather?"

"I like stuff, okay? Ever since I was a kid—if something catches my eye, my hand just reaches out and takes it."

"There has to be help for kleptomaniacs," Gracie said. "Get to a therapist. Maybe the hospital even has counselors you can talk to while you're here."

"Butt out. It ain't a problem. That stuff I took, it wasn't even worth a few bucks."

"It's a problem to those you steal from. They feel violated when you take their things. These are people who have almost nothing, and it breaks their hearts when a keepsake goes missing. Family memories are the only things most of them have."

"Bull. It's just junk."

Gracie spun on her heel and walked away from the bed.

Sandy was still curious. "I'm trying to figure out the panhandling part and your life in homeless shelters. You have a perfectly good house and a car."

Something registered in his eyes. He obviously remembered her now.

"So, why dress in shabby clothes and sit on street corners?" she asked.

"It's easier than having a job." He eased himself to sit a little straighter. "See, with a job you gotta show up every day and put in certain hours and wait 'til Friday for your pay. The way I do it, I come and go as I please. If it's raining on Tuesday, hell, I just take the day off if I want. Although I gotta tell you, people are a lot more generous when they see a guy sitting out in the rain. Those are some of my best days."

"So, panhandling is your *job*?"

"Yeah. Hey, I make a damn good living this way. I pay the rent and I got savings."

Sandy thought of the stash of money they'd found in his closet.

"But … you're not embarrassed—what do you tell your family, your friends?"

Another palm-shrug. "Ain't got many, but the few who ask me … well, to them I've got a good job that involves travel. When I say I'm off on a business trip is when I stay a few nights at the shelters. Food's not bad and it's free. When I get back, I tell the neighbor about whatever place he thinks I've been. Once I said I was in Paris—hell, how would he know? He's never been there, so I just made up all kinds of story."

"You could afford to stay in decent hotels, to actually

travel some. So, I still don't get it."

"It's a game. It's fun to watch the money come in. I grew up in a family without much. I watched my mom clip coupons and shop the bargain stores. She scrimped and saved and died of heart problems in her forties. I know how to live cheap, but I'm sure not stressing myself to death by reporting to some stupid corporate job."

No, you'll get beaten to a pulp by somebody who's either out to rob you or somebody you've cheated. Sandy kept the thoughts to herself.

"Well, good luck with your life, Ron. I hope irresponsibility and thievery sit well with you when you try to sleep at night."

She joined Gracie at the door and they left.

"Is he a whack-job or what?" Gracie asked as they rode the elevator down to the parking level.

"I'm going to call the hospital when I get home and suggest they send a counselor around. With a little background, maybe a professional can ask the right questions and get Ron to reflect on his behavior. Some little thing the counselor says might be the trigger that changes him."

"Yeah, and pigs might actually learn how to fly," Gracie said. "I think he likes the lifestyle and shows no remorse for any of it."

Sandy had to admit her friend was right.

Chapter 68

The flight into Albuquerque and the drive back to Phoenix held a dismal feeling for Pen and Mary. Watching *Corinthian* sail away, with Foster Fordyce grinning back at them from the rail, was the most intense disappointment either of them had ever felt. Exhausted, they needed to see their friends.

"I don't even need to go home first," Mary said. "Let's just call the others and see who's up for a pub evening."

Pen smiled at her from the driver's seat. "I could use some fun after the past two days, most certainly."

They chose O'Reilly's, an English-style pub in central Phoenix. Most of the happy hour crowd had dissipated and there wasn't much dinner business at the moment. By the time Amber arrived, the others had decided on ale and comfort food—the house specialty, shepherd's pie.

"Here's to giving it our best effort," Sandy said, raising her glass to Mary and Pen. "It wasn't as if you didn't go all-out to catch dear old *Orion* and *Sunshine*."

"I haven't felt so let down since my ex hid all that money and the lawyers did nothing to help me," said Mary.

"Nor I, when I couldn't convince a prosecutor to take the case of my stolen heirloom," Pen added. "But when those agents waited to get warrants, at least we felt they were trying. If I had realized the warrants were only valid while the ship was at the pier, I would have thrown myself in front of the gangway or some such maneuver."

The others laughed at the image of their sophisticated Penelope lying facedown on a metal plank.

"It had to be such an anticlimax, after you chased them down," Gracie said. "Our experience with Ron, on the other hand, was a really strange mix of comic and sad."

"Not to mention infuriating," Sandy said. "The man is completely delusional. He thinks everything he does is a big lark, a fun time, as he outwits the rest of the world."

"He really does think he's invincible," Gracie added. "If there's a name for that kind of psychological complex, he's got it."

"I hope our little talk got through to him," Sandy said. "I don't hold a lot of hope for that, though." She sat straighter as the barkeep brought their meals.

Conversation waned for several minutes as they dug into the savory mixture of meat, vegetables and potatoes.

"Anyway," Sandy said, "we're glad Pen and Mary are home again. The holidays are behind us and we can start the new year fresh."

"I'm afraid I can't let it go quite that easily," Mary said, her fists clenched on the tabletop. "I feel such anger at what they did. Ron for posing as needy when he's not, for taking things from those who can least afford to lose anything. And those religious posers. It's unconscionable how much money they must have taken while preying on people's deepest beliefs. I still feel there must be something we can do."

Amber had been quiet up to this point, but a glimmer came into her eyes. "Don't give up just yet. I'm working on something."

Chapter 69

It's going to be a very long three weeks if you refuse to talk to me the whole time," Foster said. "Baby, come *on.* We just pulled off the con of the century. This is huge! Celebrate with me instead of pouting."

"*Pouting?* Is that what you think?"

He smiled. At least she'd spoken—for the first time since Yuma, all the way across southern California, and through the process of loading the container.

"You insulted my dreams, insulted my past, present, and future." She turned her back, but he walked over to her.

"The past is done, and we can talk about the future later. Let's make the best of our *luxury* cabin and make up." He wrapped his arms around her middle and nuzzled her neck. "C'mon, we're aboard a pretty crappy old freighter, but the bed looks comfy and the room is clean enough. We have to make the best of it. And when we get to the end of this trip, you'll have all the money you ever wanted to spend."

Still in his embrace, she turned to face him. "Yeah. There *is* that."

He planted a line of kisses from her shoulder to her neck to her mouth. Suddenly, clothing began falling to the floor. They awoke to morning light from the tiny porthole in their room and went to have their first breakfast at the captain's table.

The concept sounded far more elegant than the reality. Dining at the captain's table consisted of crowding in at a small table with the wiry little Filipino, Captain Umberto Ruiz and his first mate, a Malaysian man whose name neither of the Fordyces could pronounce. Breakfast was a hearty meal of fish and rice that Melissa turned up her nose at and asked if she might have an omelet. The cook, being an accommodating sort, figured out how to make one and she was happy.

"So, I tried to get on the internet this morning," Foster told his host. "No signal. How does that work?"

"Off and on," said the Filipino with a raucous chuckle. "I tell you when. Maybe later today. Maybe tomorrow."

Apparently, the internet access Foster had been promised was somehow beamed to the ship via satellite, and there were very narrow windows of time in which to grab a little of the bandwidth. He would have to use his browsing time wisely. If he didn't have at least one or two private islands for his wife to look over when they arrived, he'd better prepare himself for the silent treatment again.

Immediately after breakfast he made his way to the crowded deck. Container number 25740 sat high atop a stack, out of his reach. That was okay, he decided. It was out of everyone else's reach too. He studied the lock and it seemed intact. It was the only thing protecting their life's savings for the next three weeks.

Daily life aboard the ship fell into a routine by the third day: a meal or two with the captain—sometimes alone, sometimes with the first mate; walking the corridors for exercise, or an occasional turn around the deck; waiting, mostly, for word that he could try to log in to the sporadic internet service. Captain Ruiz's story of a voyage when he and his crew were robbed by pirates once in the Bay of Bengal did nothing to set Foster's mind at ease, and he couldn't wait for this trip to be over.

After several aborted attempts at browsing for the island he wanted, Foster ended up finding a real-estate agent who claimed to have listings on all the high-end South Sea properties. He eagerly awaited word via email and a link or two to take a look at the offerings.

Melissa seemed strangely content aboard the ship. Foster wondered about the new laid-back attitude until one day when he found a sketchbook she'd left on the bed while she was in the shower. Flipping through the pages he saw her most recent entries—notes on a new approach she labeled as the Faith and Belief Tour.

So much for his vision of uninterrupted island life.

Chapter 70

Sandy spotted Ron on one of his usual street corners on her way to work. It was two days after he'd been released from the hospital. The facial bruises had faded and a knitted cap covered the row of stitches across his forehead, so his most apparent injury was the foot in its cast and bandages.

He seemed to be playing that for all it was worth, speaking with people in their cars and accepting their cash. He didn't glance in her direction. From across the street she could read the new cardboard sign that said: Bad accident – need help

Yeah, an accident of your own making, she thought as the light changed and she drove on. The sight of Ron continued to bother her all the way to her office. She settled at her desk, ignoring the number of emails in her inbox.

She and the other Heist Ladies had talked it over, wondering how to get the law interested in Ron and his crimes. The man deserved to be punished. His cavalier attitude about his actions, the way he felt invincible—he shouldn't get away with this.

Panhandling on the streets violated a few minor ordinances, but obviously the police didn't really follow through, Sandy thought. Otherwise, Ron and others would have been arrested long ago. The thefts at Heaven Sent most likely wouldn't draw the attention of any law enforcement agency. The values were not high enough, and in reality the victims had received their items back.

She chewed at a cuticle as she debated what to do. And then she knew. She reached for her phone and called the news department at Channel 7. "I even have the headline for this one," she told Sara Storm, the investigative reporter. "And I can tell you exactly where to find the man who's taking in thousands of dollars a month while pretending to be homeless."

The reporter's interest perked up and Sandy went on to tell her the extent of Ron's duplicity.

That night she turned on her TV in time to hear the familiar voice of the anchor person. "And later, you'll be astonished at what some street corner panhandlers are doing with the money you hand out your car window. Sara Storm has the shocking details."

Sandy texted the other Ladies—Turn to Ch 7 – quick!

When the story came on, there was Ron, sitting at his street corner, his face shocked to be facing a camera and a news reporter who knew far too much about him. The crew had shot background footage of his house and his car. Another segment had the landlord, who steered past the question about the cash rent payments and made a flat statement: "I had no idea the guy was acting homeless."

"He's not homeless, you dweeb," Sandy said. "He's living on *your* property."

Sara Storm wrapped up the piece. "I received a call from the Internal Revenue Service as we were finalizing this story. It seems our fake homeless man is probably facing charges. We *will* be following this story as further developments unfold."

Chapter 71

Pen's text messages tended to stack up during the day; as a writer she put all distractions aside whenever she was working on a book deadline. So when five o'clock rolled around on January fifteenth, she was surprised to see that Amber, Sandy, and Gracie had each suggested the Heist Ladies meet. She could hardly wait to learn their news.

She texted all of them: Come to my house. There's wine and cheese!

Within moments she had four positive responses. She bustled about, trading her well-worn old good-luck writing sweater for a fresh blouse, brushing her hair, and applying a little lip gloss before going to the kitchen to put together the snacks.

Sandy was first to arrive and was fairly quivering with excitement. "I have to tell somebody," she said. "The IRS got Ron. Tonight's news on Channel 7 will have a follow up on the panhandling story. Apparently, the city wants to send a message about anyone not disclosing cash income."

"Oh my. They've moved very quickly, haven't they?"

"Very quickly. And the best—" Sandy paused when the doorbell rang.

"Hold that thought," said Pen, rushing to admit Gracie and Amber.

Mary followed right behind. "Sorry, I left the gym a little late because there was a news story about Ron. He is *so* busted."

Sandy nodded. "I was just telling Pen. The IRS has got him on tax evasion, *and* the big news for us is … there was a reward for turning him in."

"What—wow!" Amber said.

The group had moved toward Pen's wide granite counter top where she had begun to set out plates of cheeses, meats, and olives.

"Open those two wine bottles, someone?" Pen asked. "This news is worth more than one glass apiece, I should think."

"I'm just so glad to see Ron didn't get away with stealing from the homeless. It was a rotten thing to do," Mary said, handing over the first wine bottle. "Trini was really grateful to have the items returned, and the residents … well, it was so touching to see their faces."

The women each took a glass and they toasted. "To a case successfully solved," Pen said.

"One down and one to go," Mary said. "I refuse to believe the Fordyces got completely away from us."

A wide smile came over Amber's face. "Okay, okay—I can't hold this news any longer. I know where they're going."

"Foster and Melissa? I mean, *Orion* and *Sunshine* …"

"Yes!"

"How did you—?"

"I think I mentioned right after you guys watched them sail off, the credit card activity stopped. Not surprising. So I got to thinking … what else could I track to learn what they are up to? And of course, duh, it's his browsing history. Remember, I had cracked into that at one point to locate his banking contact. So I went to his email account and set up a tracking cookie and started watching."

The rest were staring at her, clueless about the steps, but avidly listening to what she had to say.

"They must be having a hot time on that ship. He's only going online once every day or two."

"Amber! You're making me crazy," Gracie said. "Where are they going?"

"It's a little island off the coast of Bali. Well, maybe it's actually part of Bali—geography isn't necessarily my thing. Anyway, they've been in touch with some real estate person who specializes in high dollar properties, like private islands … and they've made an offer on one! They plan to meet with the guy as soon as the ship docks in Jakarta."

There was a stunned silence as everyone processed the new information. What would they do with it?

"Wow," Gracie finally said. "My big news was that my kids are back in school."

Sandy burst out with the giggles. "That's great news, Gracie. It's all great news. Do you get it? We can see this thing through. We can figure out … I don't know. We can figure out something. When does the ship dock over there?"

"A week from today," Amber said.

"I vote that we go." Pen's tone was completely serious.

"Go—to Indonesia?" Mary said it, and the others exchanged glances.

"I'll pitch in the IRS reward money toward our tickets," Sandy said.

"I just received the advance on my new book. This is a good cause for it," Pen added. "Plus, this can serve as a research trip for my next book."

"Seriously?" Amber asked, typing madly at her laptop which she'd opened on the counter. "Cause I just found empty seats …"

Mary provided the voice of reason. "We need to think this through and arrive with a plan. We missed them by such a tiny bit last time. I want to be sure we aren't racing off if there's no hope of catching them again."

Amber looked up from her screen. "Keep in mind, this time we know their actual destination. I've got the name of the real estate agent and the exact location of the island they're buying. I doubt they'll head off somewhere else. Surely they're staying, right?"

"And just to assure success, I've texted Benton with the question about whether the US agents can enlist the assistance of local law enforcement at the other end. He says yes."

"So, are we in?" Amber asked.

Nods all around. "Book those tickets!" Gracie said with a huge smile. "We're goin' … to Bali … We're goin' … to Bali …" She started doing a little happy dance around Pen's living room.

Chapter 72

The tropical air warmed them, a pleasant change after the chilly January day they'd left behind in Phoenix, and the air smelled of a curious mix of flowers and exhaust fumes. They'd arrived on Bali a day ahead of their targets, checked into the Sheraton, and enlisted the help of a friendly taxi driver to get to the shipping port.

A hoard of dock workers swarmed the area, tying off massively thick lines, wheeling a metal gangway into place while a crane stood at the ready to unload the container.

"There he is," Amber whispered, pointing toward the ship's bridge castle some fifty yards away, where the tall figure of Foster Fordyce stood beside a much shorter man. He was talking with animated gestures and a fair amount of pacing.

Pen studied the busy industrial dock. Three ships were

in port, and each seemed a hive of activity. She wanted to know that the men who were supposed to meet them were, indeed, present already. But she saw no sign of them.

Sandy, Gracie, and Mary were standing in a small huddle, all eyes on the ship and the con man.

"There's Sunshine," Amber said.

The petite blonde appeared from a doorway and went to stand beside her husband.

"I can't believe we had them so close to us in Arizona, for weeks, and we've had to travel all this way to get them," Mary said.

Pen moved nearer to the group. "This time I'm prepared to wrestle Little Miss Sunshine to the ground if I must. They'll not escape us again."

"Shall we move into position?" Sandy suggested. "It looks as though everything is in place. They could be coming down any minute."

Foster and Melissa each carried a small bag, and they started toward the gangway, talking to each other. As they walked off the ship, the Ladies could overhear a bit.

"… inspection of our container?" Melissa had asked.

"Don't worry, baby. I've got enough on me to take care of the officials and keep them looking the other way." Foster patted a tote bag with the strap slung over his shoulder.

She beamed up at him, unaware of the five women ahead of them. The moment their feet touched the pier, Pen stepped forward.

"Orion and Sunshine—good to see you again."

The stunned looks on the faces of the con artists were priceless. They stared at the women, trying to place the connection. The moment recognition dawned with Melissa she grabbed her husband's hand.

"Foster—go!" she said, tugging.

He gave a wistful look at the containers on deck.

Melissa yanked his arm and started to run, but a man in a suit stood in her way.

"Charles Blue, US Attorney's office," he said.

Pen smiled in relief.

"You can't—" Melissa began. Three other men, dressed in local uniforms, closed in.

"Actually, we can," said the agent, signaling the others to apprehend the pair. Two of the local cops whipped handcuffs from their belts and snapped them on the two suspects, while Charles Blue proceeded to read the charges—fraud, grand theft, obtaining money under false pretenses, and fleeing the United States. He read them their rights, unwavering as Foster tried to out-shout him. The third officer relieved the suspects of their hand luggage and walked across the jetty to speak with the crane operator.

Charles Blue stepped over to Pen. "We'll process some paperwork here on the island and then they'll be on the next plane back to the States. Thank you for your help, and enjoy the rest of your stay."

The Heist Ladies stepped back. Their job was done.

* * *

Frothy waves lapped at the white sand beach as the five women stared out over crystalline blue water. Already they had sighed over the fact they would be leaving in the morning.

"I still don't understand what makes people lie and cheat the way the Fordyces did," Gracie said, twirling the tiny umbrella in her drink.

"There will always be con men, trying to take what isn't theirs, to swindle someone for the fun of it." Pen had felt philosophical all day. "What's sad is how many of us are willing to go along, to hand over money to people we know nothing about, basically only on a promise or a story."

"They find followers who are willing to go along, to give huge amounts, simply because the story fits with what they already believe," Sandy said.

"Or want to believe," Pen said, "whether or not there's a shred of logic behind it. It's so sad when one is betrayed by someone they believed to have a higher calling. It's so very wrong to prey on the down-and-out, those who are desperate or in dire straights. We all must be cautious. We cannot trust blindly, simply because someone puts a religious twist on their story."

"At least we caught Foster and Melissa—Orion and Sunshine, Jimmy Joe and Billie Lynn—before they spent it all. They could have gone the way of so many other gurus, with the jet plane, a dozen Rolls Royces, mansions on several continents."

"Well, they nearly had plunked down the money for a private island and a huge house out here," Mary reminded. "I imagine the real estate agent is one unhappy guy right now."

"What will happen to the money?" Gracie mused.

Pen leaned back against her lounger. "Most likely it falls under civil forfeiture laws."

"Meaning?"

"Law enforcement uses it to continue the fight against crime," Sandy added. "I suppose if lawyers were to come into the picture, they might begin some sort of class action against the Fordyces. But it will be hard to find people willing to come forth and admit they fell for the scam. And there would be so many, most of whom gave very small amounts."

"Do you suppose there might be a reward for catching them?" Gracie asked.

More than one set of eyebrows shot upward.

"If so," Mary said. "I vote that we donate it to Heaven Sent. Trini has some wonderful ideas for bringing counselors and other types of help to the homeless who come there. She could change a lot of lives with some extra money."

"I love it!" Gracie said. There were nods and smiles all around.

Amber had been quietly browsing on her laptop, despite the way the others teased her about always staying connected. Now she let out a whoop. "I got it—the new job came through for me!"

The others turned their heads. "What new job?"

"I didn't tell you? Right before the holidays a recruiter from one of the big tech giants headhunted me for a web developer position. It's insane money, and I get to stay right in Phoenix as part of the new team that's an offshoot of the California corporate headquarters."

"You, as a corporate team player …" Mary teased. "Well, okay. I'll be eager to see how that goes."

"As long as you don't leave us," Sandy said. "The Heist Ladies wouldn't be the same without our youngest team member."

"We'll see," said Amber with a little elfin grin. "We'll see."

Gracie stood up. "Well, I am taking a dip in that balmy water. What was it my dad used to say—go for the gusto? Whatever the future brings, I'm going to say that I've swum off the shores of Bali at least once in my life."

The others abandoned their lounge chairs and dashed toward the surf and the clear turquoise water.

Thank you for taking the time to read *Homeless in Heaven*. If you enjoyed it, please consider telling your friends or posting a short review. Word of mouth is an author's best friend and is much appreciated.

Thank you,

Connie Shelton

What's next for the Heist Ladies?

It's Amber's turn to call upon the Heist Ladies for help in this wrap-up to the series. The team's youngest member has taken a computer programming job and is on her way to a promising career. But a business trip to Europe with a fun side jaunt in Paris ends badly when Amber's luggage is searched by authorities and discovered to contain contraband. Even if she can convince them she's innocent, Amber knows she's been taken in by a con artist, and, well … that's the specialty of the Heist Ladies. Will the women be able to catch this oh-so-charming bad guy before he can pull the same sleazy con on someone else?

Get *Show Me the Money* at your favorite bookseller, available spring of 2021

Connie Shelton is the *USA Today* bestselling author of more than 30 novels and three non-fiction books. An avid mystery reader all her life, she says it was inevitable that this would be the genre she would write. She is the creator of the Novel In A Weekend™ writing course and was a contributor to *Chicken Soup for the Writer's Soul.*

She and her husband currently reside in northern New Mexico with their two dogs.

Books by Connie Shelton

The Charlie Parker Series

Deadly Gamble
Vacations Can Be Murder
Partnerships Can Be Murder
Small Towns Can Be Murder
Memories Can Be Murder
Honeymoons Can Be Murder
Reunions Can Be Murder
Competition Can Be Murder
Balloons Can Be Murder
Obsessions Can Be Murder
Gossip Can Be Murder
Stardom Can Be Murder
Phantoms Can Be Murder
Buried Secrets Can Be Murder
Legends Can Be Murder
Weddings Can Be Murder
Alibis Can Be Murder
Escapes Can Be Murder
Old Bones Can Be Murder
Holidays Can Be Murder - a Christmas novella

The Samantha Sweet Series

Sweet Masterpiece
Sweet's Sweets
Sweet Holidays
Sweet Hearts
Bitter Sweet
Sweets Galore
Sweets Begorra
Sweet Payback

Sweet Somethings
Sweets Forgotten
Spooky Sweet
Sticky Sweet
Sweet Magic
Spellbound Sweets – a Halloween novella
The Woodcarver's Secret

The Heist Ladies Series
Diamonds Aren't Forever
The Trophy Wife Exchange
Movie Mogul Mama
Homeless in Heaven
And watch for *Show Me the Money*, coming in 2021

Children's Books
Daisy and Maisie and the Great Lizard Hunt
Daisy and Maisie and the Lost Kitten

Sign up for Connie Shelton's free mystery newsletter at www.connieshelton.com and receive advance information about new books, along with a chance at prizes, discounts and other mystery news!

Contact by email: connie@connieshelton.com
Follow Connie Shelton on Twitter, Pinterest and Facebook

www.ingramcontent.com/pod-product-compliance
Lightning Source LLC
Chambersburg PA
CBHW032100180726
48284CB00002B/371

* 9 7 8 1 9 4 5 4 2 2 8 9 8 *